Love Held
Captive

Center Point
Large Print

Also by Shelley Shepard Gray and available from Center Point Large Print:

The Loyal Heart
A Sister's Wish
An Uncommon Protector
Her Secret
His Guilt

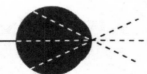

This Large Print Book carries the Seal of Approval of N.A.V.H.

Love Held Captive

A Lone Star Hero's Love Story

Shelley Shepard Gray

CENTER POINT LARGE PRINT
THORNDIKE, MAINE

This Center Point Large Print edition
is published in the year 2017 by arrangement with
Zondervan.

The text of this Large Print edition is unabridged.
In other aspects, this book may vary
from the original edition.
Printed in the United States of America
on permanent paper.
Set in 16-point Times New Roman type.

ISBN: 978-1-68324-576-6

Library of Congress Cataloging-in-Publication Data

Names: Gray, Shelley Shepard, author.
Title: Love held captive / Shelley Shepard Gray.
Description: Center Point Large Print edition. | Thorndike, Maine :
    Center Point Large Print, 2017. | Series: A Lone Star hero's love story
Identifiers: LCCN 2017035078 | ISBN 9781683245766
    (hardcover : alk. paper)
Subjects: LCSH: Large type books. | GSAFD: Love stories. |
    Christian fiction.
Classification: LCC PS3607.R3966 L68 2017b | DDC 813/.6—dc23
LC record available at https://lccn.loc.gov/2017035078

To anyone who loves westerns as much as I do.

The apostles said to the Lord, "Increase our faith!" The Lord replied, "If you had faith the size of a mustard seed, you could say to this mulberry tree, 'Be uprooted and planted in the sea,' and it would obey you."
—*Luke 17:5–6*

The past is dead; let it bury its dead, its hopes, and its aspirations. Before you lies the future, a future full of golden promise.
—*Jefferson Davis*

Prologue

There was almost nothing there. Almost.

Examining his surroundings, knowing he was mere minutes from ordering his men to take whatever this place still had, Captain Ethan Kelly forced himself to focus on his orders. General McCoy himself had given him this specific assignment, and failure was not an option.

Ethan was to make sure he and his men scoured the area and procured as much food and provisions as possible. By whatever means possible. Their efforts would make the difference between life and death for the men in their camp. The soldiers were hungry, cold, and about to be sent into battle. The Confederacy needed them to be strong of mind and able-bodied. No matter how hard it was to prey upon the South's women and children, Ethan could not allow any feelings of weakness to distract him from his goal.

His men weren't going to starve and freeze to death. They needed whatever supplies they could scrounge up.

Practically feeling his men's expectant stares on the back of his neck, Ethan steeled himself. Then he turned around to face them and began barking orders. "All right. You know what we came for. Wood. Ammunition. Food. Blankets. Fan out and be quick about it."

But instead of rushing to do his bidding, the small band of five eyed their surroundings warily.

"What about the woman, Cap?" Baker asked before Ethan could berate their slow reaction.

Caught off guard, Ethan turned to look where Sergeant Baker was pointing.

That's when he saw her. She'd come out to stand on the porch of the run-down ranch house. She was dark-haired and wore a dress that hung loosely on a form obviously too thin. A brown threadbare shawl was wrapped around her shoulders, the edges of it fluttering in the cold wind. But what struck him the most—and most likely, struck Thomas Baker too—was the way she was staring at them. As though she was mentally preparing herself for harm.

Ethan reckoned this woman looked a lot like the rest of the South. Ravaged and in pain.

Then he noticed she bore a scar. Even from his distance, he could tell it was recent. Its jagged red line tore across her temple and into her hairline. An accident?

Ethan forced himself to look away. He turned to his sergeant. Ethan could count on Baker to follow his orders, even when he didn't agree with them.

The man stared right back, bold as day. As he'd hoped, Baker's expression was carefully blank. Without distaste. Without interest. Really, without any emotion at all.

Ethan swallowed the rush of sympathy that had threatened to overtake him. And because he was afraid he might give in and decide they didn't need to search this house and barn, he turned to Baker. "Go explain to her what we're doing. Tell her we mean no harm."

"Yessir."

"But, Baker, make sure she understands we aren't going to leave until we get what we came for. The needs of our soldiers must come first."

After nodding, Baker started barking to the others. "You heard Captain Kelly. Go!"

The four other men scattered like fleas in a barnyard while Baker walked over to speak to the woman.

Ethan watched two of his men enter her storm cellar and breathed an inward sigh of relief. There had to be something down there. Maybe even some meat curing. They could take it to their unit, and for once those boys could have something to eat besides mealy hardtack.

He was warmed by that thought as he watched Baker move into the house, and his unease about the woman dissipated.

Until he noticed she was now holding one of the posts of her front porch in a death grip. She looked terrified.

He should have done the talking. Announced their intention to gather supplies for the soldiers of the Confederacy by order of President Jefferson Davis himself rather than asking Baker to do it.

Feeling far older than his twenty-nine years, he moved closer and studied her when she turned to look at him. He was sure she couldn't quite see his face in the shadows, but he could see tears forming in her eyes. She said nothing, but let go of the post and wrapped her arms and the ugly shawl around her chest and waist more securely. Almost as if she could shield her body from his men. Or perhaps he was the one she feared. He wasn't a small man, and he was also the one giving orders. His soldiers would do whatever he told them to do.

Looking at her more closely, he realized her hair was darker than he'd earlier thought. Almost black, really. It hung in thick, riotous curls down her shoulders, and when she had turned, he could see it went down her back. Almost to her waist. Her loose dress was a faded pink calico with frayed cuffs. Her feet were in worn boots that looked too big. Obviously she'd done a little bit of requisitioning herself.

But what caught his attention most was the way she continued to stare at him. Her eyes were dark. Maybe blue? Maybe green? Did it even matter? Never had someone looked at him with such stark terror.

It drew him up short. He'd supervised dozens of these raids across the South. Most of the inhabitants were resentful.

Some had been downright cordial and sympathetic, sharing stories about their own boys in uniform.

As the men brought up jars from the cellar and carried a comforter from the house, her vivid eyes turned from his and tracked every move. Another tear ran down her face when Baker carried out a sack of flour in one hand and a quilt in the other. Two privates behind him came out empty-handed.

"Where's the rest, Baker?" he called out.

"Ain't nothing more, sir."

It wasn't a surprise—it was obvious other bands of men had done their share of looting.

Knowing many homeowners hid their best belongings, even from their own troops, he hardened his voice.

"Look harder," he called out.

The men paused, but after a nod from Baker, they rushed to obey.

The woman pressed a fist to her mouth as her eyes filled with more tears.

He hated seeing her cry. It went against everything he'd been raised to be. His father and mother had taken great pains to teach him to be a gentleman, as befitting their station in Houston society. But though he felt sorry for her, a far different emotion overrode his concern.

Resentment. He resented how her weeping made him feel—as though he were stealing from her for no good reason.

Now he had no choice but to speak to her. He stepped closer, out of the shadows. Close enough for her to see captain's bars on his uniform. Probably not close enough for her to see much of his face under the brim of his hat.

"You'd best dry your tears, miss," he called out. "Our soldiers need supplies. They are fighting for our cause. Everyone must make sacrifices. Everyone. Where have you hidden everything else?"

After a brief moment her fist left her mouth, but she didn't reply. She simply continued to stare at him in silence. What was wrong with her? Had this conflict already taken its toll on her? Some women were far too delicate for the ravages of war. Imagining his mother or his sister in such circumstances, he inwardly winced.

Who had he become? A man reduced to ordering soldiers not just to fight the enemy but to raid innocents and the afflicted? His father would hang his head in shame.

"Can you speak?" he finally asked, his voice sounding unfamiliar and harsh even to his own ears.

She nodded.

"Well then, an answer please, if you will. Where are the rest of your food and provisions?" He knew his tone was severe. Impatient. But he couldn't help it. This whole situation was hellish. He didn't want to spend his day frightening young women.

After visibly attempting to regain her composure, she spoke. "There isn't anything else, sir."

Her voice was husky. Deeper than expected. It was also soft, almost melodic.

In spite of himself, Ethan climbed the steps. As much as he wanted to remain detached and hard, a part of him needed to hear a feminine voice, if only for a minute. Needed a reminder that while many hurting soldiers depended on his successful objectives, many of them were fighting for their sisters, mothers, wives, and daughters.

Well aware of his men watching and listening, he kept his voice low. "I know there is more. There always is."

"There isn't. Other men have already been here. And when they came, they

16

took everything of worth." The pain in her voice encouraged him to search her face. Once again, he eyed the scar running along her hairline on the left side. Jagged and thick, it curved from her forehead and temple, ending at the top of her ear. It was very red. It appeared to be fresh.

Deep emotion he'd tried so hard to forget existed slid into his heart and soul. Jolted him with a shock of pain as her silence and fear all made sense. Other soldiers had looted her house before. And she'd been attacked. Cut.

And now she was expecting that same of him and his men.

He turned on his heel. "Baker!" he called out. "Collect the men. We're leaving."

"But, Cap, we haven't finished searching the barn." His voice was filled with confusion.

"Silence, Sergeant," Ethan ordered in a hard voice—one he was certain Baker knew better than to argue with. When the only sound was the bitter wind blowing across the plains, Ethan made a great show of staring at the map he'd just unfurled.

Ten minutes later, they were marching back down the lane, their wagon pulled by his horse. Though the woman hadn't lied—she really hadn't had much left—they'd still managed to take what was there. But it was hardly enough to make a difference to a camp of soldiers.

Still, it would no doubt make a big difference to one woman living alone in a run-down house. Desolation coursed through Ethan as he realized what that meant. They were no better than anyone else. And maybe a whole lot worse—even if they hadn't physically harmed her.

Gasping for air, he tried not to care that he'd become everything he'd feared. He'd become everything—

"Wake up, Major!" a man said while giving Ethan a harsh shove. "You're dreaming again. Wake up!"

Inhaling, Ethan sat up. Realized he wasn't freezing. He wasn't back in Texas in the middle of winter. He was on his cot in his barracks on Johnson's Island. He was a prisoner of war, stuck in the Confederate Officers' POW camp under the desultory guardianship of Yankee soldiers. He was reduced to waiting out the remainder of the war in boredom and misery.

He was also safe and dry.

And far away from a damaged woman living on a desolate ranch.

"You okay?" Thomas Baker asked. "You were gasping in your sleep. Sounded like you were choking."

"I wasn't. I was just dreaming. I'm fine, Sergeant," he said, reverting to the man's rank. Hating that his shirt was soaked in sweat.

"Want some water? I got a canteen-full last night."

"Thanks, but I'm all right. Like I said, I was, uh, dreaming."

"I'd ask if the dream was a bad one, but of course it was. I mean, they all are, right?" Thomas asked with a wry look.

He was right about that.

"You okay, Ethan?" Devin Monroe murmured from his cot.

"I'm fine. Sorry I woke you." Realizing he had most likely awoken half the men in the barracks, he spoke again, this time a little more loudly. "Sorry, everyone."

But instead of grumbling, the rest of the men in the room remained silent.

Pure shame engulfed him. He had lost control. Struggling with how to accept that, Ethan held out a hand. "You know what, Thomas? I'll take that water after all."

When Thomas turned to retrieve the canteen, Ethan shook his head and tried to get his bearings. Then did what he always did after he dreamed about that house—prayed that woman was okay.

19

That he hadn't done any lasting harm.

But, of course, he knew he was only fooling himself. He *had* hurt her. Of course he had. He knew he was going to cause her pain and heartache the moment they stopped in front of her house.

She'd had so little, and he'd ordered his men to take what they could anyway. It hardly mattered that other men had done far worse. Pain was pain. It all hurt.

1

She never should have had her back to the door.

When it shut behind her with a sharp *crack,* Lizbeth Barclay knew she was in trouble. But though everything inside her was screaming to run, she froze while pulling on the heavy brocade bedspread in the hotel's guestroom.

And just like that, she was transported back in time. Back to another place where she should have felt safe but had been her most vulnerable.

As she heard the faint brush of clothing, a muted jangle of change in a pocket, the rustle of leather behind her back, her hands held the spread in a death grip. Frustration filled her. She so wanted to be braver. Tougher. Better.

But she wasn't. Not yet.

"You ever going to turn around?" the intruder drawled.

Her breath hitched. It made no sense, but she could have sworn she recognized the voice. It was unmistakably deep and thick and sounded much like the voice from her nightmares after

21

that day back in Castroville. Back in the middle of the war, when she was alone in her house. Alone and scared and completely sure there was no one in the vicinity to come to her aid if she screamed.

She'd been right, of course. No one had come before.

A thick bolt of dread coursed through her as she forced herself to turn. Pretending she wasn't as scarred and scared as she felt, she raised her chin and turned.

And stared directly into a pair of familiar dark-brown eyes. Confusion warred with dismay as she realized she hadn't been mistaken. She did know this man.

Intimately.

He haunted her dreams. Starred in her nightmares. She'd thought he was merely a memory. She was wrong.

"You," she whispered.

This time he wasn't wearing a uniform. He was dressed in a finely constructed black suit and highly polished black boots. But his hard jaw, the steady gaze, the way his arms hung loosely at his side . . . She would recognize him anywhere. Even now, as he stood with his back against the door. Barring it with his body.

He frowned before his expression cleared. Then, as she watched him, he turned his attention to her body. As if he had all the time in the world, his gaze slid over her. It paused on her face, lingered on her curves, then settled on her hips, covered by a neatly starched white apron.

The whole perusal made her feel dirty. Maybe he'd intended it to.

Or maybe she'd felt that way for so long she didn't remember how to ever feel clean again. By the time the war ended, Lizbeth had come to realize one never felt completely clean when one's soul—one's very being—was bruised and tarnished by pain.

Out of habit, she shrank into herself, gripping the voluminous fabric of her gray uniform. His eyes tracked her hands, following the movement of her fingertips with the interest of a predator. Perspiration dampened the fabric on her back. It fastened onto her skin, confining her movements even further.

It was becoming difficult to breathe.

"Do I know you?" he asked, his voice haughty yet curious.

Taking care to avoid his gaze, Lizbeth focused instead on his tailored suit. His cream-colored shirt. The silver pin puncturing the silk cravat at his neck. When she dared to meet his eyes again, she realized his showed no recognition.

He didn't remember her.

Realizing her cap was covering the worst of her scar, relief flowed through her. "Of course not, sir," she replied around a rush of air. "I'm just a maid here. I'm sorry I was still in the room when you arrived. I'll leave now."

"No need to do that, miss . . ." He grinned, encouraging small lines to form around his eyes. "What is your name?"

She didn't want to tell him.

"I'm going to leave now." Though she was barely able to move her limbs, she looked around for her feather duster and the little wooden crate that held her rags, the beeswax, the vinegar, and newsprint. She needed to escape.

She picked up the crate, ready to go. But still he blocked the door. Those highly polished black boots shining against the door's dark stain.

He wasn't a handsome man. Most likely he never had been, though it was hard to tell. His eyes were bloodshot and his skin was sallow. Much of the flesh on his cheeks was scarred from the pox. Everything about him screamed of dissolute behavior. But even in the midst of such disrepair, an intensity emanated from him.

He knew she was uncomfortable, and that pleased him.

It took everything she had to move forward. "Please step aside."

"I'd rather not. I'd be a fool to let an opportunity like this pass me by." His lips curved into a smile that didn't meet his eyes. "Why don't you stay awhile longer? The afternoon is still young. We can get to know each other."

She had to get out. On the other side of the door lay freedom. Relief. Air.

She had to do it. She had to find a way to get him to move aside, to allow her to turn that knob.

It was time to run. Fast.

She fought to keep her voice light and detached. "I have other rooms to clean. I need to go."

At last he moved away from the door. Clicking his tongue softly, he approached. "My bed isn't made. You haven't finished your job, have you?"

Her tongue felt thick. "I . . . I will come back. We're not supposed to bother the guests."

"Stay. You can work around me."

"I cannot, sir."

Just as she folded her palm around the door's knob, he reached for her forearm. "Reconsider."

His voice was hard. Demanding. It hurt almost as much as the memories. Images of all she'd tried so hard to forget flashed forward, making her feel weak and dizzy. She needed to get away before she passed out and made things worse.

Her lungs felt so tight, she had trouble catching her breath. She was beginning to pant. To hyper-ventilate. Hoping to regain her bearings, she grasped the crate's handle with one hand and pressed a palm to her face.

"There's no need to hide yourself from me. If you think I'm bothered by your looks, I'm not," he said with an almost-tender smile. "Don't be shy. Why, we're all marked from the war in one way or another. You'd probably be shocked to discover some of the things I've done." His tone had turned almost nostalgic, just as his gaze sharpened on her forehead.

Feeling sick, Lizbeth realized what he was seeing. She must have inadvertently slid her cap back when she'd pressed her palm to her face.

Memories threatened to overpower her. Teasing her with snippets of scattered, split images she worked so very hard to ignore during the day. But just like the four-inch scar that ran along her brow and hairline, the memories would never completely fade.

Bile rose in the back of her throat, making her gag. Her stomach churned, her vision turning spotty. If she didn't escape soon, chances were very good she was going to vomit. Right there in the hotel room.

She needed air. She needed freedom and comfort and relief. Without daring to glance his way again, she threw open the heavy door and tore out of the room.

If he complained about his service, she'd be in trouble. Though her second cousin and her husband managed this hotel, Aileen and Dallas weren't understanding. And she would never tell them who the man was.

Lizbeth looked both ways down the narrow hallway. She needed a moment to get her wits together before coming up with a decent excuse to explain herself. Quickly choosing to go left, because that end was far less occupied by guests, Lizbeth turned and hurried as fast as she could.

When she came to another junction, she glanced right and left again. Seeing both sides of that hall empty, she breathed a sigh of relief. So far, so good. If Aileen or one of her favorites caught her running like she was, they'd want to know what had happened. And they'd make her return to that room no matter what.

Lizbeth suspected Aileen would never believe what happened to her during the war. As with everyone else, she'd let her cousin believe her scar was the result of an accident. Or maybe she would believe the truth, but not care.

Aileen's parents were living in Galveston now, but she had been with them right up until she married Dallas Howard. Lizbeth's parents hadn't been the most giving or kind people. They'd thought of Aileen's branch of the family as far beneath their merit and had done little to help Aileen when she made her debut. While Lizbeth had been dressed in silks and had worn skirts filled with so many petticoats and hoops she could hardly fit through doorways, Aileen had been standing to the side. Largely forgotten.

Lizbeth had been embarrassed by that, and even offered to share her gowns. But her mother refused to let her. Aileen was just pretty enough to be competition. It was far better for their daughter to be the only one to shine brightly. Social status had counted for everything to them.

Right up until they died of an illness that had somehow spared her life.

No, she wouldn't tell Aileen this was the man who had ruined her.

She thought she heard heavy boots on the carpeting behind her, coming closer. Lizbeth's heart started beating even faster. Why had she stopped?

Desperate, she started scanning room numbers. She needed an empty room to dart into, and she needed it fast.

Just as she was about to scurry down the stairs, she realized suite 28 was just ahead. Only Major Ethan Kelly ever stayed there, and everyone at the Menger knew he wasn't currently in residence.

His suite would be perfect. It had its own bathing and sitting rooms. She could lock herself inside, splash some water on her face, and regain her bearings. Then, after a bit, she could go back to her duties. With luck, no one would be the wiser.

Rushing ahead, she set her crate of cleaning supplies against the wall and started sorting through her keys, their jingling echoing down the hallway. Hands shaking, she located the right key after two attempts and inserted it into the lock. Finally, the knob turned.

She swung open the door in relief. Feeling triumphant, Lizbeth went inside and slammed it shut behind her with more force than was necessary. Turning to face it, she laid her hands on the smooth, cool wood. She was safe.

2

After she caught her breath and turned around, the first thing Lizbeth noticed was that the major was in residence again. He must have come in late the night before. Clothes were strewn across the bed. Polished boots were lined up against the wall. Papers littered the desk, and personal belongings lay on top of the dresser.

Lizbeth was still rattled, but she found herself smiling. Major Kelly was such a mess!

Walking across the room to his bed, she ran a finger along his navy silk vest. Stopped to carefully fold his handkerchief back into a perfect square. She'd done such things more than once during the last couple of months. Unlike some other former soldiers, the major didn't seem to have retained any sense of order from his military life. Or maybe he'd had people to pick up after him during the war.

Whatever the reason, he always left his belongings scattered around. Some maids—Callie in particular—dreaded being assigned to clean his suite. It always took double the time to put it to rights. Lizbeth had never minded, though. It rather amused her to think the major, who looked every inch the dandy when he was out in public, was something of a mess in private.

Unable to help herself, she moved to the dresser. In the center was a beautiful gold pocket watch. Lying next to it was a pair of gold cufflinks. They were substantial and showy. She knew the major only by sight and reputation, but even she knew he wore them constantly.

Picking up one, she turned it this way and that. It was a carved gold knot. Beautiful, really. And far heavier than she would have imagined. For all her tidying, she couldn't remember him ever leaving the cufflinks out in the open. Picking up the other, she held them both in the palm of her right hand.

She really should put them in a safe place. Though she hoped none of the other maids would be tempted to steal them, she didn't want to test their honesty. Perhaps she should set them in a drawer. She could write him a note. Yes! That would be the best thing—

"May I help you?"

She jumped at the sound of the voice.

With a feeling of dread, she slowly turned around. And felt as though her heart had just dropped to her feet.

Major Ethan Kelly was standing in front of her. At first staring at her face, and then eyeing his cufflinks in her hand. All while standing in a pair of trousers.

In only a pair of trousers.

Though she shouldn't, Lizbeth let her gaze

drift. Like a miserly banker, she catalogued each one of his scars and battle wounds. Allowed herself to notice the way his muscles flexed when he moved his arm. The way his olive skin was smooth except for a faint line of dark hair that ran down the center of his abdomen. She noticed the line of muscles across his chest. Along his arms, his shoulders.

Last, she raised her chin and met his stare. Felt her skin flush, knew he'd just watched her look him over like a trollop in a back alley. So very like the way that other man had looked at her.

She realized now that he'd been in his bathing room. His clothes weren't on the bed because he'd changed in a hurry but because he was about to get dressed.

"It looks like you've found something you like," he finally drawled.

With a start, she realized he thought she was stealing his cufflinks. Stealing from him! Her hands went limp, and the cufflinks fell to the floor.

Clattering against the floorboards like tiny symbols of her foolishness. Or maybe just symbols of how mixed-up and confusing her life had become. Despite her best intentions, everything she did only served to make her situation worse.

After the space of three beats—or maybe after

she'd finally controlled her breathing and was able to concentrate again—Major Kelly raised his eyebrows.

Lizbeth scrambled to the floor, picked up the cufflinks, and set them back on the dresser's surface. As she stepped aside, she tried to decide how to explain herself.

She was stuck. Trapped between two men— this man, too filled with charm, and the other, the reason she had never become the person she'd always hoped she'd be. It was almost too much to take in.

She watched as his brown eyes drifted over her. Then did it again, pausing for the briefest second on her scar. To her surprise, he didn't look angry. He seemed to be assessing her, like an officer examining one of his men. Compassion might have entered his eyes. Or it might not have. She couldn't tell.

Still he said nothing. Still she waited.

When he raised one arm to absently scratch his other, he seemed to realize he was mostly unclothed. Without a word, he strode to the dresser, opened a drawer, pulled out a folded white shirt, and slipped it on. Then he proceeded to neatly button the shirt, as if what was happening wasn't completely irregular.

She needed to get out of there. She needed to simply turn and leave. Maybe, with God's help, they could eventually both pretend this moment had never happened. But just as she shifted, preparing to explain why she'd been holding his cufflinks, he spoke.

"I've seen you in the halls. What is your name?" He sounded bored as he continued to carefully slip each well-crafted button through its appropriate hole.

"I'm Lizbeth, sir. I mean, well, my full name is Elizabeth Barclay." Not that he cared. And, oh, did her voice just . . . squeak? This was only getting worse.

As he turned his attention to fastening his cuffs with the gold links, he murmured, "Would you, if you please, explain why you are in my room?"

"It wasn't to take your cufflinks, sir."

"No?"

She trembled.

Suddenly realizing he was still staring at her intently, awaiting a response, she walked toward the door. "I'm so sorry, sir. I thought this room was unoccupied. Then, when I saw your cufflinks, I thought I should put them away. For safekeeping."

"And your palm seemed like the best place?"

"Oh, no. I was going to put them in the top drawer and then write you a note," she murmured as she continued to edge to the door. "I didn't want anyone to steal them." Hearing her words, she felt even more foolish. Surely no other explanation could sound more unbelievable.

"So you came in here to do . . . what? A good deed?"

Glad that she could finally form a coherent thought, she grasped the ornate, heavily faceted knob behind her. The glass handle was cool underneath her touch and its chill soothed her. "I'm so sorry about this. If you could forget that I ever came inside, I would be so grateful." She turned the knob a quarter of an inch. "And, um . . . I'll just leave you in peace."

"Stay."

She dropped her hand. "I beg your pardon?"

He fastened a starched collar around his neck. "I said stay. Your face is flushed. Were you running? And if so, what were you running from?" His eyes narrowed. "And don't you start telling me some nonsense. I heard you darting in here like the devil himself was on your heels."

Funny, she'd felt as if that had indeed been the case. But what could she say?

"Well then?"

His voice was commanding. Authoritative. She didn't know how to not answer. "I had a small issue, but I'm sure it is better by now."

He'd tucked his shirt in his trousers and was now fastening the navy silk vest. His fingers stilled. "An issue. And what kind would that be? And please, do start talking."

Clutching her hands together, she tried to fashion a reply. But her mind went blank as he plucked a suit jacket from the back of a chair.

After slipping it on, he smoothed the fabric along his chest. If anything, he stood even taller. Right there on the expensive Aubusson rug, under a gilded chandelier and surrounded by dark ruby-colored curtains and wallpaper. He was a man used to being in charge. A man used to making decisions and commanding an audience.

For the first time since she'd arrived, his voice adopted a thread of impatience. "I am waiting for a response, miss."

Tell him, she cautioned herself. It isn't as if you have anything to gain by keeping your silence. There's no way you're going to have an ounce of pride left after this experience anyway. "I was, well, cleaning a guest's room when he returned unexpectedly."

"What happened then?"

How could she tell him she'd been so afraid? How could she when she was standing right here in the same room with the man? What was the difference between what was happening at that very moment and what had happened moments earlier? Was it because the other man was from her past?

Or was it because she didn't fear Major Kelly?

Beyond flustered now, she hedged. "It became difficult. He didn't want me to leave."

"Difficult? What is that supposed to mean?"

"I was afraid."

"Forgive me for being obtuse, miss. But am I to understand he made an untoward advance against you?"

Caught between a nod and a shrug, she kind of twitched. "Yes, sir. But it's all right, because I—"

"It's not all right. Nothing about that was all right."

No, it wasn't. But what could she say? "If you will excuse me, I'll be on my way."

"Not yet, if you please," he murmured as he turned to his dresser. Methodically, he slipped that very fine gold watch into his vest pocket. Then, just as calm as you please, he sat down on the dark-gray winged chair and slipped on his fine-looking black leather boots.

All while she stood and continued to watch him.

After rubbing his thumb along a scuff in the leather, he stood. "In what room did this occur?"

She'd already said too much. "I don't recall."

"Come now. Let us not start lying to each other."

Was it possible for one's skin to become any more flushed? "All right. The truth is that I would rather you not be involved."

"I'm already involved, though, aren't I?"

Was he? "Yes, but—"

"So what you really mean is you do not wish me to be any further involved."

"Yes, sir. That is what I mean." Just to make sure she was clear, she added, "I'd rather you not become any further involved in my business, Major Kelly."

A new, amused glint shone in his eyes. "I'm afraid it's too late to wish for that."

"It's not."

"I have to disagree." His voice lowered into a slow, languid drawl. "Don't forget, you've seen me practically naked."

She couldn't deny that. However, she could free herself from this travesty of a situation. She needed to leave. Just leave. Forget about asking for permission. Forget about how tarnished her reputation was going to be.

Yes. She needed to leave. Immediately.

She could go to her room and begin to make plans to start over somewhere else. New Braunfels, perhaps? Just as she reached for the glass doorknob again, a light knock sounded from the other side.

"Major Kelly, sir?" a high, shrill female voice called out. The woman followed with another series of sharp knocks.

As Lizbeth realized who was now standing on the other side of the door, she bit back a moan. She hadn't thought her predicament could get worse. But, as with rain, heat, and war, it seemed it certainly could.

3

After the knocks came a tentative voice Lizbeth knew all too well.

"Major Kelly? Sir, I hate to disturb you, but if I might have a moment of your time?"

Lizbeth stared at the door in dismay. Aileen was on the other side. Her employer. What choice did she have but to respond?

She looked at the major, and he narrowed his eyes just as she started to turn the door's handle. "Wait," he said, his voice once again low.

Lizbeth cleared her throat and lowered her voice as well. "Major Kelly, I do believe my cousin is knocking at your door."

"Cousin, is it?" A new light, one a lot like amusement, she was afraid, entered his eyes. "Is that right?"

"That is Aileen Howard. She and her husband, Dallas, manage this establishment."

"Yes, but that still doesn't help me understand why she is knocking so urgently."

Lizbeth realized she did understand her cousin's persistence. No doubt the other man had complained about her. But how did Aileen know where Lizbeth was? "I think it would be better for all of us if I went out to speak to her, sir."

He stepped forward, bringing with him the faint

scent of bay rum and soap. "Will you trust me? I can help you, if you'll give me your trust."

Trust him? She didn't trust any man. Not any longer. Having no words, she shook her head.

His eyes darted to the scar on her face. A flash of concern she didn't understand entered his eyes before he spoke more forcefully. Did he feel sorry for her? "I won't harm you. I promise."

But he didn't realize promises meant nothing to her. "Beyond the fact that I know you frequently leave your clothing scattered around your room, I don't know you, Major," she said stiffly. "Furthermore, we both know I am none of your concern."

"Reconsider."

One word. The same word Bushnell had said to her minutes earlier. And just as forcibly said. Both men were used to giving commands. Even more used to being listened to.

The major wasn't Bushnell, but she wasn't one of his soldiers either. She was nothing to him, and he . . . well, though he was mannerly and polite, he still symbolized everything that had ruined her life. "I would like to leave, sir."

"All right, then." Motioning with his hands, he said, "Open it up, if you will, Miss Barclay. Let us see what your cousin desires."

Desires. His choice of words took her by surprise. She pulled open the door.

Aileen was, indeed, standing on the other side.

As always, she was dressed becomingly. In one hand was Lizbeth's crate of cleaning supplies.

Lizbeth called herself three kinds the fool. In her haste, she'd put the crate on the hallway floor when she was fumbling with her keys. All the while she'd been attempting to hide, her supplies were right outside the major's door. They had been stationed there like a beacon, practically begging for her to be found.

She glanced at the major. He had clasped his arms behind him. He looked exactly like he was—a military man standing at rest.

For a split second, all three of them remained mute. Each staring at the other two. Lizbeth could only hope what was about to happen would do so quickly.

Ethan Kelly had liked to think that after four years of war, nine months in captivity, and six months of gambling in various disreputable saloons and on riverboats, nothing could surprise him.

He had been wrong.

He was now standing with two women. One whose voice was so brittle and high it grated on his last nerve. The other? Well, she was the star of his nightmares and the cause of his shame. He was torn between wanting to shield her from the rest of the world and turning his back to her in a feeble effort to retain what remained of his soul.

Impatient with the situation, he glared at the

41

woman who was standing in his doorway. She was dressed in a becoming cranberry-colored day dress, stockings, and some fine black kid shoes. When she turned her head to look at Lizbeth, he could see her dark-blonde hair was styled in a low chignon.

"May I help you?" he asked with obvious sarcasm.

"I'm sorry, sir. I was looking for this maid."

Before Ethan could say a word, Miss Barclay stepped forward. "Obviously you have found me."

"Excuse us, sir," Mrs. Howard said to Ethan before directing her maid into the hall. Miss Barclay went out, never looking back in his direction.

Ethan knew the right thing to do would be to close his door. He needed to come to terms with the fact that he had just seen the woman whose home he'd raided in the war. Maybe have a drink. Maybe then he could pretend it had been a strange coincidence that their paths had crossed again but no harm had been done. She had obviously survived, just as he had.

But despite his best intentions, he found himself unable to pull his attention away. The two women were close enough for him to still hear every hushed word.

"Why were you inside Major Kelly's room?"

"It was a mistake. I was only trying to find a quiet place to collect my bearings."

Aileen's voice rose. "In a guest's room?"

"I didn't know anyone was inside."

"It is never okay to be in a guest's room unless you were called in to clean it. You know this."

"I know. But—"

"I can only assume you were in there for another reason." She folded her hands across her chest. "Perhaps you were in search of money?"

"I wasn't stealing anything!"

Ethan couldn't deny he had thought the very same thing. Now, though, he wasn't even sure if he cared. Who was he to deny something to a woman who had already lost so much?

With an exaggerated sigh, Mrs. Howard said, "Lizbeth, why were you trying to get your bearings?"

"I had to get away from a man who walked into his room when I was cleaning. He . . . Well, it was obvious Mr. Bushnell intended to take advantage of me."

Her voice started shaking, as though she hated even uttering his name out loud.

"Surely you were mistaken. Mr. Daniel Bushnell is a gentleman."

Daniel Bushnell?

Ethan jerked his head around the doorframe, but the women didn't seem to notice.

Lizbeth shook her head. He thought he could

see tears glistening in her eyes. "I know what his intentions were."

Mrs. Howard pursed her lips. "That doesn't change the fact that you ran into another man's room while it was occupied. This is a problem, Lizbeth. My husband . . . *I* can't allow it. You know what a hard time Dallas and I have making sure we have decent, reputable maids of unquestionable character. If the other women found out I let you stay after this, they would think they could do the same thing."

Lizbeth slumped. "I understand."

"Do you? I hate to do this, Lizbeth, but you are dismissed. You can stay the night, but leave in the morning."

After nodding, Lizbeth turned and walked down the hall. Her cousin stood motionless, watching her for a moment before visibly gathering herself.

Ethan fought the torrent of emotions that boiled up inside of him. Dismay that the woman could dismiss Miss Barclay so easily. Guilt that he had somehow played a part in her dismissal. But even more powerful than that was the biting feeling of anger that flowed through him.

Daniel Bushnell, his former colonel, his enemy, was here in the same hotel. Just as Mrs. Howard started following Lizbeth down the hall, he strode after her. "Give me his room number," he ordered in a fierce whisper.

44

Aileen startled and then shook her head. "I cannot give that to you, Major."

"Of course you can, and don't you start telling me about privacy or reputations. I'm not some helpless girl in need of a job."

She flushed at his jab but lifted her chin. "I don't know what you overheard, but I really do value our customers' privacy. We wouldn't have any guests if I gave out room numbers."

"You *won't* have any guests if you don't give it to me." He hardened his voice, speaking to her in a way he hadn't spoken to anyone since he was ordering troops to retreat on bloody battlefields. "I will make sure your business suffers, and don't think I don't have that amount of influence. I assure you I do."

Mrs. Howard's expression tightened. For a split second, Ethan was sure she was going to refuse, but then she exhaled. "He is in room 240," she said before turning and retreating down the hall.

Back in his room, Ethan reached for his money clip on the dresser. He stopped with his arm in midair, staring at one of his gold cufflinks.

They were a gift from his father, given to him thirteen years earlier on his eighteenth birthday. That had been years before the war. Years before he'd realized he might have grown older but had never truly grown up. It had taken his first battle to do that.

Though he and his parents had had their

share of rocky moments, he continued to wear the cufflinks out of respect for his father. To Ethan, they were a symbol of what his father had imagined he could one day be—someone of worth.

He grabbed his money clip, walked out of the room, locked the door behind him, and headed down the hall. What he was about to do might not seem like a sign of maturity to some. Perhaps others might even consider it shameful. Revenge was an ugly emotion. But at that moment, Ethan knew he had never been more sure about anything in his life. As far as he was concerned, the Lord had brought him, Miss Barclay, and Bushnell together for one reason and one reason only: for Ethan Kelly to make sure Daniel Bushnell firmly and completely regretted his actions.

For the first time in a long time, Ethan felt as though he was finally going to do something of worth. Few opportunities had ever felt as sweet.

4

"Hello, Major Kelly," Mrs. Sandler called out with a cheery smile as she approached on her husband's arm.

It was difficult, but Ethan forced himself to stop and exchange pleasantries with the esteemed couple. "Good afternoon, ma'am," he said as he offered a small bow. "You are looking as pretty as a picture." He didn't lie. Mrs. Sandler had hair the color of mink, violet eyes, and a truly beautiful smile. She also had a penchant for wearing rose-colored gowns that flattered both her skin tone and figure.

Her smile brightened. "Thank you. I hope you are doing well on this fine day."

"Better, now that I have seen you," he said with a wink.

Obviously amused by his flirtation, she turned to her husband. "Warren, you didn't tell me the major was going to be here this week."

Warren patted her gloved hand. "That's because I didn't know. Is there a tournament this week I don't know about, Kelly?"

Warren Sandler was in his early forties and an avid poker player. Ethan had spent many hours sitting at Warren's side, back when he'd spent most of his evenings in the gambling

47

establishments around town. "No, sir. I just happened to be in the area for other reasons." He didn't see the need to mention he'd returned to San Antonio only to spend a few days at the Menger before heading to his family's ranch.

"If you plan to dine at the hotel this evening, please do join us," Warren said. "You can tell us how your family is faring."

Mrs. Sadler inclined her head. "Yes, please do join us if you are able, Major Kelly."

"It would be my pleasure." He bowed again as they parted ways.

After taking a few steps down the hall, he forced himself to stop again. Seeing the Sandlers had diffused the worst of the anger that had been threatening to consume him. He'd needed to see them, he realized. They were a gentle reminder of who he was. Yes, he was a former soldier. But he was also a gentleman. Not the kind of man to race down the hall of a hotel intending to brutally harm another person in cold blood.

Not even if that person deserved it.

Feeling more himself, he exhaled and reevaluated his mission. He needed to help Lizbeth, but even if he went so far as to kill Daniel Bushnell, would it really change her life for the better? He didn't think so. But he had to do something.

Thinking again about their meeting, Ethan realized it had taken everything he had not to simply stare at her in befuddlement. After all, she was someone out of his dreams.

Even from the back, before he had any idea who she was, he could tell she was a fetching thing. Dark, curly hair. Small waist. Not too slight. Not too petite. An armful.

But then she turned around. Her eyes? Luminous and dark green. And she had that scar on her temple.

He'd been jolted by the sight.

He'd seen that scar before. It had haunted his dreams. No, she had haunted them.

When she lifted her chin, obviously waiting for him to say something more, he was without words. Not because she invaded his room. Not because of her obvious beauty. No, it had been because of that scar.

What were the chances of another woman having such a mark along her hairline? Since he dealt in odds in his current occupation, he knew there were none. She'd been the woman whose ranch they'd raided. She was the woman who had barely said two words to them. Who had shaken like a leaf whenever any of them got too close to her. Even when he'd promised, as an officer and a gentleman, that all they wanted was food and supplies.

She was starving, scared. Completely alone. He'd still ordered his men to take everything that was of use.

And they had.

And just like that, he was lost in the past. Lost, back at a small house not too far from San Antonio.

Back in the war, when he was hungry and cold.

And so desperate to help his men that he'd done many things he was ashamed of. A great many things.

Most, he'd made peace with. The war had been difficult and far more painful than any of them had anticipated. Every man he knew had been forced to take horrible steps to survive. The ones who hadn't had died.

But even though he'd done a great many things he regretted, few came as close as his trip to this woman's home with his men.

And all he could think to do to hide his dismay was to accuse her of trying to steal from him.

Now that he'd learned she was still so alone in the world, and that very afternoon had been on the run from Daniel Bushnell—a man with whom he had a long history and thoroughly despised—Ethan realized it was time to pay his debt to her.

Miss Barclay might never realize he remembered her from the war. He hoped she didn't. It would ease his conscience. He hoped she would think of him only as someone willing to help her shoulder some of her burdens. Willing to protect her. To take care of anyone who threatened her again.

Now that he realized Bushnell was the reason for her flight. And that she was going to lose her job because of his preying on her? Well, he could only believe it was a matter of divine intervention that had brought him and Bushnell once again to the same place at the same time.

It was wrong to be feeling what he did, he knew. Wrong to be looking forward to extracting vengeance.

Why, God? he asked as he started back down the narrow passageway wallpapered with busy designs and adorned with rather uninteresting charcoal drawings of plants and animals. Why have you decided to bring us all together again?

Ethan hadn't thought of Colonel Daniel Bushnell in years. Ethan had been one of the many men who'd served under him. Frankly, if Ethan had spared him a thought, he would have assumed Bushnell had gone back to his mistress and his wife and continued to manipulate and use as many people as possible for his own selfish gains. After all, that was what he'd been so very good at.

But maybe he had been just as human as the rest of them. A lot of men had problems adjusting to life after the war and months in a prison camp. That was one of the reasons he, Captain Monroe, Lieutenant Truax, and Baker had vowed to look out for each other. A new lawlessness existed in men's hearts after the war. It was as if they were unable to give up their worst influences.

Many couldn't. After returning home and finding either their plantations or homes ruined or in pieces of rubble, they'd been at a loss for what to do. Then had come the punishment the union waged during Reconstruction. It ate upon their souls.

But now that he realized a man he loathed had accosted Miss Barclay here in the hotel, Ethan knew he owed it to her to warn him to stay away from her in the future. He hadn't been able to do anything except hurt her when he and his men had shown up at her house that day. Now, at last, he could make amends. He was determined to be her hero, even though it made no sense. He wanted retribution, and he was eager to get it. At any cost.

Situations like this—such that it was—were why he missed the army so much. In the army, there was a distinct order. His rank mattered. His disapproval mattered. Furthermore, dozens—if not scores—of men had been all too willing to do what he desired.

But this? Trying to help a gentlewoman like Miss Lizbeth Barclay? Well, that was dangerous.

Women like her made him yearn for things he'd already come to terms with never having. Like goodness and a home. Those were what he'd dreamed of and planned to have with Faye, his longtime sweetheart. But she'd grown lonely during the war and found someone else while he was in that prison camp. It seemed even majors lost some of their shine when they were reduced to mere prisoners.

That was yet another reason he yearned to do some kind of physical harm to an intangible object.

Glad he'd made Aileen Howard tell him the room number, he strode down the hall and rapped twice on Bushnell's door. He felt a pleased appreciation when it swung open immediately.

It took only seconds, but that was long enough for Bushnell to erase the shock that appeared on his face when he recognized him. "Kelly."

Ethan was thrust back in time. Back to his captivity on Johnson's Island. To Bushnell's arrival after Ethan had already been living on the premises for two months. To the man interfering with most everything Captain Monroe had put into place.

Time had not been kind to the other man. The small pox scars on his cheeks had turned red and become more pronounced. The skin on his face and neck seemed loose, whether from hard living or some kind of sickness. He also seemed to have shrunk in size. Ethan wondered if that was indeed true, or if he'd merely shrunk in importance to him.

It was obvious that Ethan's appearance caught

him off guard, but he recovered quickly. "Is it really you?"

"It was Major Kelly last time we saw each other."

"The war is over. Like in the camp, appellations don't matter much now." He raised one eyebrow. "Or do they?"

"They mattered at one time. Maybe more than I realized."

Bushnell shook his head. "It was men like me who saved the high and mighty generals from getting their hands dirty. Even your friend General McCoy."

"I never heard wind of you after we were released."

"I did what you did, I reckon. I attempted to put my life back together. I went back to Boerne."

"Ah. Yes. You had a ladybird there." Bushnell had often bragged of her beauty.

"Julianne? I did have her for a time, even after the war ended." He grunted. "But then I got rid of her, of course. I couldn't chance my wife's family discovering her, you know. After I paid her off, I went home to Fredericksburg."

"Where your wife and children live."

"Well, they did." He frowned. "My wife and son have since died, and my daughter married a blasted Yankee and moved up to Philadelphia."

"That's a pity."

"Indeed, it is." He cleared his throat. "Is there a

reason we are standing here in the Menger Hotel reviewing my life? As you must surmise, I am finding it rather tiresome."

And just like that, all the patience Ethan had hoped to adopt after meeting the Sandlers dissipated like a morning fog. He loathed this man, loathed everything about him—including the fact he had preyed on a woman who had already been through far too much.

"There is a reason," he said softly. "But I wanted to know what had become of you before I say my piece."

"I doubt I will care to hear anything you have to say."

"While that is probably true, what you want matters little to me."

"You sound so sanctimonious. Don't tell me you're going to start casting stones. You might act like you are a self-made man, but we both know you built yourself around the comfort of your circumstances. Few men can boast of such privilege."

Bushnell's words were harsh, but they were also true. Ethan was from a wealthy, old, well-connected family. Their influence was far-reaching, and their holdings were substantial. He'd never been ashamed of that. But at the beginning of the war, his relationships with his family had been strained. His father had wanted him to dodge the war. To stay back and let other men put their lives on the line for their homes and convictions. His brother, Phillip, had agreed, convinced some of the young men were needed at home to protect the women and help manage family holdings. But Ethan had refused. On the night before he left, both he and his father had said a great many things they later regretted.

But as the war wore on, as he witnessed far too many good men suffer painful deaths, Ethan was privately glad both his father and his brother were safe at home. And in their letters, both his parents shared how proud they were of him. Their letters, so full of hope and home, had helped him survive his life on Johnson's Island.

Bushnell cleared his throat, bringing Ethan back to the present. "So, say your piece, Kelly. Do it quickly now, before I slam my door in your face."

"All right, then. It has come to my attention that you accosted a woman just minutes ago."

"Is that right?" He looked amused. Leaving Ethan still standing in the hallway, he walked to a pack on his desk, pulled out a cigar, and lazily lit it with a match. As he puffed, smoke plumed from his mouth, spiraling toward the high ceiling in a lazy motion.

With another man, Ethan might have been irritated. But this small action showed that Bushnell, for all his bluster, was thrown. During the war, the man had always lit his tobacco whenever he was worried or uneasy.

Leaning against the doorframe, Ethan said, "We aren't going to play this game, are we? You know what I'm talking about."

"Do I?" Bushnell said around a smoke-filled exhale. "At the moment I don't know which woman you are referring to."

Only with the greatest effort did Ethan resist pummeling the man's face. "I am speaking of the maid you were dallying with. The maid with the dark curly hair."

He chuckled. "Ah, yes. I remember now. What of her? She is only a maid. No one of importance. Certainly no one to concern yourself about."

Bushnell's haughty manner was almost believable. Almost. His eyes gave his real thoughts away, however. They were lit with a new light that said volumes about his character. He enjoyed the game. He enjoyed both toying with helpless women like Miss Barclay and matching wits with men like him.

"Don't push me."

"Don't accuse me of things I didn't do."

Stepping into the room uninvited and striding across it, Ethan finally did what he'd been itching to do from the moment Bushnell opened the door. He grabbed him by the collar. "You attempted to violate her."

"She might have believed that. However, I did not."

"Don't lie, Daniel," he said, tightening his hold on the man's collar, nearly choking him.

To Ethan's dismay, Bushnell started laughing. "Now I understand. You aren't upset that I was dabbling with a maid, are you? You are concerned because you have feelings for her! For a maid! What is your family going to say, Kelly? Surely even they don't believe you've fallen this far from society."

"Leave my family out of this."

"You want to pretend you're suddenly just like the rest of us, bowing and scraping to get what we want and need? Well, so be it. If you want to lower yourself to fawn over a chambermaid, it ain't no business of mine." He smirked. "Just let me know when you tire of her. She might be scarred, but that won't hardly matter in the dark."

Finally, the moment he had been hoping for. He slammed his fist into the man's jaw and felt a glimmer of satisfaction rip through him as Bushnell fell to the ground with a *thump*.

Standing over him, Ethan stared at the man's face. When his eyes opened, Ethan bent slightly forward. "She is now under my protection. Do you understand?"

Bushnell's eyes narrowed and a look of extreme distaste passed through his expression before he spoke. "I understand perfectly."

Ethan was still shaking with fury when he slammed the door behind him and stood rooted in the hall.

He'd just made more of an enemy out of Bushnell. If he knew anything, it was that Bushnell wasn't going to take Ethan's assault and threat lightly. He would retaliate.

And though Ethan would have been happy never to see that man again, he now knew that wasn't an option. He would take out his retaliation on Miss Barclay because he knew hurting her would hurt Ethan too.

He needed to protect her. He also needed to discover everything Bushnell had done since the war and ascertain what his plans were for the future. He could use that to his advantage and hold it over the man. Only then would he be able to keep Lizbeth safe.

He had some choices. He could investigate him alone. He could also reach out to his brother and father. They would help him if he asked.

Or he could rely on his band of brothers, the men he knew best and knew would always have his back, no matter what the cost.

In the end, it wasn't really much of a decision. He needed to be available to Lizbeth, so he couldn't leave her alone for long periods of time. His family, while influential and powerful, would expect him to finally move back home and help run the family ranch and assorted holdings.

He'd been planning to visit them in a few days to face that reality, but he wasn't going to return for good.

He'd been putting off the inevitable since he'd returned from Johnson's Island. He hadn't been in any shape to be around people in polite society. Instead, he'd been hovering on the fringes of that society. The easy laughter and high-stakes gambling he'd found in numerous establishments around the state had been far easier to deal with. All anyone had wanted there was his money.

But he'd also been able to help the friends with whom he'd been imprisoned when they called, and now he was the one who needed help.

He decided to ride out to visit Captain Devin Monroe as soon as he could. Devin was a man of honor, thoughtful and clear-headed. He also would understand Ethan's feelings about owing such a debt.

Looking around him in the empty hallway of the second floor of the Menger Hotel, Ethan realized his own head felt clearer than it had in months.

Maybe even years.

At last, justice would be served.

5

He was too old for this.

Standing outside Julianne Van Fleet's plain but neat and well-tended home, Devin Monroe felt as though his shirt was too tight, his feet were too big, and his bearing was too hard. Nothing about him was kind or relaxed. Nothing about him was comfortable or easy.

This was a problem.

He didn't know the first thing about courting a gentlewoman like Miss Van Fleet. Actually, he didn't know much about courting women at all. He'd spent the majority of his life in the company of rough soldiers. During most of the war, he'd been a captain, and that rank had fit him like a glove.

He knew how to take orders, and he knew how to manage enlisted men. He knew what to say to push men onward and what to do when he needed them to come to heel. He had been comfortable in the army. He'd instinctively known when to speak and when to stay silent. He'd been respected. Confident. Content.

But he knew next to nothing about talking with women, and even less when it came to knocking on the door of a lady's home. Chances were better than good that he would offend Miss

Van Fleet within ten minutes of stepping foot in her parlor.

Turning away from her front door, he studied the other ten or so houses on her street. Each was one story, constructed of limestone and wood, and boasted wide front porches. The yards were carefully tended, and the gravel drives were neatly edged. It was a pretty place. Quiet. Perfect for a lady like her, but confusing for a man who was still getting used to a life out of the military.

Unease crept along his spine. He shouldn't have come. Why had he, anyway?

He knew the answer as sure as if he'd been leading a regiment of soldiers across a war-torn battlefield and his lieutenant wasn't sure whether to surge forward or retreat.

He was on Julianne Van Fleet's front porch because she was the first woman in his memory whom he'd wanted to know. Even after growing up the prized oldest son of two very ordinary people and living next to another ranch where a young lady had made no secret of her desire to be his wife. Despite his mother introducing him to every one of her friends' daughters by the time he was seventeen.

Even after all the cotillions and dances and officers' balls he'd attended, where lines of lovely women in white dresses had looked at his chest of medals with stars in their eyes. He had appreciated their beauty, but not a one had made a lasting impression.

Neither had the women he'd spent time with after his release from Johnson's Island.

He'd begun to think love and romance weren't meant for men like him. He'd killed and hurt and bled too much to even know how to be suitable company for a gently bred woman.

Then one day Miss Van Fleet appeared in his life unexpectedly. He first spied her when he was traveling to San Antonio to visit his friend and former comrade Ethan Kelly. Devin had stopped to water his horse in Boerne, and then decided to take a stroll around the sleepy little town to grab something to eat and give his horse a rest.

The action had been nothing out of the ordinary. He'd done much the same thing more times than he could count. But on that day, in that moment, everything changed.

After hitching his gelding, he walked through the town square, intending to get a dish at the local boarding house, assessing the area, as was his habit. He'd seen the courthouse. The saloon. Mercantile. A couple of men about his age lounging against the side of the bank, smoking. A mother with her brood of children. And one lady walking by herself just across the way.

She was striking. Wearing a well-fitted navy-blue gown that accentuated a nipped-in waist and an hourglass figure. Her features revealed she was likely close to his age of thirty. She was at least five feet seven and had been blessed with auburn hair and a heart-shaped face. She wasn't merely pretty. She was beautiful.

But he'd seen many beautiful women before.

Then she looked up. And he? Well, he'd been caught in that gaze.

Later he would recall other details about her. She'd worn an attractive hat festooned with ribbons. She'd been walking a dog. A book was in her other hand, and a patterned shawl was draped around her slim shoulders.

She'd been so quiet and gentle-looking. Sweet. Peaceful.

He hadn't been able to look away. She was everything he ever envisioned when he laid in too-small cots during the war. There was something about her that he wanted to get to know, if only for a little while.

He'd realized it was time. Time to stop living alone, living only for others. For most of his life, he'd done that. From his days with the Texas Rangers to the years in battle and the months in prison camp, he'd survived by putting his needs last. After what God wanted him to do. After what the Confederacy ordered him to do. After what his men needed him to do. It was time to be selfish and concentrate on his own wants, needs, and hopes.

And even though he wasn't altogether sure

what all those things were, he'd acted on his impulse.

In short order, he crossed the street and somehow managed to introduce himself and strike up a conversation with her outside the mercantile. They had talked about nothing, really. Her dog. The weather. She'd been a little shy, easing his own nervousness.

But every word she said had imprinted on his brain. And her voice, her sweetly melodic voice—it rang in his ears like church bells. She laughed at her dog's antics and looked directly at him when he spoke. She didn't simper or flirt or giggle.

He'd been charmed.

Knowing she most likely didn't want to stand talking to him outside the mercantile long, and because he still had obligations to attend to, he said good-bye to her and Boerne and went on his way. But from the moment he left her side he felt her loss. Before he was even halfway to San Antonio, he was making plans to see her again.

The second and third time he sought her out, she smiled. Once, he stood with her a full five minutes talking about Ginger, her spry little beagle. She laughed when Ginger ignored his command to sit.

Amazingly, he laughed too.

Those few encounters had brought him to this

moment. To finally behave like a gentleman instead of a war-torn, washed-up soldier.

He just wished he didn't feel more nervous than he ever had in battle. Maybe it was because he'd never feared death, but he did fear her rejection.

When a couple walking down the street gazed at him curiously, the man going as far as to stop and size him up, Devin knew he no longer had a choice. He needed to knock on Miss Van Fleet's door or he'd cause talk, standing outside her door like he was. He couldn't do that. The clerk at the mercantile had already looked at him strangely when he asked for directions to this very house.

Spurred on by that thought, he rested his left arm across the middle of his lower back, stood at attention, and rapped twice on her door with his right hand.

It opened before a full minute passed.

"Captain Monroe," she said in that quiet, melodic voice of hers. "Hello!"

He bowed formally from his waist. "Miss Van Fleet. Good afternoon."

Her eyes widened. She belatedly gave a little curtsy. Pressed her hand to her sternum. "What a nice surprise."

He smiled. Then realized something important had just happened. She didn't step backward to allow him entrance. Instead, she was looking at him curiously.

She didn't understand he'd come calling. How could that be? His aunt had given him specific instructions about the correct time to call on a young lady when he wrote to her for advice. Had she been mistaken?

His palms grew damp.

"Miss Van Fleet, I was just in the area—" No, he wasn't going to lie. Looking at her directly in the eye so he could view every nuance that passed over her expression, he cleared his throat. "The truth is I wasn't just in the area. The truth is I've come calling . . ."

Her eyes widened again, and her lips formed a perfect O. Yet she still didn't move.

This visit was not going according to plan. He should have done some reconnaissance. He should have asked more questions about courting from the men he counted as friends, no matter how much he feared their ridicule. Perhaps his aunt's directives had been antiquated. The men, once they finished laughing at his ignorance, would have gladly advised him about the appropriate way to behave.

But since it was too late for that, he had to make do with standing on her doorstep, sweating as the November sun beat on his back, and fumbling for the right words to say.

Miss Van Fleet was staring at him closely. "Calling . . . ?" she prodded.

He realized then that he'd stopped speaking

midsentence. "Yes. Calling." He cleared his throat. "For you."

All at once, amusement entered her expression. She smiled. Stepping back, she opened the door farther. "Captain Monroe, as I said before, this is such a nice surprise. Won't you please come in?"

Barely stopping himself from thanking her for allowing him entrance, Devin entered her home with a profound sense of accomplishment. While she took a moment to rearrange the skirts of her dark rose-colored gown, he took the liberty of closing the front door. As it clicked shut with a healthy *snap,* he looked around with interest.

The entryway was very small. Almost immediately upon them was a sitting room with two well-made chairs upholstered in light-blue velvet.

As Julianne guided him inside, he noticed a small desk, a matching sofa, and two other tables, each next to the padded chairs. A fine-looking lamp with a glass globe was near one of the chairs. As was a book . . . and spectacles.

She wore glasses.

"Would you like to sit with me?" she asked. "I had just come in here. I was reading." She sat down in one of the chairs.

"So I see." Holding his hat in his hands, he sat down in the space she gestured to, the chair across from hers. "You wear glasses."

She tensed before nodding. "I do. Well, I

do to read. You have uncovered my secret, Captain." She smiled, but it was obvious she was embarrassed.

He wasn't sure why. Growing tired of his ignorance, he decided to take the topic on. "Forgive me. I know a lot about ordering men about, but far too little about polite conversation. Were those spectacles something I wasn't supposed to mention? I promise I don't think they are a detraction. Quite the opposite."

"My mother used to ask me never to mention such things, but that was a lifetime ago." Rubbing her temples, she shook her head. "To be honest, I'm not even sure if I'm supposed to hide my imperfection anymore or not. We all have far too many other worries about now, I fear."

"At the risk of sounding boorish, I have to admit I am rather relieved you wear glasses. I kind of like knowing you are not completely perfect."

Her eyes widened once more. "I am certainly not that."

Just so she wouldn't think he was full of himself, he winked. "Neither am I."

Something new flickered in her eyes before she firmly tamped it down, and she stood. "Forgive me my rag manners. May I offer you some refreshment? Bula, my day maid, is in the kitchen."

He was too afraid he would either spill tea on

her furniture or ask for the wrong thing. "No, thank you."

"No? Well, all right." She sat back down. Folded her hands in her lap. Thirty seconds passed. Forty.

He started to wish he would have swallowed his pride and at least asked Ethan Kelly for advice. He was a man who always knew the right thing to say and do, at least in the company of women. Kelly's advice would have come in very handy right about then.

6

As Julianne sat composedly across from him, her pretty blue eyes patiently awaiting his next comment or question, Devin's uneasiness increased.

His mouth went dry as he attempted to think of something to say. Unfortunately, he couldn't think of a single thing of worth. He should have planned. He should have made notes. Made stratagems. Considered possible outcomes. Honestly, he never got out of bed without a detailed list of goals and possible outcomes. How could he have just taken a bath, put on clean clothes, and appeared on her porch without any more forethought?

She laughed.

He focused on her again. "Am I amusing you, miss?"

"Honestly? Yes."

All thought drained from his head as he stared at her. "Have I just committed another faux pas I wasn't aware of?"

She laughed harder. "No, Captain. I was just thinking that we are two peas in a pod, aren't we? I'm so unused to having gentlemen callers. I have no idea what to say or do . . . while you are obviously out of your element as well."

Though his cheeks and neck were no doubt turning bright red, he said, "I cannot deny my inexperience."

"A man of worth like you?"

"Like me?"

"Well, yes. After we first spoke at the mercantile, I did a little bit of checking on you. It seems you have quite the reputation, sir."

"I find that hard to believe."

"You shouldn't doubt it, sir. It seems just about everyone in these parts has heard of the illustrious Captain Monroe."

"I'm surprised."

"You shouldn't be, Captain," she said as her beagle meandered in and positioned herself under his right hand. "The stories shared describe a man of great bravery and honor."

He rubbed the soft fur in between Ginger's ears. "Such talk about a common captain seems excessive."

"I would agree, except the stories were impressive. Your reputation has preceded you, sir."

The last thing he wanted to talk about was himself. "I wouldn't believe everything you hear, miss. It's all in the past anyway."

Gazing at him with a warm look, she continued. "So even though exaggerated tales bursting about your greatness on the battlefield abound, you have not gone courting much?"

"That is true. During the war I fear I was always otherwise occupied with survival. But I must confess that I'm surprised about your lack of callers. I expected to be one of many gentlemen here today."

She shook her head. "That is not the case." Quietly she added, "You could probably tell in our earlier encounters, but I have the dubious honor of being both shy and bookish."

"It's my reward, then."

Her eyes lit up as she pursed her lips. "Captain, I'd love to know more about you. From where do you hail?"

"I grew up south of Dallas. When I got to my majority, I joined the Texas Rangers and served all over the state."

"What about your family?"

"My family?" He drew a blank.

"Yes. Were you close to your parents? Do you have siblings? Did you ever shirk your chores?"

"Shirk my chores?" He couldn't hide the incredulousness in his voice. When he spied the humor in her eyes, he laughed sheepishly. "Are you teasing me, Miss Van Fleet?"

"Only seeking to know you better."

"In that case I should tell you I had a happy childhood. My father was the foreman of a large operation. I grew up learning to mind my mother and guide my two younger brothers, and wanting to do whatever my father asked me to do at the Diamond P Ranch."

"You loved him very much."

"I did. My world was small. I loved my parents, thought every child feasted on warm buttermilk biscuits every morning, and was sure the most powerful man in the state was Mr. Pennington, the owner of the ranch." When her gaze softened even more, he felt himself relax against the cushions of the chair. "I don't remember the last time I thought about those days. About how idyllic my childhood was."

"You didn't want to return to Dallas? Boerne seems awfully far away, both in size and consequence."

"It is. But not only do I currently live near San Antonio, not here in Boerne, I have no reason to go back. My family . . ." He paused, surprised that after all this time, speaking of them still brought pain. "They are all gone."

"All?"

He nodded. "My father signed up to fight even before Texas followed Jefferson Davis. My brothers, Colin and Will, perished at Antietam."

"And your mother?"

"Yellow fever."

"And Mr. Pennington?"

"You know what? I haven't thought about him in years." He rubbed a hand along his jaw, wondering how he could have forgotten about the fine man who had done so right by his family. "I hope he did survive. That would be a blessing."

"I hope he survived for you too."

Devin wasn't sure how to respond to that. Her compassion was unfamiliar and stirred him in ways he hadn't expected. It also made him uncomfortable. "How about you?"

"Me? I have no exciting tales or experiences to regale you with."

"You might be surprised by what I find interesting."

She smiled, charming him. "Not all of us can be heroes, I'm afraid. I've lived all my life in Boerne," she said, running her hand against the smooth grain of the table next to her.

"So you grew up around here."

Her smile brightened. "I grew up in this very house."

"Is that right?" He surveyed the room, looking a little bit harder for signs of other inhabitants. "Who lives with you now?"

"No one."

He stilled. "No one. You lost everyone as well?" For some reason he didn't want to think of her suffering the same losses he had.

"Oh, no, Captain Monroe." Her pretty smile turned brittle. "My sister married, and then my mother moved in with her and her family. In Amarillo."

Obviously there was a story there. But what

kind of story was it? He debated, curious as to why she had stayed while everyone else left.

It seemed odd and vaguely alarming. Women of good breeding didn't live by themselves. It was also too expensive for them to do so. Especially in these lean days after the war.

Was she that wealthy?

The house, while not terribly large, was finely appointed and well cared for. Her gown, while not all that fancy, was of obvious quality. She looked fresh and well rested. Healthy.

But if she was that wealthy, why wasn't she living in one of the bigger cities? A beauty such as hers would always attract a following. She could have had her choice of suitors.

A new wariness entered her eyes. "It's good you were a soldier, Captain, and not a poker player."

"Is my expression that transparent?"

"I'm afraid so. I can practically see the wheels turning in your brain. You are wondering about my circumstances."

He didn't bother to deny it. "Yes. Even though it is none of my business, I must admit I am curious."

"You deserve an explanation. But, before I give it, I want to thank you for this."

"For what?"

She waved a hand in the air, somehow managing to encircle the entire room. "For being so attentive and gentlemanly. For calling on me. It has been flattering."

He wanted to smile, to say she was finding worth in something that shouldn't be out of the ordinary for her.

He certainly couldn't relay that he'd waited his whole life to come calling on her. He didn't know much about courting, but he knew enough to sense that such . . . well, enthusiastic devotion was unseemly.

He made do with reassuring her. That was something he knew how to do. Not all men who fought were gifted soldiers. The majority were clumsy in battle and unsure of themselves. Or lonely. Or afraid. He'd spent more hours than he could count reassuring men of their worth. "Miss Van Fleet, though I don't have a great deal of experience with women, I am no stranger to life. I can't imagine taking exception with anything you could tell me."

"I hope that is indeed the case, but I have my doubts."

Instead of responding, he leaned back against his chair and folded his hands on his lap. And waited.

Looking pained, she started speaking. "During the height of the war, around '63 or so, my circumstances were far different from what they are now. I was hungry, so very cold, and out of options."

He was stunned.

"Were you alone?"

"Almost. My grandmother lived with me."

"What of your parents?"

"My father had already died in the war. My sister married days before her husband left to fight. Weeks later, she discovered she was with child. It was a difficult pregnancy. That's when my mother went to live with her."

"Leaving you responsible for yourself, the house, and your grandmother."

"Yes." She swallowed. "It was very . . . challenging."

"I imagine so."

"My grandmother was ill. In fact, she was wasting away because we had so little food. I asked my mother for help, but for one reason or another she never had funds to spare. That was when I knew I had to do whatever I could." Looking more agitated, she averted her eyes. "One reason I was alone, I'm afraid, is that I hadn't quite grown into my looks. That, along with my shyness and bookish nature, made me something of an oddity on the marriage market. I didn't take."

"Men don't always see what is right in front of them."

Instead of smiling, she cleared her throat. "Eventually I did grow into my features, and I learned to keep my glasses hidden. That seemed to help." She took a breath. "Anyway, when some of the young women I knew confided they were going to travel to San Antonio to attend an officers' ball in the hopes of making a match, I thought maybe I would do that too."

"So you did?"

She nodded. "I . . . well, I couldn't think of any other option. A friend offered to stay with my grandmother. I put on my best dress, went with those girls, and made sure I outshone them all."

"And did it work?"

Eyes still shadowed, she nodded again. "At first my social graces weren't much different from what they'd always been. I fumbled through conversations and stumbled through dances. But then I met a man who seemed different. He didn't seem to care that I loved books or that I didn't know how to flirt or be especially charming. He didn't even seem to care that I wasn't wealthy. He wasn't very handsome, but I didn't mind. I was sure I had met the perfect man for me."

"Ah." She'd been married. He relaxed. That was her secret? He hadn't known she was a widow, but the mystery officer asking for her hand made perfect sense. She was exactly the type of woman he would have wanted to marry quickly, and many, many men had done the same thing.

"You shouldn't be embarrassed about that, Miss—or should I say Mrs. Van Fleet? Women need protectors and men need to protect. I'm sure your husband was thankful to have someone to think about when he was far away from home, and you needed someone. All I can say is he was a lucky man."

Chewing on her bottom lip, she shook her head. "No, I'm afraid it wasn't quite like that, Captain. This man called on me several times. He was everything proper and very wealthy. Each time he visited he brought gifts for both me and my grandmother. I was sure I was in love." Her hands clenched. She cleared her throat once more. "I thought he was going to propose, you see."

His mouth went dry. What was she about to tell him? "He did not?"

"Oh, no. He admitted he was already married."

Devin was shocked by what an officer had done to her. "What a scoundrel. I'm sure you were devastated."

"Yes, I was. I was ruined, you see . . ."

He shook his head. "Miss Van Fleet—"

"This is very hard. I need to finish, please." Gazing at a point just beyond him, she said quietly, "One evening he said he was joining his regiment the very next morning. Still thinking he was going to ask me to be his wife before his departure, I let him . . . spend the night. It wasn't until the next morning I learned he was married, and that he wasn't going to his regiment for a week. I was upset and desperate, and this man, this colonel . . . well, he knew it. He did make me an offer, but it wasn't to be his wife."

He knew he shouldn't ask. He knew he shouldn't make her say it. But he wanted to be clear about what she was saying. Just in case he had misunderstood. "Miss?" Was his voice as hoarse as he feared it sounded?

She raised her head and looked him directly in the eye. But whereas before there was light in her expression, nothing remained but flat resignation. "You didn't misinterpret what I said, sir. Daniel Bushnell asked me to become his mistress. And though I no longer had stars in my eyes where he was concerned, I knew I had little choice in the matter. I said yes."

His body protested each word she said. "You were Colonel Bushnell's mistress?" he said slowly. She'd belonged to Bushnell. One of the slickest, most corrupt officers he'd ever had the misfortune to know.

Pain entered her eyes. "I was. I felt I had no choice. My financial situation was dire. My grandmother and I were literally starving. I had to do something."

"And that was all you could think of?" he asked, his voice harsh. Scathing.

She drew back. "I had no other options, sir."

"Really? Or did you not want to be patient? I imagine many a man would have come up to heel in a few months."

"That wasn't going to happen. No other man had shown any interest in me, and as I told you, we were already starving. And now I was ruined." She shrugged. "I don't suppose it really matters. I entered an agreement with him that morning."

"You agreed to continue to lie with him for money." He didn't bother to hide the disdain in his voice.

"Yes." Her face was a mask of control now. "He said he'd married young, and neither he nor his wife was happy. He was determined to find happiness elsewhere."

"And you believed him?"

She lifted her chin. "Do you want the truth, Captain? The truth is no, I didn't believe him. I thought he'd lied to me, taken advantage of me, ruined my innocence, and erased the dreams I'd had. But I had no choice."

"What about your grandmother? What about your mother? Your sister? Surely they advised you against it."

"My grandmother was happy to have food and firewood. I don't know if she even realized how it had all come to be. If she did? Well, she pretended she didn't understand. When he was here that night, she was already fading . . ."

Pain flickered in her eyes. It was obvious she was hurt that he was forcing her to talk more about this. "At first my mother said she understood. Eventually, though, my reputation became too much for her to bear. I don't know what she told my sister, but I stopped hearing from both of them. I only know they are well through a friend."

"Yet you continued that alliance."

"It was a great many things, sir, but an alliance it was not."

"Perhaps it was more of a *dalliance,* instead," he said before he thought better of it.

"Well, I lived here, kept this home afloat, and opened the doors to the colonel whenever he came." Her voice softened. "With that money, and because that money allowed me to engage Bula, I was able to care for my grandmother until she died, and pay for her funeral as well."

He knew he was being judgmental. He knew sharing this wasn't easy for her to do. She could have simply turned him away at her door or kept up a pretense. Yet she'd elected to tell him her true standing.

He should leave, but he couldn't seem to stop himself from prying even further. "Are you still Bushnell's kept woman?"

She looked surprised. "I am not."

"What happened?" he asked, hating that he even cared.

"Eventually the war ended. He, of course, went back to his wife." She looked out the window. "Or maybe he found someone new. A woman younger."

"So he was the one who ended it."

"I'm not sure if that is always the case, but yes, Captain, in my case, that is how my 'association' with this man ended. He gave me an envelope of money and told me he would not be back." She sighed and at last looked at him again. "I used part of it to buy sewing supplies and started making clothes for some women in the area to support myself and keep this house in good repair. Even if more women had been able to afford new clothes during the war, I couldn't sew when my time and energy were reserved for caring for my grandmother. The rest I put away for safekeeping." She sat back in her chair. "So that is how I came to be living here on my own."

"Does anyone even associate with you? Beyond your sewing customers?"

She paused, as if she was attempting to regain her composure. When she spoke, her voice was arched. "What do you think, Captain?"

It all made sense now. Why he'd only seen her walking alone, never with other women or companions. The reason she had no other callers and was surprised to see him at her door.

She was nothing like the gentle lady he had imagined. She was used. She had traded in both her respect and her reputation. She said her circumstances had been dire, that she'd only been trying to survive. But was that true? Had Miss

Van Fleet simply wanted more comfort while the South was at war?

Suddenly realizing he was sitting in the chair Bushnell had no doubt occupied many times, Devin sprang to his feet.

She watched him with wide eyes.

"I knew Colonel Bushnell," he said coldly.

With great deliberation, she stood as well. "Then you know what Daniel was like."

"I know the type of man he was. I not only served under him during the height of the war, but we were interred in the officers' prison camp on Johnson's Island together."

Surprise flickered in her eyes. "He hated that camp so much."

"I'm sure he did. I certainly hated being stuck there with him." With far too many memories of the man fresh in his mind, he continued. "He was the worst sort of man. Entitled. Lazy. Mercurial." He could have gone on and on. Described how he'd used people to his benefit. How he was sure the man would have sacrificed his own mother if it would have benefited him.

Julianne looked shaken, but she didn't dispute his words. "So you did know him," she said softly.

"You knew these things too? You knew these things and still allowed him . . ." He couldn't even finish his statement.

She reached out a hand and gripped the edge

of the chair behind her. Only then did she sit back down. "I came to know more about Bushnell's ways than either of us would care to discuss. Good day, Captain Monroe," she said after she arranged her skirts. "I trust you can see yourself out."

Indeed, he could. He turned on his heel and strode out of the room. He was shutting her front door firmly behind him mere seconds later.

Heading toward his horse, sharp indignation flew through him. After waiting for most of his life to find a prospective bride, he'd centered on the most unsuitable woman.

What a fool he'd been!

He had devoted so much time to her. He'd dreamed about her. Imagined how pure and sweet she was. Had concocted a story in his head about how she'd been waiting for him too. How he hadn't been the only person to believe in fate and the value of patience.

He couldn't have been more wrong.

This is nothing you don't deserve, Devin, he told himself. You ignored scores of perfectly lovely women, sure that none of them was the right match. And because of that, you've lived alone, only taking comfort in dreams. You should have dreamed less and lived more.

Mounting his horse, Midge, he rode off her street, out of her town. Determined never to return.

He only hoped he could forget Julianne Van Fleet just as quickly.

But just like the worst moments on the battlefield, he had a feeling the moments in her company would be forever seared into his brain. A constant reminder of his faults and the danger in believing in dreams.

7

Julianne was alone in her house once again. Nothing she wasn't used to.

So why did she feel so lonely?

Her breath caught in her throat as she stared into the entryway, at the door that had just closed in her face. It wasn't a surprise, but it still felt like one.

It had been two years since she'd seen Daniel. Two years of blissful freedom.

Contrary to how Devin obviously viewed it, she most definitely had not entered into her arrangement with him lightly. It had been exactly as she'd told the captain—a decision born out of fear and hunger and a willingness to do whatever it took to survive.

Though it hadn't been what she wanted, she knew women who had suffered far greater pain and injury than she had, especially since she hadn't seen Daniel all that much.

After entering their agreement, he'd gone back to his regiment, returning to her only a few times. He spent most of the next two years in battle, and then in his confinement on Johnson's Island.

When he was gone, she didn't have to endure his abuse.

And she'd tried to make him out to be better

than he was. She wanted to believe he was a brave man, responsible for hundreds, if not thousands of men. He'd been captured and then fought for survival while in the hands of the enemy. He deserved her loyalty, didn't he? Especially since all he asked of her during his absences was correspondence.

She wrote to him. Dutifully, twice a week. Tried to think of entertaining stories about her days, most of which were greatly exaggerated. When he wrote her back and asked if she missed him, if she longed for him, it was easy to lie and say she did. After all, it was because of his funds that she hadn't starved.

However, she learned something about survival. She learned there was a great variance between being respected and being shunned. As word of her arrangement became public knowledge in Boerne, people of good faith began to avoid her. Eventually decent women wouldn't even look her in the eye. She didn't blame them. After all, there had been a time when she would have treated someone like her the same way.

After her grandmother died and she could leave home more often, the minister still permitted her in church. But she felt his disapproval. Once, she was fairly sure she was the subject of his sermon.

It had been hard. At first she'd been bitter. But then, as the months passed, she decided she needed to do something besides sit by herself in her home. She took some of Bushnell's money, bought chickens and seeds, and planted a large garden. Worked on it painstakingly. Then shared as much of her bounty as she could with anyone else in need. She'd volunteered at the hospital, working with injured soldiers.

By the end of the war, she had no friends, exactly. But she wasn't nearly the pariah she'd been before. She could go to the mercantile for supplies easily enough. Even sit in the back of the church without others turning to stare.

She almost—*almost*—pretended she was respectable again.

Then he came back.

She still felt sick when she remembered how awful he looked. He was so terribly thin. His skin sallow, two of his teeth rotten. And he wanted . . . well, what he came for.

She'd had no choice but to give him that. For one week.

He'd been rough—more than before. He'd hurt her. Scared her. At times he was cruel.

War had changed him, from bad to worse. And by the time he was finished with her, bruised and pale—desolate—she realized she'd been a fool to think accepting that arrangement had been right.

No, it had been everything wrong.

She'd prayed for his abuse to stop. Prayed for any kind of relief. Then, miraculously, her prayers were answered. He told her he had no use for her anymore. He gave her an envelope of money, said he was returning to his wife, and left. She was free.

She didn't know where he was now, and she didn't care. All she had known for some time was that she didn't need much to survive. Until today, when she'd been almost courted by Captain Devin Monroe. That was when she realized she couldn't have been more wrong. She needed peace and acceptance and happiness. But those things were going to once again be out of her precious grasp. There was nothing she could do about it either.

She never thought her future would be so cruel.

Late the next morning Julianne forced herself to get up and perform her usual preparations. She looked in the mirror and tried to care about the smudges under her eyes and the lines of strain around her lips.

After brushing her hair a hundred times like her mother had long ago taught her, she pinned it up, slipped on a warm dress made of blackberry-colored soft wool that she'd made two months earlier, and then put on her cloak. She needed to get out of her house. More importantly, she needed to banish Devin Monroe and the silly, girlish dreams he'd brought out in her from her mind. He wasn't going to come back, and he wasn't going to change his mind about her.

The longer she dwelled on what she couldn't change, the more depressed she'd be. Deciding that her walk was as much for her well-being as anything else, she left a note for Bula, who was out shopping. Then she set off toward Boerne's only diner for an early lunch. After all, she hadn't had any breakfast.

The temperature had dropped overnight, and the cold had made the dirt roads hard and the air crisp. It felt exhilarating, and it improved her mood and outlook. She hoped her brisk pace combined with the cool air brought some needed color to her cheeks.

As she walked the few short blocks to the town square, several people nodded in her direction. A few even stopped to exchange pleasantries. Oh, how things had changed from when she was known to everyone as only Bushnell's ladybird.

Now, though some sticklers made a great show of walking to the other side of the street when she approached, most folks in town seemed as determined to move on as she was. Time—and the fact that she now lived so visibly alone— had done miracles for her reputation. She might always be whispered about as a woman with a questionable past, but she was no longer treated with overt contempt and scorn. It was a welcome relief—and a welcome reminder after Devin's departure the day before.

Once she arrived in Bonnie's Café, she greeted

the owner, then walked to her usual spot, the corner booth in the back of the room. She would have some soup and a piece of their roasted chicken, then walk back home, maybe even taking the time to stroll around the town square.

When she was halfway through her bowl of vegetable beef soup, a young man and lady approached her. Well-dressed and extremely proper looking, they were a handsome pair. They also looked apprehensive about speaking to her, but determined too.

She looked up at them and smiled slightly. Perhaps they were lost or needed directions.

"Miss Van Fleet?" the woman said.

"Yes?"

After the man gave what could only be described as an encouraging nod, the woman spoke again. "My name is Abby Bernard. This is my brother, Carl. May we join you?"

"I'm sorry, but you have me at a disadvantage. Do we know each other?"

"We do. Well, we do, after a fashion," Carl said.

"I'm afraid I still don't follow."

"That's what we want to talk with you about," Abby said. Gesturing toward the two empty spaces across from Julianne, she said, "May we join you? I promise we won't take up too much of your time."

She was curious now. "All right."

As the pair got settled, she eyed them

93

inquisitively. Upon closer inspection, Julianne realized their clothing wasn't quite as good quality as she first thought. Miss Bernard's gown was well fitted, but there were marks from frequent alterations. The ends of the blue ribbons on her bonnet were slightly frayed. Her brother had on a smart-looking brown suit, but it had turned-in sleeves and cuffs.

Her first impression had been that they were in their early twenties, but now she determined their ages were closer to late teens, perhaps eighteen or nineteen. The boy's build was still lanky, all arms and legs, and the girl still had the full cheeks of youth. Both looked very much like the siblings they were, with fair skin and thick brown hair—only the girl's eyes were dark blue while the young man's eyes were a caramel color.

She thought of a number of ways she could begin the conversation, but none seemed right. Then, too, was the fact that she was still exhausted after Devin Monroe's visit. She decided to simply sit and wait.

After another moment of awkward silence, the boy spoke at last. "Miss, I'm afraid there's no delicate way to begin . . ."

The girl nodded, looking rather embarrassed.

As the time stretched out again, Julianne began to grow impatient. "Perhaps you could simply start at the beginning. That usually works for me."

"All right, then," Miss Bernard said. "As you might imagine, we were children during the war. Our parents lived over near New Braunfels."

New Braunfels was not far, but at least several hours by horseback. "Is that where you reside now?"

Carl shook his head. "When the war broke out, our pa went off to fight. When he left, our mother, well, she had a tough time of it."

"She was with child, you see," Abby interjected.

Julianne fought to keep her expression neutral. Though their history was mildly interesting, she could sense nothing that pertained to her. "Ah."

"She ended up dying in childbirth," she continued. "God rest her soul."

"I'm, uh, very sorry. And your father? How did he fare?"

"He didn't survive either. He died in the war."

"So you two have had your share of hardship." Again, she felt sympathy for their past, but nothing in their story was unfamiliar. One would be hard-pressed to find a single person in Texas who hadn't lost either a parent or sibling.

When they both nodded, she tried to think of another reason why they wanted to speak with her. She couldn't think of one. Feeling vaguely uncomfortable, she said, "While I certainly feel for your loss, I am not sure how it pertains to me."

Carl cleared his throat. "Of course not." He

95

began to speak more quickly. "You see, after our mother passed, we were on our own. So we were sent to live with a relative here. Our aunt, Dora Feldman."

"Dora?"

Miss Bernard sighed. "Yes! You knew her quite well, I believe?"

"Indeed I did." Now that the connection had been made at last, Julianne felt immeasurably better. "You're kin to Dora? Well, that is something. She was a lovely lady."

"I don't know if you remember, but you took care of her, and therefore us, during the last years of the war."

She shook her head. "I think that is putting it a bit thick."

"You brought her food every week."

"Nothing much to speak of," Julianne pointed out. "Sometimes it was nothing more than eggs or greens."

"It was everything. Those items were how we survived."

A knot formed in her throat. "I didn't know that." Remembering what a dark time that had been, she whispered, "I don't remember much about those years except trying to survive." She coughed. "After the war? What did you do?"

"Aunt Dora took us over to Fredericksburg. She had a cousin who was willing to take all of us in."

"So you went there."

"We did, miss." They exchanged looks again. "After a few months, Aunt Dora passed away, but our cousins couldn't have been kinder to us. We . . . well, we both have a very nice life now."

"I'm glad to hear that." Their gratitude made her feel inadequate. She hadn't done much. Maybe she could have done more. "Thank you for letting me know you are doing well."

Miss Bernard leaned forward. "Thank you, but that isn't the purpose of our visit. You see, we have been meaning to come see you for some time now. But we weren't sure if we should . . ." She blushed as her voice drifted off.

They weren't sure about seeking her out because of her reputation. "I understand," she said quickly. She wasn't about to make them refer to her tainted past out loud. Or to have it presented to her face.

The girl looked at her quizzically. "Do you? I don't."

She looked sincere, but Julianne knew better than to believe anyone could be so naïve. She began to resent their intrusion almost as much as she resented the reminder about her past.

She folded her hands in her lap with care while she took a fortifying breath. "It is no secret that I was an officer's kept woman, Miss . . . Abby," she said, her voice like ice. "Most people don't want to associate with me because of that."

When Carl averted his eyes and Abby blushed again, she fought back the temptation to snap at them both. How dare they allude to her past, but then act as if it was too much to deal with!

Frustrated, she pressed her lips together and began to hope this unexpected visit would soon end.

As if Carl was sensing her dismay, he said, "What we're trying to say, Miss Van Fleet, is that your past doesn't matter to us. We were reluctant to come see you because we didn't want to bring up that time in your life. On account that it is no doubt painful to remember."

"I appreciate your visit. Thank you." Now she wished they'd leave.

"I haven't spoken to you to simply express my gratitude, Miss Van Fleet. I came in the hopes that I might one day be your friend," Abby said. "So I might seek permission to call on you at your home."

Her friend? "I beg your pardon?"

"I would like to visit you from time to time. That is, if you wouldn't mind my company." Softly she added, "You see, I recently became affianced to Preacher Timothy. I am very excited about the match."

"I wish you much good fortune," Julianne said haltingly. "However, I must stress that you mustn't feel obligated to visit. You don't owe me anything."

"That is where you are wrong, Miss Van Fleet. We owe you everything," Carl said. "Please don't say no."

"I won't say no." She did her best to ignore the tears that had just formed in her eyes.

Abby's smile was nearly blinding. Or perhaps it was simply beautiful. "I'm so glad. Thank you, Miss Van Fleet."

It was time to let down her guard. It was obvious that God had brought these two people to her for a specific reason. They'd come to remind her that faith, hope, and trust were not pretty, antiquated words that meant little or pertained only to other people. No, God had brought them into her life so she would believe in a future again. And maybe that was the essence of it too. It didn't matter that the future wasn't promised to be perfect or free from hurt. What mattered was that she was going to have one. Yes, it was time to stop subsisting in near isolation, bearing all the shame of her past, and start living again.

And since she was well aware that faith, hope, and trust did exist—though she'd given up imagining they existed for her—she held out a hand. "Please, if we are going to be friends, you might as well call me by my Christian name. Julianne."

Immediately, Abby slipped her hand into hers and clasped it tightly. "I would enjoy that. Thank you, Julianne."

"And I as well," Carl said.

Thirty minutes later, when she was alone again, Julianne wondered how the Lord had known she'd needed Abby and Carl. They'd come at the perfect time, just when her heart had been breaking over the loss of Devin Monroe.

Just when she'd been at her lowest point.

How had he known? Was it simply because he was God and all-knowing?

Staring at the road out the café's front window, she decided it didn't matter after all. For whatever reason, they had come, and their kindness had transformed her. She felt lighter of spirit, fuller of heart. Her cloying depression had lifted.

That was enough. More than enough.

8

It turned out Aileen really hadn't minded if Lizbeth stayed the night. And an hour after firing her, she came all the way up to Lizbeth's room to say her husband would compute her final payment in the morning. He'd been sidetracked by attempting to wrangle a group of disreputable gunmen in the hotel's bar.

She also told her Bushnell had made no complaint, but she and Dallas still thought it was necessary for Lizbeth to go because of her interaction with Major Kelly. She'd had a strange look in her eye when she said that, but Lizbeth didn't have the energy to ask why.

Aileen told her all this after she made Lizbeth promise she would stay in her room like a wayward child. Lizbeth felt so fragile, she would have agreed to anything as long as she didn't have to leave the hotel immediately. She'd lain down early in the evening and tried to sleep, but every time she closed her eyes, memories of being alone in her house on the ranch invaded her thoughts.

Just as she had been pulling out a sheet of paper to begin listing all the options for her future she could think of, Callie knocked on her door.

Lizbeth answered it with mixed emotions.

Callie was her closest friend in the hotel, and talking to her usually brightened her day. But Lizbeth was afraid this conversation would only reinforce how hard it was going to be to completely change her life once again.

To her surprise, Callie didn't look full of questions. She was wearing a concerned expression. "Oh good. I was afraid you weren't going to answer the door."

"Is something wrong? What do you need?"

"I don't need anything," Callie said in her breezy way as she sauntered inside. As usual, she'd taken off her white maid's bonnet and stuffed it into a pocket. Therefore, her brown hair was on display. Today it was artfully arranged into an elaborate configuration of braids. It always struck Lizbeth that Callie's penchant for a fancy coiffure, in stark contrast to her rather plain features, was an effort to present herself as more than a maid in a fancy hotel.

But Callie knew that's all she was. Lizbeth, on the other hand, had recently remembered her previous life made her more than that. Inside, she was still a lady.

Taking note of Callie's expectant expression, Lizbeth arched an eyebrow. "You came up here to say hello?"

"Of course not. Downstairs, we all got to talking about what happened to you. I was elected to come up as the representative." She smiled, looking very pleased with herself.

"So you came up here to check on me?"

"No. I came up here to give you this." She held up a canvas tote bag. "See? We all got together and brought you something."

Stunned, Lizbeth took the tote from her. "Thank you."

"Go ahead," Callie said, gesturing with her hands. "Open it."

Lizbeth pulled open the heavy tote and nearly gasped. Inside were two wrapped sandwiches, a container of cookies, and a Mason jar of lemonade. "This all looks wonderful. Thank you."

Callie lowered her voice. "We heard how Mrs. Howard warned you to keep out of sight. It's just her way to forget that you need to eat and drink, same as anyone else. You'd think she wasn't related to you."

Lizbeth didn't comment on that. She had a feeling Aileen had other concerns on her mind.

Callie waved her hand. "Keep digging. There's more."

After carefully setting the sandwiches on her bed, she pulled out a large envelope. Inside were several notes . . . and a large collection of coins. "What is all this?"

"Come now. You know what it is. It's some money for you."

"I don't know what to say." Tears were threatening to prick her eyes, which would be a mistake. Callie was never a fan of emotional women.

But to her surprise, Callie reached out and clasped her hand. "You don't need to say a thing. Though it ain't a big surprise that you're getting fired on account of some horrible gentleman guest, it's still terrible."

"Please thank everyone for me. This . . . this is so very kind."

"I'll pass on your thanks, though it's a real shame you aren't allowed to come downstairs and do it yourself."

"I'll be all right. No doubt I'll catch up on my sleep."

"That would be a treat, wouldn't it?" After squeezing her hand again, she said, "Do you have any idea what you're gonna do now?"

"No. The only plan I've been able to come up with so far is to get a room in one of the inns in the area for a while."

Callie's eyes widened. "Which one? Some of them have terrible reputations."

"I'll stay at whichever place has a room for me. I'm not going to try to find work yet. No one is going to hire me without a recommendation." Carefully putting the sandwiches back in the tote, she said, "I've saved some money. That, along with what y'all have so generously shared, should be enough to give me a few weeks' reprieve while I decide where to go next."

"So you're planning to leave San Antone."

"I don't have a choice." Lizbeth needed to get as far from Daniel Bushnell as she could.

She also needed to distance herself from Aileen and Dallas. She didn't know what to think about her cousin. They weren't close, but Lizbeth had thought she meant more to Aileen than she obviously did. After everything they'd both been through during the war, Aileen was still putting the needs of the hotel above her cousin's. But she also knew Aileen wasn't about to upset Dallas. A husband had been hard to come by during the war.

Callie nodded. "I understand. I'd want to leave too, if I were you." She sighed. "I'm sure gonna miss you, though."

Realizing she was going to end the battle with her tears, Lizbeth crossed the small room to her side. "I'm going to miss you too. You've been a good friend."

Callie hugged her quickly and then hurried to the door. "I best get back to work. You enjoy the sandwiches now. And don't leave town without saying good-bye to all of us, okay?"

"I won't." She smiled bravely until her door closed again. She figured it didn't matter anymore if she cried or not, and she at last gave in to tears.

It wasn't as though there was anyone around to see them fall.

● ● ●

Now this morning, Lizbeth shook off the memory of her talk with Callie the night before and left her room, her cloak around her shoulders and her bag in hand. Just as she was walking through the lobby, about to claim her last paycheck from Dallas in his office, Major Kelly appeared at her side.

She was relieved he wasn't Bushnell, but still, he made her flustered. Her cheeks were no doubt burning bright red, but she forced herself to greet him. "Good morning, sir."

"And good morning to you," he said as he curved a hand around her elbow. "I'm delighted I located you so easily."

"Sir?"

"Miss Barclay, may we talk?"

Yet again he was standing so tall, so well dressed, and so debonair. Though she wasn't wearing a maid's uniform, her dark-brown dress made her feel like a plain wren next to him. Then there was the fact that his easy smile and charm affected her too much. Being around him made her think of things she had no business thinking about. He was everything she shouldn't want in her life. Everything that was beyond her grasp, even if she did want a man like him.

No, it was much better to work on putting some distance between them, which meant she needed to do what she could to get him to turn away.

Attempting to tug her elbow from his clasp, she said, "I think we've said everything there is to say, sir."

"I happen to disagree." Instead of loosening his grip, he tightened his hold on her. It wasn't painful, but it also didn't leave any room for her to refuse to walk by his side.

"Come along," he said easily as he guided her into a hall. He didn't look down at her. Instead, he kept his hand on her arm and escorted her into one of the private lounges some of the wealthiest guests reserved from time to time.

For a moment she considered simply leaving, but then she decided to listen to what he had to say. The truth was she didn't fear him. She also no longer had anything to lose.

After she perched on the edge of a plum-colored velvet chair, he sat down across from her. "Do you know what you are going to do now?" he asked, obviously not wanting to waste another second.

He knew she'd been fired? Aileen had probably told him. Or maybe it was obvious because of the bag she'd been carrying. Glad that she had a plan, she nodded. "I do. I have some money saved up. I'm going to stay in one of the local inns for a few weeks while I look for work."

He frowned. "You plan to stay at an inn by yourself?"

"Well, yes."

"I don't think that would be wise, Miss Barclay. A young woman, living alone? That isn't safe."

She almost laughed. "It's dangerous for a woman on her own everywhere. Even here."

But instead of looking chastised, he seemed pleased that she'd brought up that point. "That is why I wanted to speak to you. I'd like to help you."

She stared at him guardedly. He seemed sincere. But even if she completely trusted him—which she did not—she couldn't imagine there was any way he could help her.

"Help me? How? Find employment? If so, I should tell you I don't intend to stay in San Antonio."

"You mean to move? Where?"

"As far as I can." She shrugged. "Maybe Fort Worth. Or, I don't know . . . Maybe I'll head to Galveston."

"That's very far, Miss Barclay."

"That's the point. I need to start over someplace where no one knows me."

"Doing what? Cleaning guest rooms?" His voice was thick with contempt.

"Maybe." Embarrassed, she said, "Or perhaps I'll try to find employment as a nanny or governess."

"Those jobs are around children."

She laughed. "I realize that, Major. I happen to like children."

Looking at her intently, he said, "I have a better idea."

"And what is that?"

"Allow me to intervene."

"I beg your pardon?"

"Miss Barclay, let me find you a new job. With my connections, I'm sure I could find you something better."

She would have rolled her eyes at his heavy-handedness if she wasn't fairly sure he probably could find her a better job than she could on her own. But that didn't mean she had to accept his offer. "Sir—"

"Let me help you," he pressed. "If you don't want my help finding employment, at least let me help you find a suitable place to stay. You need to be someplace safe, where you won't be fending off men like Bushnell. I know he was the one who accosted you. I knew him in the war. He was no better then."

He must have eavesdropped on everything she and Aileen said in the hallway outside his suite, but she decided to let that go when she noticed he was staring at her scar again. And that's when she realized he really did pity her. He wanted to find her someplace where she could be safe and secluded. Alone. Where no one would ever stare too long at the scar on her face. Or say anything unkind.

"You know I can't let you do that, sir." If

she accepted his help, she would owe him.

"You could if you wanted to." He stared at her, his eyes filled with so many turbulent emotions she thought she could read his mind if she were so inclined.

"But I don't." She smiled slightly, needing to take the sting out of her words, though she knew there was no real reason to do so. "I need my independence. It's important to me."

He looked tempted to object but shook his head. "I don't want to argue with you."

"We agree on something, then." She stood. "Now, thank you for your concern, but as you can see, I am fine."

"You are very far from fine, Miss Barclay."

Her cheeks heated again. "Even so, I am not downtrodden. Not yet. Now, if you'll excuse me—"

"Hold on." He got to his feet. "I have been wondering something."

"Yes?"

"Forgive me for asking, but does this sort of thing happen often? Do men accost you in rooms often?"

"No."

His eyes narrowed. "I'm starting to realize you are a gifted liar."

"I'm not a liar, sir."

"Then tell me the truth. Do men accost you often when you are working?"

Had it happened before? Of course it had. They were in Texas, barely two years after the end of a long and bloody war. Everyone's morals were in upheaval. Women no longer expected to be cosseted. And men? Well, most of them had become hardened. Some were now cruel, as if all the softness and compassion in their hearts had been emptied on the battle-fields.

But how could she say anything about that without including the major in that group?

Maybe it didn't even matter. " 'Often' is a relative term, sir," she said stiffly. "I have been accosted before, but never, um, in the way Colonel Bushnell did."

The muscles in his jaw tightened. "You need a protector."

"I need a new life, Major Kelly. But since that isn't forthcoming, I am going to settle for a new job."

"Will you at least allow me to escort you to Harrison House?"

Harrison House was a small inn just a few blocks on the other side of the Menger. Though she'd never been inside the establishment, she'd walked past it many times. It had the air of a comfortable relative's house. It also was known to have an exclusive clientele. "I can't afford to stay there. And even if I could, I wouldn't be welcomed." It went without saying that Mrs.

Harrison would no doubt look down at a mere maid's attempt to stay there.

"I know Mrs. Harrison. As a matter of fact, I went over and talked to her about you early this morning. She has a room for you."

"Still, I can't afford to stay there."

"She offered to give you a room at half price."

Her eyes narrowed. No one did things like this without wanting something in return. "Major, why—"

"She feels for your situation, Miss Barclay." He leaned a little closer, bringing with him the fresh, clean scent of milled soap. "Bushnell seems to have left the hotel, but we can't be sure he won't return. Don't say no. It's all arranged."

She closed her eyes. Her pride wanted her to refuse, but the rest of her was so very grateful. Major Kelly was exactly right. Harrison House was safe and reputable. No one would bother her there. And she certainly did not want to see Bushnell again if she could help it. He might remember he'd been the one to . . . She shook the memory out of her mind. "Thank you."

"Let's be on our way, then."

"I would appreciate your escort."

His smile was blinding. "I'm delighted to hear you say that. Especially since it didn't include ten minutes of argument."

"I only argue when it's necessary."

"In an effort to keep the peace, I'll refrain from commenting on that."

"I need to claim my paycheck from Mr. Howard. He should be in his office."

All traces of that sunny smile vanished. "Indeed you do. Well, let's go take care of that."

Though she imagined a part of her should protest his coming with her, Lizbeth was relieved to have the major with her. Right before the lobby, she turned down another, narrow hallway. The hotel's private offices were there. Just beyond was a private section of the hotel. It allowed guests who didn't wish to be seen to come and go with a measure of privacy. She'd never actually seen anyone who was staying in the rooms, but she'd heard rumors that both Grant and Lee had slept in those beds.

After knocking on the door and announcing herself, Dallas beckoned her inside. He abruptly got to his feet when he realized the major had accompanied her. "Major Kelly?"

"I came with Miss Barclay to ensure she received her monies without issue."

"We're not swindlers, Major." He opened the top drawer of his desk and pulled out an envelope. "Here you are, Lizbeth."

"Thank you, Dallas." For a moment she wondered if she should say something else. But what else was there to say? She turned back to Major Kelly. "I'm ready now."

Ethan's eyes warmed. "Let's go, then."

The moment the major followed Lizbeth out of Dallas's office, he held out his arm for her to take.

She stared at it. Hesitated, because it felt as if he were offering her something more. It felt as though they had a relationship, or, at the very least, an agreement.

It felt too forward, too fresh.

But in the end, she decided it felt right as well. Realizing she'd already gone too far to back up now, she rested her hand along his forearm. She felt his muscles tighten from her touch, sending a spark of awareness traipsing up her arm and reminding her that no matter how much she protested, she wasn't immune to his charm.

Major Kelly looked pleased when he slipped on his Stetson. "Shall we proceed?"

Walking by his side through the back of the hotel and out one of the side doors, she felt as if she wasn't just stepping outside; she was stepping back in time.

Back before the start of the war, when she and her parents lived on the ranch, she'd gone walking with quite a number of gentleman callers whenever they went to town to visit friends. Her worries had centered around her appearance and whether she would make an advantageous marriage. How silly she'd been!

After they'd walked one block, Major Kelly

spoke. "This is nice, Miss Barclay. I've been hoping for this day for some time."

"To escort me to Harrison House?"

He laughed. "No." Sounding far more serious, he continued. "I've been hoping to do something of worth for a while now. You are giving me the opportunity to do that."

Being his charity case didn't feel good, but she resolutely pushed the feeling away. She couldn't change her circumstances. At least one of them was finding something good in her situation.

It was rather cold. She had been meaning to buy a new dress for the winter but hadn't wanted to part with any of her precious funds. In light of the recent events, Lizbeth realized that had been a wise decision.

But it also meant she felt the bite of the cold more intently than she wished to. When a burst of wind blew across her cheeks, she shivered.

Major Kelly looked down at her in concern. "You are chilled."

"A little."

He stopped. "Here. Take my coat," he said as he began peeling off his suit jacket.

"Absolutely not."

"Because?"

"Because entering Mrs. Harrison's inn wearing your coat will not improve my reputation."

"Mindy won't care."

He was on a first-name basis with Mrs.

Harrison. For some reason, that knowledge pinched. Maybe it was because it was yet another reminder of how different their circumstances were. "Of course she will care. I promise you, no innkeeper wants a boarder of questionable repute."

"That would never be you."

Lizbeth didn't bother to argue anymore. The fact was, she knew how society worked, both from a society lady's and a maid's perspective. Major Ethan Kelly—with his money, good looks, and heroic reputation—didn't have a clue.

He looked far more somber when he escorted her into Harrison House. After he stated their names, the maid who answered the door led them into a small parlor decorated in shades of rose and gray.

"Mrs. Harrison, Major Kelly and Miss Barclay have arrived," the maid said to an elegantly attired woman sitting on a chaise lounge, calmly knitting what looked to be a long and intricately designed shawl.

She looked up with a smile. "Major Kelly. You have arrived."

He bowed formally. "Mindy, may I present the young lady I told you about, Miss Elizabeth Barclay. Miss Barclay, please meet Mindy Harrison."

"Ma'am," Lizbeth said, dropping a curtsy. She'd seen Mrs. Harrison before, but they'd

116

never had the opportunity to meet properly.

Laying her knitting aside, Mrs. Harrison stood and practically glided over to them. "I have so been looking forward to meeting you, Miss Barclay. I hope you will be happy during your stay here."

Lizbeth felt completely tongue-tied. Was this how Mrs. Harrison greeted all her guests, or was she being especially cordial since the major was held in such high esteem? Neither possibility seemed correct. "I'm not sure if you understand who I am," she began. "You see, I was a maid over at the Menger."

Mrs. Harrison waved a hand. "Oh, I know. Ethan told me all about what has happened to you. I know it will be hard, but I hope you will put that all out of your mind. After all, that part of your life is over now."

Major Kelly was standing tall and proud, and looking extremely pleased with himself too. After giving him a pointed look, she smiled again at Mrs. Harrison. "Thank you, ma'am."

"Of course." She turned back to where she'd been sitting and rang a small bell. "Miss Fletcher will take you up to your room now. Be sure to let her know if it will be suitable."

"I will. I mean, all right."

"Please send for me if you need anything, Miss Barclay," the major said. "And if you leave this establishment for any reason, please do be cautious. A certain man could very well still be about the city."

"Yes. I mean, all right." Oh, what did she mean?

"If you would follow me?" Miss Fletcher murmured from behind her.

Following the maid to the stairs, Lizbeth knew her life was indeed about to change again.

She sincerely hoped it was for the better.

9

Now that Lizbeth was safely settled at Harrison House, Ethan felt he could take some time to visit Devin Monroe. Ethan knew he was still living in that small place on the outskirts of the city.

Since the war, Ethan trusted few people, and rarely dared to rely on anyone other than himself and his three remaining best friends from the prison camp. He knew, deep in his gut, that he needed advice. His emotions around both Lizbeth and Bushnell were too intense for him to see clearly. Every time he tried to make sense of his plan for them, he became distracted by either Lizbeth's pretty face or how much he loathed Bushnell.

Devin Monroe would help him see things much more clearly. He felt sure Bushnell would show up again, and he'd need a plan. Bushnell was not the type of man to take Ethan's attack lightly. He was also not the type to seek vengeance only on Ethan. Ethan feared Bushnell would choose to take out his revenge on someone who couldn't fight back—Lizbeth or some other innocent woman Ethan might be acquainted with.

But short of killing the man, Ethan had no idea how to permanently end this threat. He needed Devin's clear head and reasoning to put together a plan to keep Lizbeth safe and himself out of jail for cold-blooded murder.

At the Menger stables, he saddled up Gretel and headed west. He rode for two hours, enjoying the November air. Even after two years, he couldn't help but contrast Texas's relatively balmy climate with Johnson's Island's bitter temperatures and unrelenting wind. He doubted few other places would ever feel as cold or barren. He also doubted he'd ever again consider a Texas winter unbearable.

Perhaps it was because his incarceration had begun at the beginning of winter. He'd been captured and eventually taken to northern Ohio by train in November of 1863. When the guards motioned them along, much the same way one would herd cattle, Ethan had been bleary-eyed and exhausted. The wounds he'd sustained in his chest and shoulders had begun to heal, but he'd suffered nerve damage. He'd often felt as if his insides were burning hot trails of pain down his arms.

When they arrived, snow lay thick on the ground. It was icy and gray, a sign it had been there for some time. The guards forced them to walk on the ice of Sandusky Bay, and he'd been afraid it wouldn't bear their weight.

The drafty barracks, desolate landscape, and long, gray days threatened to drain their spirits. Later, they all came to grips with the new reality of their situation. Only prayer and other men's support made the conditions bearable.

As prisoners, they were kept in a constant state of discomfort and insecurity. When there was no snow, a cloying dampness still hung in the air. It sunk into a man's bones and teased him. Making every injury he'd ever incurred ache as though he had only recently received it. Sometimes the morning would be filled with a fog so thick he wondered if it was ever going to clear.

Hours passed far too slowly. Small enjoyments began to take on greater meaning. When his family was able to send him cigars, he would stand against the fence and watch the fog dissipate. For those few minutes, the scent of tobacco would fill the air and he'd be transported to another time and place, one where he was safe and comfortable.

Other days he would watch Thomas Baker stare off into the distance, lost in his daydreams. He'd been envious of the man's ability to lose himself in his own thoughts. He'd been able to transport himself to anywhere else on the planet anytime he chose.

Gretel neighed, bringing him back to the present.

And back to how empty his life had become.

Now he had all the comforts he could desire, but with his freedom he'd also lost his home.

How had he plunged into such a situation? After

visiting his family briefly when he was released, he realized that, though they'd overcome their differences about his service in the war, he didn't have much in common with them anymore. How could he? He'd spent years putting both his life and the men who served under him on the line. He'd buried dozens of soldiers and mourned countless others. Then, of course, there were all those lonely months on Johnson's Island.

When he first returned home and was in a room by himself, he hadn't even been able to sleep. He felt too alone and had been plagued by flashbacks. He eventually told his family he needed to leave to work through his demons. At first his mother had cried, but then even she realized he wasn't the same man who had left their home in a resplendent gray uniform with visions of glory in his eyes.

When he left the ranch again, the feelings among them all were bittersweet. They loved him, of course. Just as he still loved them. But love hadn't been enough for him to feel as though he belonged.

In the end, he had taken a portion of his sizable inheritance, deposited it into the bank, and then gone about reinventing himself.

But, of course, he didn't know how to do anything but order men to kill enemy soldiers. That reality hadn't set well with him, and he'd spent much of his time gambling in smoky saloons and riverboats, all while waiting to be needed from time to time by the only people who felt real to him anymore—his three fellow former prisoners.

But lately he'd felt as if he had changed again. He was ready to make commitments. Ready to lean on others again. Ready to be himself.

Lizbeth's arrival in his room had been a turning point for him as well—and he hadn't even realized he'd needed one. She needed a hero in her life. And he? Well, he needed to make amends for his sins, and he knew she was someone he had wronged, even if she never realized he was one of the men who'd scavenged her home during the war.

Out of all the blood and gore of the battlefields, the stench of death and infection, the men he'd lost, the loneliness of being held prisoner for months, that was the moment that haunted him the most.

Before he knew it, he and Gretel had arrived. Just over the bend was his captain's temporary home. It wasn't much. Just a simple stone-and-clapboard house next to a thicket of abundant pecan trees. He remembered Devin saying once that he liked living next to a constant source of food that could be brewed into coffee in a pinch.

That was Devin Monroe, Ethan supposed. A man who leaned toward both the practical and the worst-case scenario.

But what did surprise Ethan was that the captain lived so far from other people. He'd been a sociable man both during the war and in the prison camp. He'd also had something of a tender heart, though he probably would have threatened to maim anyone who dared say it. Ethan had always assumed the day Devin Monroe returned to civilization he would find himself a lovely woman to bind himself to.

As if the captain had been looking for him, Devin was standing in front of his house by the time Ethan dismounted. He was dressed in his usual attire of faded denims, a pure white shirt, and black boots. It seemed he wasn't concerned about the Texas November chill either.

"Captain," Ethan said. He outranked Devin, but he used the title as a form of respect. Devin had earned every bit of his rank, while Ethan's family's money had paid for his.

Devin clasped his hand. "Ethan, this is a welcome surprise. It's good to see you."

"I'm relieved to hear that. Sorry to show up unannounced."

"You know we are beyond worrying about such niceties. Do you have any news?" he asked, his voice smooth yet betraying a touch of concern. "Is Baker all right?"

"Yes," he said before realizing he'd probably

spoken too soon. "I mean, I haven't heard anything from him. I'm assuming he's enjoying wedded bliss."

Devin chuckled. "I hope so, though it's hard to imagine him staying out of trouble for too long. What do you think the chances are of him keeping his head down for a while?"

"Married to Laurel? I'd say real good."

"Me too."

Ethan smiled, thinking of their sergeant who could once only be described as a loose cannon on the best of days. Now he was far more circumspect and married to a beautiful woman with golden hair. And a fondness for cattle.

"What brings you out here? You in trouble?"

That caught Ethan off guard. He knew Devin would want to know how he was doing. But he'd hoped they might be able to ease into the point of his visit. "You still don't beat around the bush."

"No need to with you. Is there?"

"No." Realizing it would be futile to postpone the inevitable, he said, "I came to get some advice, if you have some time to listen."

"Always. Why don't you take care of your horse and then come join me?" Looking a little embarrassed, he said, "Even though the temperature is probably in the fifties, I've been feeling the cold today. I've been in the kitchen making chili. You can come in and chop."

Ethan hadn't touched a kitchen utensil since he'd been freed from captivity. "You still don't have a maid to do that?"

"No. I guess after living among men all my life, I don't know how to live with women. I get tongue-tied." A shadow filled his expression before he carefully wiped it away. "Matter of fact, I've recently come to the conclusion that I'm not real good around females at all."

This confession startled Ethan. Devin Monroe was one of the most confident men he'd ever met. "I find that hard to believe."

"You shouldn't. We all have our gifts. Mine do not lie in understanding how women's minds work . . . or in conversing with them."

After settling Gretel, Ethan followed Devin into the simple house. The captain had told him a friend was letting him use the house for as long as he wished, and as one might have expected for a bachelor, the interior was plain. Nothing decorated the walls, and there were no knickknacks or frames on any surface. It reminded Ethan of their quarters at the beginning of the war. Back then, they'd had relatively comfortable spaces but nothing that wasn't needed or necessary.

The kitchen was in the back. It was really nothing more than a small room where the captain obviously prepared his meals, but it had a black cook stove, a wooden table, two chairs, a line of beautifully made cabinets, and a large basin for washing.

The room's simplicity suited the captain well. It had enough to satisfy his needs, but nothing extra.

Devin walked directly to a cast-iron pot on the cook stove and started stirring. "Ethan, slice those peppers and onions on the table."

After washing his hands, Ethan rolled up his sleeves and got to work. Back before the war, he had only ever thought of a kitchen as someplace to sneak into when his servants weren't available to bring him food.

All that had changed during the war. At first they'd had various enlisted men take cooking rotations. Toward the end, their ranks were so ragtag and he'd spent so many nights by himself, he learned to cook just about anything. He received a greater education in culinary arts when they were incarcerated on Johnson's Island. They had nothing but time on their hands. And since food was so precious, each of them had taken to learning how to prepare it.

That said, he certainly hadn't missed kitchen duty.

"This reminds me of cooking at the camp," he said as he lopped off the top of a pepper. "I got pretty good at slicing carrots and potatoes."

"We ended up doing all right once we started our garden, didn't we?"

"All of us except for Baker. He couldn't grow a batch of thistles."

Devin laughed. "That he couldn't. He was worthless at anything domestic. 'Course, that might have changed now that he's found Laurel."

"Did that surprise you?" Ethan asked as he turned the pepper on its side and began slicing. "That he found love while working in a chain gang?"

"You know what I mean. Thomas Baker is as rough a man as I've ever known. His wife is his complete opposite in every way." Devin shrugged. "Perhaps on paper the alliance might not make much sense. But I'm not surprised he found a woman to love him. Underneath all Baker's bravado and insecurity is a good man."

"Which Laurel discovered, even though he was wearing a prisoner's uniform when they first met."

"You are right. She discovered Thomas's best qualities in spite of a prison uniform." Devin looked at him quizzically. "*You* sound surprised. Why is that? You knew Baker even before I did."

"I'm not disparaging Thomas," Ethan said quickly. "Of course I'm glad he's found love and happiness."

"Then what's bothering you?"

"I'm just, I don't know, thinking about how two such unlikely people became enamored with each other. It's curious, don't you think? I never understand how and when the Lord chooses to bring people together."

"That's why we have God. We trust in Him so we don't have to try to understand such things ourselves." Grabbing a handful of the peppers and onions Ethan had chopped so far, Devin tossed them into his pot. "Is that what this visit is really about? Have you found yourself a woman, Major?"

The question startled him. "What? No." Then, as an image of dark, curly hair and the sound of a soft, sweet voice came to mind, he amended his words. "Well, maybe. But, um, not in that way."

As he should have expected, Devin latched on to his last two words. "What other way is there?"

Suddenly tongue-tied, Ethan stared at him. How did one answer that? He had no earthly idea.

10

Though his mind was no doubt racing with a dozen questions, Devin allowed Ethan a few minutes to gather his thoughts. He continued working on his chili, his movements sure and easy. As if there was nothing unusual about either Ethan's unannounced visit or what they were discussing.

Lulled by Devin's matter-of-fact movements, Ethan finally relaxed. Then he told Devin about Lizbeth's sudden entrance to his room at the Menger and how her cousin had fired her rather than take her concerns seriously.

Devin's expression had turned dark at the mention of the colonel's name. "Bushnell. That man was always a scoundrel."

"I want to help Miss Barclay because of Bushnell's involvement. But I must confess I have other reasons as well."

Devin put down his spoon. "Which are?"

"I think . . . well, I know she's from my past."

Devin watched him carefully. "Which past? Your home or from the war?"

Ethan swallowed. "I met her—more or less—during the war. On a requisition raid."

Devin stared at him. "That is surprising, but not unheard of, I reckon. After all, we all met

130

our share of women. Some during dances, others when we were marching through wherever we went."

Ethan knew what Devin meant. They'd marched or ridden their horses through several states. Arkansas. Tennessee. Kentucky. Texas. "Like I said, I met this woman on a requisitioning raid. At a place near here."

"Ah. You haven't said. Did she recognize you?"

"Apparently not. It would be different for her, though. She probably only remembers groups of men in gray and gold stealing her belongings."

"Or men in blue. We weren't the only ones searching for supplies, Major."

"Probably so."

"No, I know so."

Realizing Devin Monroe had never talked about raiding homesteads, Ethan searched his face. "Did you ever do that?"

"Requisition supplies for our troops? You know I did."

"Did you ever feel guilty about it?"

"Truth?"

"Of course."

"Not at the time." He shrugged. "Come to think of it, I still don't feel guilty about those runs. We didn't have a choice. Our men were dying. Starving and cold, wet and hungry. It was our duty to provide for them in any way we could. Our duty as officers."

"I know."

Grimacing, Devin continued. "Early on, we visited a horse farm in Kentucky, and I almost got poked with a pitchfork because I wanted a pair of champion breeders. That blasted man wanted all of us to bleed and die on the battlefields while he raised horses and waited for the war to be over. I've never forgotten that. What kind of man prefers for other men to defend his home?"

"I agree with you there. But this woman? Well, her circumstances were different."

After inspecting his chili again, Devin said, "How so?"

"Back when I was still a captain, Baker, five other men, and I were covering a block of land, trying to get some wood to burn and food. The men were starving. And freezing."

"I remember."

"Anyway, we came upon this ranch house. It had obviously been a pretty house before the war. It was run-down, but we were sure it was going to give us at least some of what we needed. The woman I now know as Miss Barclay met us at the front." Realizing his friend had turned and was listening intently, Ethan tried to form the right words without breaking down. "She was alone. And skittish."

"And scared."

Ethan sighed in relief. He was glad he didn't have to explain in too much detail about her state of mind. "Yes. She was petrified of me and my men." Raising his hand to his temple, he continued. "She was also scarred from her ear to her hairline. Men had come to her place before, you see."

"Ah." Devin turned to his stew pot. After a couple of additional stirs with a wooden spoon, he spoke again. "The story is sad but not surprising, Ethan. Those were dark times for everyone. Desperate. What did your men take?"

Ethan knew what Devin was asking. "We took everything we could, but it wasn't much. When we left her homestead, I knew she didn't have anything left." Shame choked his words, but he continued anyway. "It's my fault too. I ordered the men to scavenge."

"You can't judge the past by today's standards. Our circumstances were different back then. We would spend days fighting and killing before spending weeks burying the dead and tending to the wounded." Devin shuddered. "I thought I was never going to get the scent of blood out of my head."

"I hear you."

"Good. You must also remember that it wasn't only our war. We were all under orders. Even esteemed captains." Looking a bit amused, he added, "Even elusive majors."

Ethan would have saluted the sarcastic quip if he weren't so in need of guidance.

Impatiently, he said, "My point is that . . . this woman I'm concerned about? Well, I did help her with Bushnell."

"Ethan, before you tell me what you did, are you sure she's the same one? That raid took place a long time ago, right? It had to have been almost a year before we were imprisoned."

"I'm as sure as if I'd visited her home last week. I knew I'd never forget her. Plus, that scar that has haunted my memories is on her temple." Sighing, he said, "When I found her in my suite, she was in danger again. Running from Bushnell after he'd cornered her when she was cleaning his room."

Devin cursed under his breath. "Our world keeps getting smaller and smaller."

"You're right. He is one man I would have been happy never to cross paths with again."

"What did you do?"

"After I heard her cousin fire her—Lizbeth is her name—I made the woman give me his room number and I went there."

Devin stared at him intently. "What did you do?"

"I threatened him." And he might have bruised his face a bit.

"Ah. And later, how did Lizbeth react when you relayed how you remembered her?"

"When I saw her again, I didn't mention it. Or tell her anything about my encounter with

Bushnell. Only that she needs protection and assistance and I am willing to give her that."

"You didn't see the need to tell her you raided her home?"

Though he was mentally cringing at the dismay in his friend's tone, Ethan attempted to excuse himself. "Lizbeth has no idea I was with that band of men. I don't want to tell her."

"Of course you don't. You would become less of a hero, wouldn't you?"

This time Ethan didn't bother to hide his discomfort. "Your contempt might be no less than I deserve. But if you were in my position, you might find yourself doing the very same thing."

"Maybe. Or maybe not."

"I am not ready to tell her everything, but I still feel the need to do something. She can't keep living on her own. She's going to get hurt." *Again,* he silently added.

"You're right. She very well might. But her problems aren't yours."

Hardly hearing him, Ethan revealed what he'd been turning around in his head. "I think they could be. I might not want to admit being at her house, but I still feel guilty about it."

"What does your guilt have to do with her?"

"Everything. If I make things right, I might be able to find absolution too."

Devin sighed. "Ethan. That isn't how it all

works. God grants absolution. God will help you find solace."

Ethan knew Devin had a deep faith. But his didn't run that deep. "I can help her and help myself, too, if I take Bushnell on. She needs a protector. It might as well be me. Late last night I even contemplated marrying her."

Devin started laughing. It abruptly stopped when he noticed that Ethan didn't even crack a smile. "Wait a minute. Are you serious?"

"I am. It will solve a lot of her problems." All of them, as far as he could tell.

"It will also create a whole slew of them for you," Devin said with an uncharacteristic note of derision. After glancing at him again, he walked to a back cabinet, opened a door, and pulled out a crystal bottle of whiskey. After filling two shot glasses, he handed one to him. Before waiting, Devin tossed back a good portion of the contents.

Only then did he speak again. "Ethan Kelly, have you lost your mind?"

"Not yet." He took a sip of the whiskey. Realized how fine it was, then took another sip before setting it down.

"That might be a matter of opinion."

"Look, I know I'm not responsible for her problems, but I couldn't do anything about what happened to her during the war. I can help her now."

"You may think you are helping her. But if you

encourage her to marry without love, where does that get her? Trapped in a loveless marriage, I tell you."

"She's alone. Bushnell could have raped her in that hotel room."

"But he did not."

Just as he was about to confess more of his worries, he noticed Devin looked extremely agitated. Something more was troubling him than just his idea about marriage. "What did I say?"

"Other than you are considering giving up your life for a maid in a hotel?"

"No, there's something more afoot. Is it the mention of Bushnell?"

Devin hesitated. "Partly."

"Why? What do you know about him that I don't?"

"I recently met the woman who was his ladybird during the war."

Surprised, Ethan picked up his whiskey and drained it. "I remember him speaking of her." Closing his eyes, he recalled Bushnell bragging.

"So do I," Devin said, looking pained. After taking another sip, he seemed to gain control of himself. "So you remember Bushnell speaking of her? Was it at Johnson's Island?"

"He did then too, but I'm thinking of another time. It was when we were traveling south and spent the night somewhere in the middle of Tennessee." Thinking back, Ethan remembered how appalled he'd been by Bushnell's tales. Deciding to tread carefully, he added, "He said she was beautiful. Deceptively beautiful, whatever that means."

"She is." A muscle in his jaw tightened. "Auburn hair and blue eyes. She's . . . well, she's striking."

"Ah. You know her well?"

"No. I only recently met her. She, um, she practically lives in isolation now. Her alliance with him ruined her reputation."

"That ain't surprising."

"It's not, but I've been thinking. She had good reason to do what she did," Devin said with more force. "She was desperate. Hungry. Had a grandmother to care for." His lips thinned as he stared off into the distance again. "Actually, I would go so far as to say her actions were justified."

Since Ethan had come for advice, he decided to bring the conversation back around to him. "Lizbeth has suffered too. She's all alone, except for a miserable excuse of a cousin."

"You look as if something else is weighing on you. What is it? Is there something you aren't telling me?" Devin stepped forward. "Did you hurt her in some way but don't want to admit it?"

"Of course not." He hadn't, except when he'd taken all her provisions and left her starving and alone.

"Then her pain is not your problem."

Everything Devin said made sense. But Ethan was starting to realize sometimes a man had to do what didn't make sense.

"What should I do about Bushnell? I didn't just threaten him. I knocked him to the floor. He's checked out of the Menger, but I'm afraid he's going to come back to retaliate—by hurting Lizbeth. My friend Mindy Harrison agreed to let Lizbeth have a room at her inn, but will she really be safe from him even there?"

"That would be like him." Lips pursed, Devin stared at their pair of empty shot glasses. "I need to take care of some business, but then I'll come find you at the Menger. We'll hunt down Bushnell and confront him together. Maybe find out more about why he was even in San Antonio. He's from Fredericksburg, right?"

"Yes, but there's no need for you to do that. I didn't come here to ask you for help. Just advice."

"I need to be there, Ethan."

"Do you think the two of us talking to him will make any difference?"

"If it doesn't, we'll come up with a plan to make sure he takes our warnings seriously. In the meantime, don't do anything rash. Don't offer that woman marriage yet."

As they walked into Devin's cozy living room, Ethan said, "I'm glad I came here."

"Are you? I don't think I helped you much."

"You helped more than you know. You helped me remember I'm not alone."

Leaning back on the couch, Devin nodded, his cool blue eyes looking almost empty. "You've done the same thing for me. You also made me realize I may have been a fool. Honestly, Ethan, I think you might have helped me more than I helped you."

As that statement lingered in the air, Ethan leaned back in his chair and exhaled. He'd come hoping to solve his problems. But if he wasn't mistaken, he'd just uncovered several more issues. Issues he was certain weren't going to be solved with a threat or a thrown punch.

11

Johnson's Island, Ohio
Confederate States of America
Officers' POW Camp

The hour was late. It was long after dark, long after the time most of the prisoners had returned to their barracks for the comfort of sleep.

Devin Monroe wasn't one of them.

He was leaning against one of the barracks' outside walls, unsuccessfully attempting to come to grips with what Colonel Daniel Bushnell was saying.

Correction. What Bushnell had been saying for the last ten minutes, ever since he, Bushnell, General McCoy, and Major Ethan Kelly had decided to have an impromptu meeting about yet another grave that needed to be dug. Well, their "meeting" was actually an argument between Bushnell and Kelly. Devin and the general had stuck around in case blood was shed.

Usually Devin didn't put too much emphasis on their military rank at the camp. No one did, for there was no need. From the time they'd been forced to march across the ice to their prison, each of the men had come to realize his life was no longer his own. They had no power. Definitely no control of their needs or their wants. No man's rank would ever change the fact that they were all at the mercy of their enemy.

Because of that, usually Devin would have no reason to stay outside and listen to an argument between two other men. He figured he'd broken up enough fights during the war for a lifetime.

But tonight? Well, Bushnell was being more of a pompous jerk than usual. And Ethan was taking greater offense to the man's words than he usually did.

"Once again, I will not allow it, Major," Bushnell blustered, his voice deep and foreboding. "That private shouldn't have even been on these grounds in the first place. I won't allow him to be buried in the officers' graveyard."

"Private Gluck was a good man. His being here was a clerical error. Nothing more, nothing less," Ethan retorted. "And it's not like it matters anyway. He's dead. Everyone he'll be buried next to is dead as well."

Bushnell turned to Devin. "Is that the truth, Captain?"

Since he was forced to be involved, Devin decided to have a bit of fun at the man's expense. "Are you speaking of Gluck's ranking? His being here in the first place? Or are you possibly dwelling on the very fact that he's dead and so it doesn't matter anymore?"

142

General McCoy chuckled. "I was wondering the same thing."

Bushnell visibly attempted to keep his temper in check. "You know what I am speaking of. Did you pull strings for Gluck to be here? Because I know you did for Baker."

At the mention of Baker's name, all traces of amusement left Devin. "Baker is not at issue. He is alive and well."

"He is also no officer. He should be in one of the other POW camps, one for noncommissioned personnel."

Devin raised a brow. "Because we shouldn't mix with the men who have been doing the majority of the fighting?"

A vein popped out on Bushnell's forehead. "That is not what I meant and you know it. Just answer the question. Did you sneak Gluck in here?"

"Gluck was placed here by accident. I had nothing to do with his assignment. And that is the truth."

"Perhaps."

"I wouldn't start questioning my integrity, Colonel. I am a loyal Southerner and a gentleman."

Bushnell grunted. "Don't act so surprised, Captain. You have been the champion of developing your own rules. Unlike your sergeant, for example. A sorrier soldier I've never had the displeasure of meeting."

"Baker rode behind enemy lines and put himself at great risk doing so," General McCoy said quietly. "The South is in his debt."

Bushnell's expression tightened, but he didn't argue with generals.

"Is this discussion done?" Ethan asked.

"No. We still have not resolved our dilemma."

Devin gritted his teeth. For a moment he wished Sergeant Baker was in the vicinity. Then he could have counted on Thomas to have uttered something disparaging. Thomas called everyone pet names. Most were derogatory, but right on point. Which was why Bushnell was often referred to as Blowhard behind his back.

As it was, Devin knew better than to be overtly disrespectful. Not only did he need to conduct himself in a way befitting his rank, but his men needed him to do that as well. That, however, didn't stop him from sneaking a look at General McCoy.

McCoy raised his eyebrows at Devin. Telling him everything he needed to know. The general was just as irritated by Blowhard's insistence about poor Gluck's burial as he was.

Very well, then. "You are right, sir," Devin said stiffly. "This matter of Gluck's final resting place has not been decided. The fact is I disagree with your directive, Colonel. We may have ranks, but they were earned on the battlefield and in the company encampments. Here on Johnson's

Island, we are all Johnny Rebs in the eyes of the enemy. Because of that, we all sleep in the same barracks, eat the same food, and line up the same way. Consequently, we all are the same in death. Military ranking doesn't signify in death."

Bushnell tensed, then turned to Ethan. "Are you holding firm to your decision? Or do you agree that we should bury him on the other side of the barracks?"

The colonel wanted to bury Gluck near the latrines.

Devin held his tongue, but only barely.

Sitting on a boulder, Ethan crossed his legs. The major was so elegant, he somehow managed to look at ease anywhere he was. Only the look of distaste in his eyes hinted at what he thought. "It would be detrimental to our group's morale to bury Gluck without our usual fanfare. He deserves it. He was a good man and an honorable soldier."

"The men here need to be reminded who is in charge," Bushnell said. "If we start acting as though we are all equals, discord could erupt."

Ethan froze. "We are all equals in the eyes of God, and in this prison encampment, sir. The fact that I am a major means next to nothing here."

"That's been patently obvious. After all, I've seen you follow Monroe's directives without hesitation."

"I would be the first to admit that not every

145

soldier's ranking comes from merit. For example, my commissions were purchased with a respectable amount of silver and gold."

Bushnell sniffed. "I should have known."

Ethan uncrossed his legs, seeming to pause to pick off a piece of lint from his trousers' cuff. "That reminds me of something I've never asked. How did you obtain your rank, Daniel? Was it through bars of silver and gold like me . . . or through other means?"

General McCoy coughed.

And Devin? He was exhausted. If they'd been back on the battlefield, he would have given in to temptation and jabbed Ethan in the ribs so he'd shut up. He settled for muttering his name under his breath. "Kelly."

But it was doubtful that his utterance was heard. Ethan was staring intently at Bushnell. Practically egging him on with its intensity.

And the colonel? Well, Bushnell looked mad enough to snap in two.

Not another second passed before he jerked to his feet. Glaring down at Kelly, he bit out, "You sound as if you feel no respect for either me or my rank."

"I'm saying I feel no respect for your ranking, sir." Ethan grinned suddenly. "Though, of course, I will honor it here as much as I am able." His voice turning cold, he said, "Unless we are discussing the dead bodies of good men."

Bushnell's hands clenched. "I take offense to your words."

"What do you want to do, sir? Fight me at dawn?"

"Ethan, control yourself," Devin said.

"And you? Sit back down and stop being such a popinjay," General McCoy said to Bushnell.

"Sir. You had to have heard him. We cannot allow—"

"I can and will do whatever I please. I'm languishing on an island in the middle of a lake! Have you forgotten?"

Bushnell sat down. "No, sir."

"I hope not. Now, calm yourself. This fight you have wanted to win is over and you lost. Take it like a man."

"Yes, sir."

"Good." With a groan, the general lumbered to his feet. Devin, Ethan, and Daniel Bushnell got to their feet as well. After rubbing his thigh and cursing under his breath about Yankees, stray bullets, and sawbones in battlefield tents, the general glared at the rest of them. "Gentlemen, tomorrow we will get into formation, walk to the officers' cemetery, and dig a grave for Gluck. There will be no further discussion. Understood?"

"Yes, sir," Devin said.

"Glad to hear it. Now, Captain, you have been on this island double the time I have. Do you foresee any problems with our guards?"

They would need to be bribed, but he knew how to take care of that. "No, sir."

"Good. Good night, then," the general said as he strode away, his gait uneven and painful to see.

With McCoy out of sight, all Devin wanted to do was seek the privacy of his cot. Well, and hope that Thomas didn't snore too loudly for once.

But before he could take his leave, Daniel sneered. "Look at you both, jumping to your feet even though you just explained how the lot of us are all one under the eyes of the Lord."

"Perhaps I simply respect him," Ethan drawled.

Bushnell laughed quietly. "Fool yourselves with your high and mighty words, but I know what's really taking place. You jump to his pleasure as quickly as my mistress does when I call for her. You owe him."

"I didn't realize you had a ladybird," Ethan murmured. "Do you keep her near your wife?"

Surprisingly, Daniel laughed. "Of course not. I've got her off in another town, just outside San Antone. She's perfect. Gorgeous, even, with blue eyes and auburn hair. Real grateful for my money too."

After he left, Ethan sat back down and stretched his legs. "There you go, Devin."

"What are you speaking about?"

"Well, I know you enjoy looking for everyone's weaknesses. Now, next time we're all sitting around, wishing we were somewhere else, we can think about how there's someone in this world who's got things a far sight tougher than we do."

"Bushnell's mistress?"

"Absolutely. Just think. Somewhere out there is a woman hidden in a little hovel, whose whole existence is dependent on the likes of Daniel Bushnell." He shook his head. "Can you imagine a worse way of spending one's day? Jumping to the wishes of a man like him?"

Though Devin could imagine far worse things, he conceded that Ethan did have a point. "I hope she gets paid well."

"Whatever she gets paid, Captain, I'm telling you right now, it ain't enough."

An hour later, lying in his cot next to Thomas, who was blissfully silent for once, Devin closed his eyes and said a prayer for that woman. Ethan had been right. War was hard. So was imprisonment. But to be imprisoned the way that woman was—dependent on a man like Bushnell for her very survival?

That was something he wouldn't wish on his worst enemy.

12

Her coffee had grown cold. Yet instead of getting up and refreshing her cup with warm liquid, Lizbeth simply sipped at the cold concoction. She would much rather stay in her comfortable chair and continue to appreciate her new situation and surroundings at Harrison House than get up to refresh a drink.

The moment was simply too sweet.

She figured she needed this time too. Though she'd been at Harrison House for two days, she'd spent the first doing little more than sleeping. It shouldn't have been a surprise, for she'd been both mentally and physically drained.

Being a maid had been exhausting. Working for her cousin and feeling constantly beholden to her and her husband added another type of strain. When she added Colonel Bushnell's scare and the subsequent interactions with Major Kelly and Aileen?

She'd been on the verge of collapse and she hadn't even realized it. Her body had craved rest, and she'd been more than happy to comply.

That morning, however, she'd awoken feeling rejuvenated. Now she was gazing around her surroundings as though she were a brand-new visitor to San Antonio. Indeed, everything in the area looked rather unfamiliar.

Sitting on a cozy wicker chair on a wide front veranda while wrapped in a lavender-scented soft afghan was to be savored.

Unable to help herself, she stretched her legs and leaned her head against the plush cushions behind her. Took time to count her blessings. And she did, indeed, feel blessed.

She was no longer working on her feet before dawn, racing against the clock to do Aileen and Dallas's bidding. No longer living in dread of being in the company of strange men. No longer afraid of being approached by people she didn't know.

For the first time in ages she was in charge of her day. She could do whatever she wanted. It wasn't a one-time thing either. She could very well live like a lady of leisure for quite some time. Well, at least until she ran out of funds.

It made her giddy.

That had been the first thing she'd thought of that morning when she awoke far later than she usually had on her days off. After lazing about under the comfortable down comforter and watching the last of the embers extinguish themselves in her room's fireplace, she gave in to the day and got dressed. Then she ventured downstairs to the kitchen at the back of the house and poured herself a large cup of coffee.

Next to the coffeepot on the stove had been a container of muffins and a note inviting guests to take as many as they would like. Feeling decadent, Lizbeth helped herself to two.

She didn't know if she would ever take such things for granted again. After living in her small room at the top of the Menger and having to follow Aileen's directives about what she could and couldn't do, being able to help herself to a steaming cup of coffee was a wonderful experience. Even the kitchen staff at the hotel hadn't been allowed a beverage except at designated times of the day.

Curling her feet onto the chair, Lizbeth continued to watch the world go by. A pair of mockingbirds squawked merrily as they signaled for their mates. A trio of squirrels played tag on the pine trees that lined the property. Their noisy chatter made her smile as they raced up and down the tree limbs. Below them was an orange tabby cat. She was lounging on the top of a wide stone fence, her tail lazily swinging like a metronome.

No doubt these things had happened all day everyday both here at Harrison House and right outside the Menger Hotel. Maybe they happened everywhere? All she knew for sure was that she'd been too preoccupied with work and worries to appreciate them. She silently promised herself not to let that happen again.

As the minutes passed, Lizbeth directed her sight toward the road just beyond her. Little by little, it filled with horse-drawn wagons and buggies. Men and women walked on its dusty sides. Some were striding intently, obviously hoping to finish a great many errands in a short amount of time. Others were simply strolling. They were speaking in cordial tones to each other, going about their routines. Other guests at Harrison House came up the steps and greeted her before going inside.

As she continued to watch all those people move about, Lizbeth realized she'd been concentrating on surviving for so long that she'd forgotten to remember one very important point. She *had* survived. Even though she'd endured many hardships, she was still surviving. She hadn't given up.

And while that was good, she also knew she hadn't been living either. Not really.

She knew if she stopped each one of the people out for their walks and asked about the war, they would share stories filled with as much heartbreak and longing as hers were. She had not been alone in her suffering. She was not the only woman to have experienced a great many hardships at the hands of others. She was certainly not the only person to have lost her home. Others also bore scars. Men lost limbs, eyes. Their very being.

Many women had also experienced pain at

men's hands. She knew she was not the only one to have nightmares or to fear being alone in the dark.

So why was she still pining over the fact that her life was different than it had been before the war? Different from what she'd anticipated? Why had she not felt the need to stop often and give thanks?

She should have.

Nothing about that made her proud. Her grandparents would have expected more from her.

"Lord, please forgive me," she whispered. "I have been so blinded by my pain that I've neglected to realize I have so many things to be grateful for. Instead of remembering that, I took them for granted. I promise I'll do better."

Closing her eyes again, she concentrated on the warmth of the sun on her face . . . and a new sensation. It was a feeling of completeness. As if God himself was taking time out of his busy day to reach out to her. To let her know her words had been heard.

She was stunned. She'd thought her faith was true. Strong. But like her daily attempts of survival, she had only seen part of the whole picture.

Feeling stronger than she had in months, maybe years, she reached down to take another sip of her coffee. Then turned when the French doors that guarded the side entrance to the verandah swung open.

"Good morning, Miss Barclay," Mrs. Harrison said. "I trust you slept well last night?"

"I did. Thank you."

Just as she moved to stand, Mrs. Harrison waved off the motion with a hand. "Please, don't get up. I came to sit out here with you for a few minutes."

"All right." Lizbeth smiled, but her insides began to churn. Was something wrong? Had Mrs. Harrison changed her mind about allowing her to stay there?

She yearned to ask those questions, but she forced herself to continue to sit quietly. She swallowed the last of her cold coffee and watched her new landlady settle herself on the chair by her side. Her morning gown was especially attractive. It was a deep shade of plum and sported a wide ruffled hem that no doubt fluttered with each step.

After folding her hands neatly on her lap, Mrs. Harrison spoke. "I hardly saw you yesterday. I was worried you were ill."

"I thought at first I was. But then I realized I was simply tired. The excitement of the last few days caught up with me."

"I imagine so. As you know, Major Kelly shared your situation. I don't know if I found it more disturbing that you were accosted while making a bed or that your cousin blamed you for running into what you thought was an empty room to protect yourself."

"Both were rather difficult to deal with." Not wanting to be seen as only a victim, she said, "However, I am better now. I plan to buy a newspaper and start combing the ads from some of the surrounding areas. I aim to get a new job by the first of the year."

Instead of looking relieved, however, Mrs. Harrison merely looked contemplative. "I see. Well, I am relieved you will be waiting until after Christmas to leave us. It will be nice to have you here."

"Thank you." Still feeling awkward, she moved to stand. "I was just about to get another cup of coffee. Would you like one?"

"Thank you, but no." Looking a little embarrassed, she added, "Before you refill your cup, may we talk about something first? I must confess there's another reason I came out here to speak with you."

"Oh?" Here it came.

"Yes. Major Kelly sent word to me early this morning that he'd like you to call on him at the Menger. At your convenience."

"He didn't want to call on me here?"

"It doesn't seem so." A wrinkle formed in her brow. "I feel rather awkward delivering his messages."

"Of course you do. I would feel the same way." But at the same time, she wondered why he hadn't sent word directly to her. Perhaps he suspected she would still be asleep.

"All right. As soon as I put on a bonnet and a proper cloak, I'll be ready to go."

"I'm sure you could have that cup of coffee first. I don't think it's that urgent."

"No, if the major is waiting for me, I don't want him to have to wait longer than necessary." Besides, she knew the relaxing moment had passed. She wasn't going to be able to rest until she discovered exactly why Major Kelly had summoned her.

After hurrying up to her room, Lizbeth put on her best felt bonnet and then put on real stockings and her best kid boots. After slipping on her cloak, she carefully locked her door and slipped the brass key into her bag before walking back down the stairs.

She spied Mrs. Harrison sitting at a writing table in the front parlor. "Thank you again for letting me know about my appointment, ma'am," she said politely.

"Would you like me to accompany you? The streets are awfully busy right now."

"I don't mind walking alone. Thank you for the offer, though."

After sharing another smile with Mrs. Harrison, Lizbeth ventured out onto the road. The lady had been right. Even more people were out walking and riding in carriages than when she'd been observing before.

Lizbeth felt very strange going back to the Menger, especially when she entered the hotel through the front lobby doors instead of the servants' entrance.

Several people looked her way, and, hoping she looked more composed than she felt, Lizbeth nodded at a few of the women. When she felt some of the staff stare at her in confusion, she pretended not to notice. Though she did feel awkward and on edge, she had nothing to be embarrassed about.

She really did need to remember that.

She started for the reception desk, relieved to still not see Bushnell anywhere around. But then she almost ran into Aileen.

"Good morning, Lizbeth," she said with a puzzled frown as she rushed to her side. "Do you need something?"

Lizbeth realized Aileen seemed concerned about her. She was beginning to wonder if fear of Dallas's disapproval had been what had pushed Aileen to dismiss her.

But though she was still hurt, Lizbeth realized she was also in a better place. She might not know what the future held for her, but she hadn't been happy being a maid at the Menger. "I am meeting Major Kelly here," she said. "He, uh, sent for me. Have you seen him, by any chance? I was just about to ask if he is in his room or—"

"He's in the parlor, standing in front of the fireplace." Looking at her curiously, Aileen added, "Is everything okay?"

"I don't know." Smiling tightly, she said, "I guess I'm about to find out."

Lizbeth shook off her doldrums and walked into the parlor, where the major stood with his back to her.

"Major Kelly, good morning."

After turning to her and smiling, he bowed. "Miss Barclay. Thank you for joining me here. I regret that I couldn't come to you, but my appearance at Mindy's establishment might have only caused talk."

She realized he was right. Though, from the interested stares around them, Lizbeth knew this meeting would be on the tongues of many people as well. "It was no trouble. I'm sorry for the delay. I'm afraid I was lazing about on Mrs. Harrison's verandah this morning."

"You have nothing to apologize for. We had nothing scheduled. After being gone most of Saturday and yesterday morning, I did quite a bit of lazing myself. Only inside where it is warmer." He smiled and gestured toward two chairs that faced each other. "Please sit down. May I order you something to drink? Hot tea, perhaps?"

Lizbeth didn't think she'd ever feel comfortable

enough in the Menger Hotel to be waited on by the rest of the staff. "No, thank you."

After Major Kelly seated himself, he said, "How are you finding Harrison House?"

"Wonderful." Unable to help herself, she smiled. "I think I will enjoy living there for the next couple of months."

"Ah. Well, yes." He cleared his throat. "That is why I wanted to speak to you."

"About my living at Harrison House?"

If anything, he looked even more pensive. "That, and other things. I have been doing a lot of thinking, you see."

She didn't.

"Thinking? About what?"

"I feel bad about your circumstances."

"How so?" Before he could reply, she added, "Sir, you secured a safe place for me to live until I can find employment. Mrs. Harrison is very kind. Already she's made me feel like I'm an honored guest."

But instead of looking relieved, his jaw tightened. "Perhaps we could talk about your job search for a moment."

"Sir?"

He looked as though he had to struggle to formulate his words. "Are you still hoping to look for work somewhere else?" When she nodded, he leaned forward. "As what? A maid?"

"Well, yes." Lizbeth felt a little stung. He

was acting as if that wasn't respectable work.

He frowned. "Don't you want something more than that?"

"I've learned what I want doesn't always matter."

"I think it does."

She almost laughed. Didn't he realize it wasn't just the men who had been changed by the war but the women too? "Times have changed, sir. I'm no longer the woman I used to be."

To her surprise, pain entered his eyes. "That may be true, but you don't have to give up all your dreams."

His comment, while sweet, was misinformed. She certainly did have to give up all her dreams. But more importantly, she'd realized that she was okay with that. "Major Kelly, something happened to me this morning."

Before he could say a word, she leaned forward, eager to share her epiphany. "You see, the strangest thing happened when I was sipping my coffee on the verandah. It occurred to me that I am not the only woman who suffered during the war."

When Ethan stared at her in confusion, she flushed. She needed to explain herself more fully. "I mean, of course I know thousands of men died or were grievously injured. The women in their lives grieved for them. I know that. But, well, I think a small part of me felt that no one had gone through quite what I had. I assumed that was why they were able to pick up the pieces of their lives and move on."

"When you weren't able to?"

She nodded, glad he understood. "Yes. I decided I've been a bit selfish, only focusing on myself and my own hurts. I need to start thinking about other people. And I am going to!"

But instead of looking pleased, Major Kelly only appeared more taken aback. "Don't make light of what you've gone through, Lizbeth—may I call you Lizbeth?"

She nodded, flattered he would want to.

"Others might have suffered," he went on, "but what happened to you was terrible."

"I know . . . but what I don't think I had completely appreciated was that I had been so used to being in pain and hurt I forgot to look at everything good in my life." Seeing the interest flicker in his eyes, she straightened with a smile. "I decided to start telling the Lord how grateful I am instead of asking him for things that cannot happen."

"Such as?"

His prodding was making her feel self-conscious. Stuttering a bit, she said, "W-well, things like marriage and children—and a home again."

And just like that, the tense set of his jaw eased. He shifted. "Lizbeth, it seems my timing is perfect, then. I asked you here to speak of those very same things."

"Do you know of a governess or a nanny position?"

"Uh, no."

Racking her brain, she tried to think of another job she might be suitable for that didn't involve either cleaning a house or caring for children. "As a companion?"

"No." He shifted. "You see, I don't like you working so hard, from sunup until sundown. It isn't right."

She may have given him permission to call her by her given name, but she was starting to feel as though he was completely overstepping his bounds. "Forgive me, but I must point out that what I do with my time really isn't your concern."

"But it is."

She was tired of his riddles. "Why?" she blurted.

"Because I've decided we should marry."

She almost started laughing. Almost. But then she looked into his eyes. He was very far from making a joke.

"Major Kelly, thank you for the honor, but I—"

He clasped her hand, startling her. "Miss Barclay, would you do me the very great honor of becoming my wife?"

His words were beautiful. His voice was fluid

and strong. No hesitation. No doubt in his tone. No flicker of unease in his eyes.

It was more than she'd ever hoped for. It was more than she deserved. To say no would be giving up so much.

Tears filled her eyes. Wanting to treasure the moment, even if it was for just another second.

13

As she did each morning, Julianne wrote in her journal, taking special care to write down the date. Today it gave her pause.

Four days had passed since Captain Devin Monroe walked away after entertaining a brief but misguided infatuation with her. Three days since Abby and Carl Bernard had rushed into her life like twin tornadoes, already upsetting everything in her daily routine and turning it on its side.

Amazing how God presented her with so much joy and so much pain at the same time. Amazing how she'd been able to bear both almost easily.

Abby hadn't been speaking lightly when she said she wanted to begin a friendship with her. Abby had visited her home on both Saturday and Sunday. She first brought her fiancé, Timothy, along with Carl. Julianne had been so surprised by the preacher being in her home that she had been flustered. The whole time they were talking, she'd been on pins and needles. She had been sure that, just when she relaxed, the preacher would choose to lecture her about the choices she'd made.

Timothy couldn't have been more different, though. He'd been friendly and open. As open in his conversation as his fiancée had been in her heart.

The second time Abby came alone. Carl was making a Sunday-afternoon call on a young lady.

Julianne was delighted with Abby. She was so chatty and friendly, and brought back memories of another time in her life. Back when she had little to worry about beyond what to wear to parties she was invited to. When they'd taken a stroll together, she was surprised to see their friendship was already doing miraculous things to her standing in town. It seemed seeing her with a companion was all anyone had needed to take the final step in setting her past firmly behind her.

As they drank tea when they returned, Julianne commented to Abby that she'd never expected to be so well received.

Abby brushed off her surprise. "It isn't as though you have a man living in your upstairs rooms right now, Julianne. Actually, even my aunt Dora was hard-pressed to remember a time when you did anything to cause talk. She said you conducted yourself like a lady at all times."

Had she? All Julianne could remember was being both alone and lonely. Except for when Daniel visited her. Then she had been at his beck and call until the moment he left, telling Bula her services were not needed when he was there. And when she had been a slave to him? Well, she'd been an emotional wreck. Sometimes a physical one too—especially when he took out his wartime misery on her, hitting her for some imagined slight.

Those had been dark days. She'd been embarrassed by what she'd done and scorned by others. The money the man gave her always felt tainted. Only when she used it to help her grandmother—and to buy chickens and garden seeds to help others during the war—was she reminded that everything she'd done had been for a good reason.

"If I haven't told you before, I am grateful for your kindness. It says a lot about your character to befriend a woman with my reputation. You are going to do Timothy proud, Abby."

"I hope so, though I want you to know I didn't befriend you for any reason beyond my explanation when Carl and I first introduced ourselves to you, Julianne."

"I am glad we are getting to know each other," Julianne said, feeling self-conscious.

Abby beamed. "Now that you've gotten that off your chest, let's talk about something far more interesting."

"Which is?"

"How we should go about finding a husband for you."

Julianne was thankful she hadn't been about to take a sip of tea. If she had, she would have probably choked on it! Instead, she laughed, determined to keep the moment light. "As much as you try to champion my honor, some realities cannot be overlooked. My past with the colonel is one of them. I simply am not marriage material."

"I heard a handsome man called on you the other day. Was that not the case?"

"Well, yes, a man did. A Captain Monroe. But that was a few days ago, the day before I met you and your brother. Nothing became of it, though."

"Maybe he'll call on you again. Men get busy, you know."

"He might be busy, but it doesn't signify. He won't be returning."

"Are you sure?" Abby must have noticed the expression in her eyes, because she softly added, "Did it not work out?"

That was one way to put it. "It didn't work out."

"But you liked him, though. Didn't you?"

Julianne was tempted to lie, but there was no reason to. "I did. I liked him very much."

"Maybe he'll change his mind and return."

"I'm afraid not. But that's all right, Abby. I've learned some things can never be changed. The past is one of them."

Abby nodded. "I'm starting to realize the most disappointed people in the world are the ones who cannot come to terms with that reality."

Since she knew disappointment well, Julianne decided truer words had never been said.

• • •

When she was alone again, buoyed by Abby's words of wisdom, Julianne decided to call on a woman she had talked to at church several times. She had always been kind and friendly, but Julianne had been the one to keep a small measure of distance between them. She realized now that she'd been unconsciously distancing herself from a potential friend.

She'd told herself it was so she wouldn't taint anyone with her reputation. But after Abby's talk, Julianne realized she had been the one putting up barriers. While honorable men like Devin Monroe might find her to be a less than suitable bride, it seemed others were not as judgmental in whom they befriended.

Miss Blake was gracious and welcoming when she tentatively knocked on her door. She invited Julianne into her parlor and served her tea and cake. In turn, Julianne did her best to be a friendly and entertaining guest. She shared stories about her gardening mishaps and the war she'd been having with some wily squirrels.

After visiting a half hour, she started for home. Between Abby's visit and her own call, Julianne couldn't recall having a more social, conversational day. The idea that it might be the first of many days made her smile.

As she entered her street, she drew up short. Just beyond her house was a proud-looking man on a black stallion. His back was to her, but she knew both his bearing and the horse as well as she knew the contents of her linen closet. It was Daniel Bushnell.

Her first reaction was to stop in her tracks. Heart racing, she scanned the area, looking to her left and then right. She ached to dart off to the shadows and hide. There weren't many options. A thicket of evergreens. The Conners' shed. But she was willing to take a chance on anything. Anywhere would be better than being out in the open. If he turned around, he'd spot her immediately. But just as she started walking, Daniel and his horse sped up and disappeared out of sight.

After waiting another moment, Julianne hurried to her house. As she approached the front door, she scanned the yard, examining the area. For what, she wasn't sure. Maybe she couldn't imagine Daniel leaving her house without leaving his mark as well? When all seemed quiet, she unlocked her door and started to step inside.

Then she saw it. A small bouquet of flowers. No doubt the cost had been dear. Flowers in November would be. Daniel had been forced to lay them on the doorstep. He was going to be so angry that she hadn't been there to receive them!

She picked up the bouquet. Fingered the rose petals absently. She was going to have to take them inside. Display them for anyone to see. Her heart started pounding as she wondered how she was going to explain their appearance to Bula. Or to Abby and Carl.

Then, with a start, she realized she didn't have to accept the flowers. She could leave them on the doorstep or even toss them in the trash. She wasn't Daniel's mistress anymore.

But instead of feeling better, she was confused. Because while she wasn't his anymore, her insides didn't seem to realize the difference.

Even now, after all this time, a part of her was still under his control.

14

It was cold. Dressed in his overcoat, boots, and felt Stetson, Devin still felt the bite of the cool wind on his skin as he leaned against the side of his house. He should probably go inside. He had a good steak he'd bought from a nearby rancher. He should cook it up with a couple of eggs. Maybe even open the book he'd purchased on a whim the last time he visited the mercantile. It was a rag highlighting the escapades of the notorious outlaw Scout Proffitt. Perhaps it would be entertaining enough for him to forget about Julianne Van Fleet for a couple of hours.

Yeah, right.

When Ethan was here two days ago, he'd promised to ride to San Antonio as soon as his other business was done—not just to find and confront Bushnell for the honor of Lizbeth but also for the honor of Julianne, even if he'd never see her again.

But he doubted he'd ever forget the look she gave him when he coldly told her he was leaving. She'd been crushed, yet also unsurprised.

And that was what had stayed with him. She hadn't expected to be treated better by him. She'd grouped him in the same category as a blackguard like Bushnell. That had hurt. Worse, he feared she might have been right on the mark.

Because the fact was he had behaved abominably. When had he decided he was fit to judge others?

For that matter, when had he become so cold? Hadn't she told him Bushnell had deceived her? That she and her grandmother had been suffering? Hadn't she told him she'd practically been forced to accept his offer because she'd been ruined and they'd been cold and hungry?

What did it really matter if she had done what she had to do to survive? Was that very different from some of the things he'd done during the war?

Julianne was lovely. When she was desperate, she used what the Lord had given her, just as he used his gifts to lead men into battle.

He'd left her feeling ashamed, but he knew that, in actuality, he had shamed himself. Tainted much of what he was.

No, turning his back on a woman wasn't who he was. Especially when he was already half in love with her.

He had to go back.

Once he'd made the decision, it was suddenly so easy. Not only would he see Julianne, but he'd also follow through on his promise to join Ethan in San Antonio and hunt for Bushnell. Although

Ethan could have already resolved his dilemma with Bushnell. Or perhaps the scoundrel had even left the area after Ethan threatened him. But he'd made a vow never to let his friends down when they needed help, and he wasn't going to start now.

Within fifteen minutes, he had walked to the barn, saddled Midge, and started toward Boerne. Pleased that he had a goal to accomplish, he felt better than he had in days.

Once in Boerne, he rode directly to Julianne's, even though the late-afternoon light was waning. He wasn't sure how he would be received, but he was willing to chance her displeasure for the opportunity to apologize.

When he got to her door, he knocked before he could talk himself out of it.

Almost immediately, he saw the curtains in a front window move. She had seen him.

Minutes passed. Then several more. He knocked again.

At last the door opened and Julianne stepped out onto the porch.

She was dressed far differently from the last time he saw her. She was wearing her glasses, her rich auburn hair was confined in a loose knot on the top of her head, and she was wearing a brown dress that was so shapeless it not only washed out her complexion but made her appear a bit like a baked potato.

Behind the glasses, he could see shadows under her eyes. There was a new wariness about her. Almost as if all her joy had been suctioned out of her.

"Yes, Captain?"

"Miss Van Fleet," he began after he bowed slightly. "May we talk?"

"I don't believe we have anything more to discuss, sir." Her hand was curved around the edge of the door. He knew he had mere seconds before she closed it in his face and turned around. With that same certainty, he knew he would not get another chance. If he could not smooth things out between them at once, she would never acknowledge him again.

"Miss Van Fleet, please reconsider. I won't take up much of your time," he continued in a rush. "Perhaps we could even talk out here." Even though it was getting colder outside.

She sighed. "Captain, I don't know what you want from me."

"Just your time."

"I gave you that, and it ended badly." Before he could apologize, she continued. "You seem to forget I never sought you out. I was also honest about my past."

"You are exactly right. I sought you out. You are beautiful, that is true. But there was something more that struck my fancy. I wanted to get to know you better."

"And you did." Wrinkling her nose, she murmured, "You don't have to feel any kind of misplaced guilt, sir. I didn't expect you to understand my circumstances."

"But that is why I am having such a difficult time. I know I disappointed you. But I disappointed myself as well." He straightened, holding himself so stiffly he might as well have been standing at attention. "I expect better of myself, you see."

"So this is about you."

"No."

"Are you sure about that?"

He felt his cheeks heat. Oh, but he was handling this badly. "It was wrong of me to leave the way I did. Please forgive me."

Her expression softened. "You are sincere, aren't you?"

"Very much so."

"I . . . I appreciate your words. But I feel I must remind you that nothing has changed. I can't change my past, Captain."

"I can't change mine either. Please don't give up on me yet."

She wavered, then opened the door farther. "Obviously I'm not dressed for callers."

"You look fine."

Placing her glasses in a pocket, she almost smiled. "Not so fine. If you would like, you may come inside. It's too cold for me out here."

"I would like to come inside. Thank you."

She smiled then. "I just made a pot of hot chocolate. Would you like some?"

He would consume anything she offered if it meant he could stay near. "Of course. Thank you."

"Entertaining again, Julianne?" a caustic voice called out behind him.

Julianne stiffened, and Devin turned.

Before he even realized what he was doing, Devin stepped in front of Julianne and faced the one man he'd hoped he'd never see again—even though he was planning to go to San Antonio to help Ethan find him.

Bushnell looked to be taken aback by his presence, but only for a moment.

"Sniffing after my castoffs, Devin?" he asked as he sauntered closer, finally stopping a few feet away.

Behind him, Julianne gasped.

And for the first time in memory, Devin acted without forethought. He punched the man hard in the jaw.

Bushnell flew back on impact. Then, sur-prisingly, he righted himself quickly and fisted his palms.

When he heard Julianne's cry behind him, Devin struggled for control. He could not lose his temper again, not if he ever wanted a chance with her. If Bushnell wanted to fight, he would fight him, but someplace far from Julianne. "You deserved my fist for what you just said about Miss Van Fleet," he said. "But if you think we're going to continue this discussion here, think again."

Daniel smirked. "What? So I'm supposed to just take that and walk away?"

"That is your choice. If you want to fight, I'll gladly do that. But I don't intend to beat you to a bloody pulp in front of Julianne."

"Like she matters?"

Comments like that were why Devin was so eager to pummel him into submission. "I'm warning you. I won't take kindly to you disrespecting her."

"Disrespecting her?" Bushnell spit on the ground. "She was my mistress, Devin. Nothing more than that. She lay on her back for my money."

Seeing red, Devin stepped forward. It seemed it was inevitable. He was going to have to beat this man on Julianne's front porch and pay the consequences later.

Just then Julianne placed a hand on his shoulder. "No, Devin. Please, don't trouble yourself."

"See? She knows what she is." Bushnell smirked.

Devin suddenly wished they were back in the army. At least then the strict code of conduct would have forced Bushnell to watch his mouth—or Devin to curb his temper.

Instead, he looked at the other man coldly. "I am advising you now to stop any and all interest in Miss Van Fleet. She is no longer your concern."

"Or else?"

He should have known that was coming. "Or else I'll make sure everyone knows about the secrets you sold during the war."

"What secrets? I was no traitor."

Devin knew he wasn't. But he also knew—thanks to what had happened to Phillip Markham in Galveston—how easily information could be twisted and misconstrued. "Good luck convincing everyone of that. One word from me and there won't be a man in the state who will give you the time of day."

Bushnell glared. "You have made a serious mistake, Monroe. I won't forget this."

"Neither will I. I can promise you that." Devin stood motionless, never taking his eyes off the man until Bushnell walked away, mounted his horse, and left. His only regret was that he'd not determined where he and Ethan could find him next.

Devin could hear Julianne breathing hard a few steps behind him. He moved to stand in the doorway until Daniel Bushnell was out of sight. Only then did he step inside, close the door, and face her.

As he suspected, she was in tears and pale. Staring up at him, her blue eyes looked murky with worry and dismay.

And, it seemed, fear.

That hit him hard. "Don't be afraid of me," he said, stepping forward. "I would never hurt you."

"What have you done?"

He drew up short. "I kept you safe." He'd also been marking his territory, establishing his regard, and setting ground rules. Now if Bushnell ever contemplated approaching Julianne again, he would think twice. And maybe he'd done enough to keep him from Ethan's Lizbeth as well. When the man calmed down, he was bound to realize he and Ethan were still friends, still in touch. Maybe the thought of the two of them coming after him would be a deterrent—at least for the time being.

Julianne shook her head. "He is very powerful, Captain Monroe."

"Not so much."

"He has powerful friends. And a lot of money. I have no way to fight what he wants or anything he tries to coerce me with."

"Yes, you do."

When she stared at him in confusion, he murmured, "You are not alone anymore, Julianne. Please. Calm yourself and don't worry."

"Don't worry. You make that sound possible."

"It is. He is not going to bother you again. I know he is not."

"You don't know that. Besides, what am I going to do when you leave and he comes back?" Her bottom lip trembled. "Now he's going to think we are more to each other than we are."

Her bitter tone. The way her arms were curved around her middle, as though she was attempting to comfort herself. Those words. That lack of belief in him . . . It all came together. Made something snap.

And so he did what he shouldn't do, what she was no doubt afraid of, what was undoubtedly a very bad idea.

He took the last four steps to her side, grasped her upper arms, and pulled her into his embrace.

She stumbled forward and braced her hands on his chest.

He almost smiled. That was exactly where she needed to be. Exactly where he wanted her.

"Captain—"

"I'm not your captain," he said, his voice rough. "My name is Devin. Call me by my name." Then, before she could protest again, he bent his head and claimed her lips.

She gasped. He took advantage and deepened the kiss. Then did what he had been dreaming about since the first moment he'd spied her across the town square. He pulled her closer and kissed her again. More thoroughly. And when she melted against him, he felt such a thrill that he groaned and continued.

Her hands reached up, curved around his neck. Her touch was so sweet. So precious. So exactly what he'd been imagining that he lifted his head to smile.

When he looked down into her face, what he saw there made all the pain and suffering in his life worthwhile.

Because Julianne Van Fleet was gazing at him in wonder. Her lips were slightly parted, and her blue eyes were bright with passion.

She'd desired him too. He felt triumphant.

Until she slapped him. Hard.

Hard enough that he flinched in response. Rubbing his hand along his jaw, he studied her curiously. "What was that for?"

"Need you ask?" Fire, mixed liberally with condemnation, burned deep in her eyes.

She was upset with him. Blamed him. Had he hurt her?

Horrified, he drew back. Dropped his hands from where they'd curved so perfectly around her waist. "I thought you wanted that kiss as much as I did. Julianne, I swear I didn't think I forced you." He knew he hadn't. He was enough of a man to know when a woman welcomed his touch.

Enough of a man to know when she didn't.

She was trembling now. "Please leave."

"Leave?"

Breathing heavily, she nodded. "And do not come back."

After that kiss? After he'd confronted Bushnell about her honor?

Then, finally, he noticed she didn't look frightened of him. No, it was more as if she was frightened of the things she was feeling. Maybe she was just unsure of his intentions, or what she meant to him.

"Julianne, I know you enjoyed that kiss as much as I did."

She inhaled. "I . . ."

He almost smiled as he continued. "Don't deny it." Lowering his voice, he murmured, "Maybe, like me, you are hoping I will hold you in my arms again soon."

She paled as disappointment flowed from her. "Is that why you came here today, Devin Monroe?" she asked quietly. "Did you come to claim my charms? Have you decided to become my new keeper?"

"Of course not."

"I have no desire to be another man's mistress."

He would have laughed if he hadn't been so disappointed that she thought he would ask her to do such a thing. "I did not come here to ask you that. I don't want a mistress."

"Oh? Is that simply how you greet all women you know?"

"Of course not." Becoming frustrated, he said, "Don't twist my actions into something dishonorable, Julianne."

She blinked. Her posture eased. "Maybe you could explain yourself."

She didn't sound as mortified now. How could he begin to explain the mixture of emotions he felt toward her? It was likely impossible.

But still he tried. "I came here for the very reason I told you when I first arrived on your doorstep. I wanted to apologize. I was wrong. I hold you in high regard. But then, that blasted Bushnell came and you were crying . . . and—"

"And you decided to kiss me without my permission?"

For the second time in ten minutes, his temper snapped. "Julianne, as much as I respect you and have worthy intentions, let's not start pretending you are an innocent miss."

She gasped. "Sir—"

"Let me finish. Listen to what I have to say. I don't want an innocent miss. And for the record, that wasn't my first kiss either." He edged closer. Close enough to smell the faint scent of roses in her hair. "But no kiss I've ever experienced was like that. It was perfect."

Her eyes were stormy as she gaped at him.

"Do you disagree?"

For a second, he was sure she wasn't going

to reply. But then she shook her head. Almost imperceptibly.

Making him feel triumphant again.

Glad his emotions were coming in check, he said, "I wasn't going to tell you this because I didn't want to scare you, but I aim to marry you one day soon."

"Marry? Captain—"

"Devin."

"Devin, you don't know what you're saying. I cannot . . ." Obviously flummoxed, her voice drifted off.

"Finish that thought, Julianne. I want to hear what you have to say."

She pressed her fingertips to her lips. "But . . ."

He decided to make it easy on her. "I think it's time for a bit of space. I am coming back in one week. Please plan for me to take you out to dinner."

"We can't discuss marriage. We hardly know each other."

"That's exactly why I'm coming back. And if Bushnell returns, don't answer the door."

"I hardly know what to think."

He laughed. "Good. Now you know how I've felt from the moment I first saw you. I don't know what to think. I don't know how to act. All I know is that I want to know you better. I want you in my life."

"Devin . . ."

"If I'm going too fast, well, I'll slow down. I'll wait until you are ready. But I'm not going to change my mind about us."

"You sound so sure."

"I haven't been this sure about anything in quite a long time. Trust me, Julianne. Believe me when I say I am coming back and that my intentions are honorable." Staring at her hard, he said, "Okay?"

Tears pricked her eyes as she gave a purely feminine, adorable shrug. "Well . . . um, okay."

Pleased that he'd gotten his way, his tone gentled. "Good. Now, don't forget about Bushnell. Stay away from him."

She nodded. "I will."

"Good."

"You don't have to leave this minute. Would you like to come sit down?"

She was too tempting. So tempting, he knew he needed advice. He needed to go see Ethan. "I cannot. I need to go to San Antonio. I've got an old friend there, a fellow former prisoner with whom I need to confer about some personal business." Such as how to ruin Daniel Bushnell. "Major Kelly is a bit of a gambler now, but I know of no finer man. He's staying at the Menger Hotel there."

"Will you promise to be careful? Daniel was so angry . . ."

"Always." Reaching out, he cupped her cheek

186

with one rough palm. "See you in one week."

Before she could ask any more questions or think of another argument, he bowed and then strode out her front door.

If all went well, he would be in San Antonio by nightfall and seeing Ethan Kelly shortly after. Hopefully, he could already shed some light on Bushnell's present occupation and usual whereabouts. Then, together, they could decide what else needed to be done to get him out of their lives—and out of their women's lives too.

It was time.

15

Devin took care to follow the curve of the river as he rode east toward San Antonio. Though there was a bite to the air, it felt exhilarating. Fresh.

He knew, of course, the elements outside weren't what made it so. No, his response to the weather had everything to do with his state of mind.

At long last, he was hopeful about the future. His time with Julianne had been transformational. Not only had they mended their rift, but he had new goals in mind. He intended to one day marry Julianne Van Fleet and find a way to remove Daniel Bushnell from her life.

Both missions were daunting. Neither was sure to be a success. But it was because of those plans that he felt uplifted.

While keeping a careful watch for other riders in the distance, Devin allowed his mind to drift back to when he'd been a cavalry officer.

Oh, not to the bad times. Not back when all of them were bloody and hurting and exhausted. Or when everyone had been injured, suffering from stomach ailments, or hungry. But back at the beginning of the war. When he'd first enlisted and been so cocky and full of himself. Back when there was so much hope and excitement in the air it was almost impossible to think of anything else.

Because of his father's influence and his natural ability to lead, handle a rifle, and ride, he'd been able to gain commissions as a second lieutenant. Over the first year, he'd easily slid up the ranks. He'd been so gratified when he'd made captain. So comfortable with that rank that he'd stayed there.

Scanning the horizon again, he relaxed slightly as he saw a collection of lights in the distance. He would be in the Menger Hotel soon. Once there, he was going to spend a good hour at the bar. Indulge in a shot of whiskey. Maybe two. Talk to the other men sitting around the bar who were usually amiable, often ready to trade stories about nothing that mattered. That was something he was looking forward to.

And get down to business with Ethan. He needed to tell him what happened with Bushnell at Julianne's.

"Not long now, girl," he murmured to his mare.

Midge whickered softly. Then, as if she'd understood his words, increased her pace.

Soon they were trotting across the cold surface of ground that had already settled in for a long winter. The wind brushed his cheeks, curled tight around the skin on his neck like a kerchief. His tan duster—stained, worn, and frayed at the edges—felt like a warm companion. Enveloping him with warmth without asking for much.

He realized he was happy. At last, he had been pulled from his inertia. Julianne was going to allow him to court her. One day he'd bend down on one knee and ask her to honor him by being his wife. And when she said yes, he knew he would push her to the altar as quickly as he could. No doubt, she'd protest. Maybe even remind him she was no innocent, blushing bride.

But she was perfect for him.

He'd have to remind her that he'd seen too much, done too much bad to be the right fit for someone too sheltered.

He smiled, imagining the conversation. No doubt, she'd shake her head. Say—

Crack.

The force of the bullet hit his shoulder with enough emphasis to make him gasp. His mind blanked. Only the memories that lay deep in his muscles allowed him to keep his seat in the saddle. Only the horse's knowledge of war and battle enabled her to continue forward without getting spooked.

When he heard another gunshot, he hugged his mare's neck and spurred her on, allowing her to run hell for leather. Though he figured the Lord had gifted him with more years than most soldiers ever deserved, he wasn't ready to die. Not yet.

He turned to look behind him. Needing to see

how much distance he'd gained. Needing to see who had been so yellow as to shoot him from behind.

The rider loomed in the distance. He was wearing a pale Stetson, a black duster, and was keeping his pace. His familiar gray appaloosa was a fine piece of horseflesh. He was galloping steady, solid.

After another few seconds passed, Devin glanced behind him again. That's when the rider's head lifted. When Devin caught sight of who had shot him. He'd been right.

Bushnell.

Cold calculation settled in Devin's soul. As Midge continued to zig and zag and direct him to safety, as Devin's blood no doubt stained his tan duster more, he fostered that anger.

To keep his bearings, he planned his revenge on Bushnell. And though it didn't make him proud, he knew he was not going to regret giving the man his due. No man was going to live long enough to attempt to kill him twice.

Not if he could help it.

16

Sitting on one of the bronze velvet chairs in the main parlor at the Menger, his marriage proposal looming awkwardly between them like an unfamiliar relative, Ethan had stared into Lizbeth's eyes.

What he saw hadn't been reassuring. Pain and worry distorted their green color. Made them look a little murky. Darker than they were.

Or maybe that had been his imagination.

It didn't really matter all that much. All that mattered was that she was about to say no. But without a word, she had risen to her feet and walked out to the lobby. He didn't have to follow her to know she was returning to Harrison House.

Ethan had expected a refusal. Lizbeth Barclay had more integrity in her fingertips than he did in his whole body. No doubt, she probably had more integrity than most of the men he'd served with and fought beside during the war.

She was certainly more upright than most of people he'd been spending time with of late. She would never marry him just to help herself. She especially wouldn't agree to a match between them if she thought he might later regret it. He was beginning to think she wouldn't promise to love and honor someone if she didn't—certainly not in a house of God. Maybe not even to herself.

The only people he'd held in such high esteem were his band of brothers. Monroe, Truax, and Baker were his best friends in the world. Their bond had been forged on scarred battlefields, in desperate fights, and during forced captivity.

And now, after he'd spent all day trying to determine where Bushnell had gone, trying to convince himself it would be wrong to pursue Lizbeth further, she had returned. When it was almost dark. They were sitting on a brown velvet settee in the lobby this time. But she wasn't saying anything. And neither was he.

As the silence stretched between them, he wondered how that could be. How could he feel so close to a woman he just met when it had taken years of pain and suffering to feel as close to other people?

Under his regard, she began to look uneasy.

And why wouldn't she? He was staring at her intently. So far, he'd done nothing in her company that was worthy of her.

But he wanted to. He wanted to change. To become better. He thought he might have a chance if he had her by his side.

And that was the heart of why he wanted her. It wasn't just that he felt he owed her for his part in her trials. It wasn't just that he ached to do something of worth again. Something that he could go to sleep at night feeling pleased about.

More than that, he yearned for someone good in his life again. Someone pure. No, not innocent. He didn't need innocence. He needed a pure heart and kindness far more.

It was selfish. He knew that. But he had long ago come to terms with the fact that he wasn't nearly as good as some thought. He was a study in missed opportunities and multiple faults.

That made him realize he was going to have to do something harder than just about anything he'd done in a very long time. He was going to have to show his real self to her. Not the slick gambler who bent rules. Who used his looks and charm to get what he wanted. He needed to show her the man he was underneath the layers of gold cufflinks and silk vests. The man he'd been for the Confederacy, when having honor and integrity had mattered so much.

He was going to have to allow her to see a man of whom she could be proud. A cold chill swept through him, one that had nothing to do with the lobby door opening and allowing the frosty air to worm its way inside. He had to start talking.

"Don't say no," he blurted, defying all his good intentions.

Her expression turned even more pained. "Major—"

"It's Ethan. Call me Ethan."

"Yes. All right. Ah . . . Ethan," she began. "Your

proposal shocked me this morning. You and I met only days ago, but that was no excuse to leave as I did. I simply had to . . . think. I did not want to offend you, because I do appreciate the sacrifice you are willing to make for my safety."

"It's not a sacrifice."

She kept talking. "What's more, you honor me, but I cannot accept. *Of course* I cannot accept."

Tears were now in her eyes. She was rattled. He'd upset her that morning, and she was still upset. "Please, let us discuss this," he said quietly. "Please know I don't propose lightly. I do not intend to make a mockery of these vows. I will honor them."

Glancing around the lobby, she stiffened. No doubt she was as aware as he that they were being observed. They were causing a scene. "Sir, how could I think otherwise? We don't know each other. And . . . and, Ethan, I'm just a maid."

"You are more than that and we both know it."

"But—"

"And I know enough." He'd told himself he wouldn't, but he persisted, using all the skills he'd learned to press his suit. "Don't forget that marriage is for a lifetime. We'll have years to get to know each other."

"But that isn't how it's supposed to happen. Is it?" She stood.

"Does it even matter?" Getting to his feet, he held out a hand. "Please. Sit down again so we can talk about this." When it looked as though she was going to refuse, he murmured, "Don't I at least deserve your time?"

She sat back down, but her back was tense. "Of course you do, but I don't see what can change." Taking a deep breath, she said, "As I thought about your proposal all afternoon, I was reminded that marriage is the culmination of a romance. It's the crowning glory, the opportunity to make promises and say vows honored by God. It is not the beginning."

Her words were pretty. But he also thought they were far too fanciful for the violent, desperate times they were living in. "Lizbeth, for others, perhaps that is how marriage comes about. But we both know that isn't what always happens. Sometimes a couple marries because it makes the most sense. Think of all the unions that formed before men went off to war."

"Ethan, perhaps I should have spoken more clearly. While others might venture into such a union, I will not."

"Lizbeth, if you consider it for a moment, you will see you need a protector."

"I need a great many things, Major. A marriage of convenience is not one of them."

"Not even for protection?"

"Not even for that."

He couldn't help it. He smiled. She had so much fire. She was so earnest. Intent. "You could be wrong. Have you considered that?"

"Even if I am, it doesn't matter. I won't repay kindness by shackling a man like you with a woman like me."

"Don't speak as if we are worlds apart. You have much that I desire."

Her cheeks were now flushed. "You are embarrassing me. People are listening."

Feeling brash, feeling desperate, he shrugged. "Let them listen. I don't care. Aren't you going to allow me to explain my reasons? That's hardly fair."

"Do you have reasons?"

"Of course."

She still looked skeptical. "Real ones?"

"First, to be completely honest, you need me, and I need to do this. Lizbeth, Miss Barclay, there is more to me than you are aware. There is more to me than I've allowed you to see."

"Why is that?"

Because he'd been afraid. Afraid to revisit the memories. Afraid to admit he had changed. Afraid to share he had as many scars in his soul as he did on his body. He was marked, and sometimes, in the middle of the night when the things he'd done haunted him, he was very weak. "Maybe, like you, I need time. And I need to be able to trust."

A new light of vulnerability shown in her eyes. "You too?"

"Especially me."

"If you need to marry, a great many willing and desperate women are available. I suggest you set your sights elsewhere."

"For reasons I cannot explain, the bride needs to be you. Please consider it. I promise you will not be disappointed."

She was weakening. He could feel it. Felt it as sure as if he were sitting at a poker table and knew the man across from him was holding a straight flush in his hands.

Just as sure as if his enemy had a flaw, a gap he could identify.

He was going to get his way. It was all he could do to not smile.

Then the door swung open. In walked a man with blond hair in a tan duster. Hair cut short by necessity and bleached by wind and sun and years. A man with eyes so light in color that one might imagine they were gray or silver. But they were light blue.

They also looked filled with pain.

Concerned, Ethan surged to his feet. "Monroe!" he called out to get his attention. "Are you all right?"

Captain Devin Monroe turned to him, started forward, then stopped again, as if the step was too painful. "No."

By now Ethan was at his side. He reached out, intending to support him, but instead he ended up enfolding Devin in his arms. Realizing the other man had passed out, he eased him to the lobby floor.

"Ethan?" Lizbeth cried. "What happened? Who is that?"

"Get a doctor. Fast," he barked as he started pulling at Devin's duster. Blood stained his hands, sunk into the crevice of his fingertips.

It had been years since he'd seen a wound like this. Devin had been shot with a high-caliber shotgun. And, if he wasn't mistaken, he was staring at an exit wound. Devin Monroe had been shot in the back, just below his shoulder.

"Someone's already gone for help," Lizbeth said as she knelt next to him. "Use this."

Grabbing the soft fabric, Ethan realized she'd given him one of her petticoats.

Folding it tightly in his hands, he pressed it against Devin's wound. The fabric turned red in seconds. So much blood.

When Devin groaned, Ethan leaned closer. "I'm here," he whispered. "You are not alone."

"I'm . . . I'm okay."

Glad that Devin had spoken again, though weakly, Ethan felt a burst of anger surge through him. It was unimaginable that this friend, their captain, could survive so much only to be felled now. "Who did this?" He knew Devin would understand. If he didn't survive, someone would need to avenge him.

Even if it took the rest of his life, Ethan knew right then and there that it needed to be him.

"Bushnell," he whispered.

17

"Bushnell?" Ethan repeated, leaning closer to Devin, ignoring the blood seeping through the linen cloth against his friend's wound and staining his hand. Surely he had misunderstood.

"Colonel Bushnell did this?" Lizbeth asked faintly. "How . . . how could that be?"

It didn't make any sense to him either. But he didn't doubt that Devin had spoken the right name.

He was aware that Lizbeth was upset and standing directly behind him, but Ethan forced himself to ignore her needs. He ignored the questions forming in his mind too. Only one thing mattered at that moment—ensuring Devin's survival.

"What is going on? Oh!" a feminine voice exclaimed behind him. Ethan glanced over his shoulder and saw it was Aileen Howard.

"This gentleman has been shot, Aileen," Lizbeth said quietly. "A doctor has been sent for. At least, I hope so. We need a room to place him in."

"Yes, well . . ."

"Immediately, ma'am," Ethan bit out. "And get someone outside to see to his horse."

"I'll take care of this, Aileen," her husband said

as he joined them. "Go see if the physician has indeed been sent for." After a pause, he knelt on one knee by Ethan's side.

Though he resented the intrusion, the tone of Dallas's quiet voice reassured Ethan something was about to get done. "I need to get him off the floor this minute."

"I have just the place. Lizbeth?"

She stepped closer. "Yes, Dallas?"

"We're going to put this man in the Mockingbird Suite. Take my keys and open it, if you please."

As Lizbeth took the keys without a word, Ethan's admiration for her grew. Here she had just discovered the man who threatened her had tried to kill his friend. Furthermore, she was having to interact with her cousin and her husband, both of whom had treated her shamefully.

But instead of asking dozens of questions or breaking down into tears, she was calmly assisting them as if she were used to such things happening all the time.

"I'll help you carry him to the room, Major," Dallas said. "It's a private suite just down the hall here."

Ethan was hesitant to move Devin, but he figured it was the lesser of two evils. At least six or seven men were standing nearby, looking on. No doubt far more men and women were observing from more distant spots. This was no way to treat a war hero. "All right," he said at last. "I'll take his shoulders if you can take his middle."

"I'll help you carry him," another man said as he came forward.

Ethan eyed him closely and then nodded when he realized he recognized him from some of the better local gambling halls. The man was a former soldier and had always seemed competent enough. "Thank you."

The three of them bent down, surrounding Devin. As Ethan slipped his hands around Devin's upper torso, he gave a silent prayer of thanks that he was again unconscious.

"On my count of three," he barked, slipping into the tone he'd used in the army. It was forceful and allowed no discussion. "One. Two." He inhaled. Prayed they were doing the right thing. "Three," he said around an exhale.

And together, the three of them lifted Devin's form in unison. Devin wasn't a small man. Easily six feet and solid muscle. Ethan was glad the third man had offered to lend them assistance.

"We'll take him about ten feet, then turn down that hallway," Dallas said.

Ethan started walking backward. He was vaguely aware of another man motioning everyone who was gawking to get out of the way.

They turned and continued their slow pace. Blood from Devin's wound soaked Ethan's hand and dripped on the carpet. Each drop made him worry all the more. His friend was losing a great amount of blood. This was also too close to some of the worst battles he'd been involved in. He began to feel a little dizzy and light-headed as the metallic, coppery scent of blood invaded his space and brought him suddenly too near memories he always tried very hard to forget.

"Not much farther, Major," Dallas said.

Ethan nodded. Hating the sudden weakness he felt, he forced himself to focus on the present and gazed down at Devin. His eyes were still closed, his mouth slack. His face deathly pale.

What was he going to do if they lost him?

"Here's the room," Dallas announced. "Lizbeth, is everything ready?"

"I believe so. I found Callie in the corridor. She's bringing hot water and clean linens to treat the wound."

"Good. That's good," Dallas said easily as he guided them toward the bed.

Just as they were about to set Devin's body down, Ethan noticed Lizbeth had placed an extra blanket over the coverlet.

Though it was awkward, the three men managed to lay Devin on the mattress with a minimum of jostling. Only when he was lying still but looking no worse did Ethan feel as though he could take a cleansing breath at last.

"Thank you," he told the gambler. "I'm sorry. I don't recall your name . . ."

"Harold Neidig," he said. "Formerly a sergeant out of Virginia."

The description, said with a small amount of pride, spurred a smile from Ethan. "I'm indebted to you, Mr. Neidig."

"Is that Captain Monroe, by any chance?"

"It is."

Mr. Neidig studied him closely. "I heard stories about him, but I never thought we'd meet."

"God willing, you will soon."

"I'll pray for his recovery," Mr. Neidig said, executing a small bow before exiting.

Right then a small maid carrying a wooden bucket of steaming water and a pile of linen against her chest entered the room. Lizbeth rushed to her side. Together, they emptied the water into a basin.

After the maid left, Dallas walked to the door. "I'll go see where the doctor is," he said. He closed the door again, giving them privacy.

Ethan found he was incapable of moving. "I'm afraid he's about to die," he said at last.

"I know you are, but we mustn't give up hope," Lizbeth said as she walked to the foot of the bed. "Let's take off his boots and make him comfortable."

Glad for something to do, he worked with Lizbeth to move Devin's leg enough to allow them to pull off the snug-fitting boots.

Devin groaned under his breath.

Amazingly, Lizbeth smiled. "See? We haven't lost him yet."

Her irreverent comment brought back his hope. Lizbeth was right. They hadn't lost him, and what's more, Ethan was going to do everything he could to make sure they didn't.

Determined to do something, anything, instead of allowing his fears and the memories of war to overtake him again, he pulled out a knife and carefully cut along the seam of Devin's tan duster, then his jacket.

When only a linen shirt covered Devin's skin, Ethan felt dizzy again. The fabric was soaked with blood. Some of it even looked like it was stuck to his flesh. He stared at the linen, unsure whether it was better to leave the fabric in place or clean the wound as quickly as possible. "We need that doctor," he said to Lizbeth. "Could you see what his status is?"

"Of course." But just as she was about to leave, Aileen peeked inside.

"Major Kelly, Dr. Palermo is on his way. He should be here very soon."

"Palermo, you say?"

Still hovering at the door, Aileen nodded. "Yes. He's Italian. Very knowledgeable."

"Thank you for coming to tell me yourself."

After Aileen exchanged a look with Lizbeth, she closed the door again.

Lizbeth walked to his side. "Major Kelly, all we can do is pray and wait."

Her words made sense, but he needed to do more than that. Devin's face was deathly pale. After feeling for his pulse again, he made the decision. He was going to pull off the last of the fabric and care for Devin until more help arrived. It's what he had done on the battlefield, and it was what he needed to do now.

After taking off his jacket, Ethan removed his gold cufflinks and rolled up his sleeves. "I need to bathe his wound. Get me some more warm water, soap, and more cloths."

"Of course." She turned and walked out the door without another word.

Glad to be alone with his thoughts, he took the cloth Lizbeth had placed by the basin and dampened it. Then he carefully removed what was left of Devin's shirt. As he had known it would, the wound started bleeding again.

Steeling himself, he pressed cloths to the wound, hoping his efforts would staunch the flow of blood. As he did, he also inspected the rest of Devin's torso, looking for any further damage he had inadvertently overlooked.

Devin's skin was as marked as his own. A product of the Rangers, then the cavalry, Devin looked as though he had survived as many close calls as any other veteran of the war. Funny how Ethan had never taken the time to think about Devin being a survivor like the rest of them. For some reason Ethan had always regarded Devin Monroe as impervious to cuts, bruises, bullet holes.

Stunned, he sat on the side of the bed. He'd seen Devin sleep, of course, but the captain never looked completely relaxed. His body had always had a certain tenseness about it, as though he were only moments from springing into action and taking charge of most anything.

Now he only looked vulnerable.

Ethan realized his hands were shaking. Not from fear for himself. No, it was from fear of failure. Fear that he wasn't going to be able to help Devin. That Devin could die in this room.

When the door swung open again, Lizbeth entered, along with another maid. He heard Lizbeth call the young woman Cassie. They were carrying a pitcher, a floral basin of steaming water, and several cloths. After the other maid set the basin on the dresser and left, Lizbeth spoke.

"I know you don't want or need my help, but could I stay in here with you?"

He was about to refuse, but he did need help. "I'm, uh, attempting to bathe him. But I can't seem to do that with this wound in such bad shape. I need to keep pressure on it."

"I can bathe him."

"Thank you, Lizbeth."

Without another word, she dampened another cloth, picked up one of Devin's arms, and carefully began cleaning his hand. His fingers were stained with blood. It was obvious he'd been applying pressure to his wound himself.

But instead of looking shaken by the blood and grime she was removing, Lizbeth seemed calm. He recalled that she hadn't flinched or launched into hysterics like the other women in the lobby had when Devin appeared. She'd been surprised and upset, of course, but seemed more intent on helping him than giving in to vapors.

"This wound doesn't seem to faze you," he said quietly. "Is it because you've seen bad wounds before?"

"I have."

"From the war?"

"Yes. But while growing up too." She moved to her left so she could clean the last of the blood from Devin's skin. "Growing up on a ranch, well, all sorts of accidents occur."

He was intrigued by the thought of Lizbeth working a ranch. Hoping to concentrate on anything other than the chance of failure, he murmured, "Any happen to you?"

"Yes. Once I knocked into the blade of a scythe

that had been recently sharpened. Before I knew it, I had a sizable cut on my calf. My grandmother stitched me up."

"I bet your wound was painful."

She smiled faintly as she smoothed a fresh rag across Devin's brow. "Being stitched up hurt worse, I can tell you that. My grandmother wasn't an especially gentle nurse."

"And your forehead? Did you get stitches then?"

"No." Her voice was tight and distrusting. He realized she was upset that he'd even brought it up.

He probably shouldn't have. She was helping him. The very least he owed her was to respect her privacy. But he couldn't bring himself to apologize. He needed to know about her, and what secrets she had.

"Do you remember how you got that scar?"

Her hand stilled. "Of course I do."

He waited, hoping she would expound upon it. When she didn't, he prodded again. "Was it, by chance, a ranch accident?"

"It was not."

Her voice, usually rather tentative, was as hard as the red dirt in the middle of summer. "What happened?"

"This scar isn't something I speak about."

He should have said he understood. After all, he didn't like talking about anything that happened in the war. Instead, he kept pushing. "Have you ever talked about it with anyone?"

"No."

"Perhaps it would help."

She turned to rinse out her cloth. "Help what? The scar has healed."

He swallowed, half feeling as if he was talking as much to himself as he was to her. "I've heard that talking about painful topics makes them easier to bear." He wasn't lying. He had heard about that. But all the same, he felt like the worst sort of charlatan. He could barely handle the smell of blood now.

"Talking about this won't help."

He should leave it alone. Devin was bleeding, they were waiting on a doctor, her whole life had just been turned on its side, and they hardly knew each other.

But her voice had sounded so tight, so filled with pain, Ethan knew he had to say something. If nothing else, he owed it to her. After all, he'd seen that scar when it was fresh and he'd hurt her anyway. "I am used to hearing confidences," he said. "I wouldn't betray your trust."

"Sir—"

He talked right over her. "Holding something like that inside can be harmful to you." He drew in a breath. Stared at her pretty green eyes. Tried to make his words softer, more meaningful. "Take it from me."

"Whom did you speak to about your scars and injuries, Major?" she whispered softly. "And how did it help you heal?"

"I am surprised by your sarcasm."

"And I am surprised you think I am so naïve as to imagine that speaking to anyone about something that can't be changed would change anything for me."

He knew she was right. But she was wrong too. "I shared my pain and worries with my comrades at Johnson's Island. I complained about my wounds and injuries to the men I fought beside on the battlefields. I talked about my fears with the men on the cots next to me in the hospital tents."

"You aren't lying, are you?"

"I'm not lying."

Her voice lowered. "And when you shared your hurts with them, what happened?"

He knew this question was important. That it meant everything. Therefore, he struggled with how best to answer. Finally, he simply spoke from his heart. "I was free. Even there, in a prison barracks, behind enemy lines. Their acceptance freed me and made me almost whole."

She blinked. A hint of wonder lit her eyes before she firmly pushed it away.

But he had seen it.

And he knew then that she believed too.

18

Had a morning ever been so gloomy? Julianne stared out on the horizon and searched for a glimpse of blue sky. But only dark clouds hung there. They seemed weighted by precipitation yet too stubborn to give up their precious water.

She could understand that. Part of her felt more than a passing kinship with those clouds. From the moment Devin had left the day before, she'd felt a heavy ache in her chest, convinced he would not return as promised. Experience had taught her a good cry could ease her pain and alleviate the pressure there. But she was so tired of crying. It didn't help, anyway. All her tears ever seemed to do was make her eyes red and her mouth parched. She was done crying over whatever she wished were different.

Instead, she realized bitterly, she seemed happy enough to stand out in the cold and look out into the distance. Wishing a certain man with light-blue eyes and blond hair would appear, already back from his visit to San Antonio and eager to see her again.

Folding her arms over her middle, she rested her head against one of the posts holding the porch railing. Sighed. And finally cautioned herself to stop making a spectacle of herself.

Just as she was ready to turn around, she caught sight of a carriage. Holding a hand over her eyes, she peered into the distance. Her pulse began to race. Maybe Devin *had* come back early. Maybe he was bringing a carriage to take her on an outing today.

Then she realized it was Carl and Abby Bernard. Today's appearance was a blessing. She'd grown tired of her mournful thoughts. Their company would be a welcome change of pace. At the very least, she wouldn't be looking out into the horizon for hours on end.

When Carl parked their carriage, Julianne opened the front door and let her beagle, Ginger, outside. Ginger looked delighted by their visitors and scampered ahead, her soft ears flapping in the wind.

The moment Carl alighted, Julianne raised her hand. "Good day, Carl."

After a second's pause, he smiled broadly. "Indeed it is, Julianne. I trust you are well?"

The proper response would be to say she was, indeed, very well. But she was as tired of pretending as she was of her doldrums. "I've been better, if you want to know the truth."

He looked at her closely, then seemed to be waging a war with himself as he extended a hand to help his sister down from their carriage.

Julianne fought back a smile as Abby accepted her brother's gesture, but then practically jumped out of the conveyance as though she were on a newfangled pogo stick. Her brown hair was artfully arranged in a high chignon. It flattered her features. That, and her sparkling eyes, made her appear almost fairy-like. Julianne reflected once again that Abby's pastor fiancé had no doubt been charmed from the moment he spied her.

"Hello, Julianne! And Ginger too!"

Ginger barked while Julianne laughed. "Hello, Abby. Would you care for some tea or coffee? It's rather dreary out here."

"I would, indeed. I dressed in layers, but I still find myself chilled to the bone." She trotted up the steps and gave Julianne a hug.

Startled, Julianne wrapped her arms around the girl and tried not to think about how long it had been since she'd been the recipient of such a warm gesture. After Carl joined them, she led the way inside.

The fire was still burning in the parlor. "Please, do make yourselves comfortable. Bula is away today, but I'll return with tea—"

"Please, allow me to help you," Abby said, interrupting. "After all, we're more than mere guests by now."

Carl scratched his chin. "Well, now, I don't know if that is how one should behave . . ."

When Abby's cheeks flashed bright red, Julianne decided to save the conversation. "Of course you both are more than mere guests now. Abby is right. You are friends."

As they followed her to the kitchen, Carl said, "Is that why you were honest enough to share that something has been upsetting you?"

"Perhaps," she allowed. "Or I might have come to the conclusion that no good would come with me pretending otherwise."

"What happened?" Abby asked as they entered the small but well-appointed kitchen.

Though it was on the tip of her tongue to make up something inconsequential, Julianne decided to err on the side of honesty. "Captain Monroe came to visit me again. Yesterday, late in the afternoon."

"But that is good, yes?"

"It would have been, except it was rather, um, tumultuous." She supposed that was one way to describe Daniel's visit and Devin's reaction.

"I'm sure you'll make things right again," Abby said. "I've had difficulties with Timothy before. But we've worked it out."

"This is a little different, I'm afraid. He, uh, was confronted with the consequences of my past. It wasn't pretty." She turned her back and fussed with the water pump, taking far more interest in priming it than necessary. Then there was his kiss and the way she'd responded to him.

"I am sorry to hear that," Carl said.

"Thank you. I am sorry about it too." After she

filled the teakettle, she turned back to the siblings. "He did say he would return to take me out to dinner in a week, but I've been wondering if he really will. Thank you for listening. Speaking of it actually made me feel a bit lighter in spirit."

Abby nodded. "Speaking about problems does help." She pulled out one of the kitchen chairs and sat down. "Julianne, I guess you have two choices, then."

"And what are they?"

"You can wait and have faith he will return. Or you can go after him right now. Do you know where he's gone?"

Julianne laughed, sure Abby was making a joke. When she realized the girl wasn't, she felt more than a little tongue-tied. "Run after him in San Antonio? Just like that? That would be one way to finally dissolve the rest of my reputation."

"What does that matter if it means you will be happy?"

Abby was serious. "Well, I, um, I don't know. But that's beside the point."

"Why?"

"Well, I don't know if I can."

"Why couldn't you?" Carl asked. "The stage can take you there."

Was it their youthful enthusiasm that made them act as though anything was possible? Or was it more the fact that they had never been on the receiving end of rejection? When Ginger padded in, Julianne leaned down and petted the beagle. Then she got her a fresh bowl of water.

Anything to give herself some time.

"I'm afraid it isn't that easy. Besides, he told me he needed to visit a friend on personal business. Someone he knew in the war. I would never wish to interfere."

Both her visitors stared at her expectantly. It was obvious they wanted to hear more about what had transpired between her and Devin. But no matter how kind Carl and Abby were, Julianne wasn't about to share everything that happened. Instead, she kind of sighed, hoping they'd let the matter drop.

And they did. With a small smile, Abby walked over to the stove. "How about I help you with the tea tray?" Before Julianne could refuse the offer, the girl poured the hot water from the kettle into a teapot. After she added tea to steep, she opened a likely drawer and pulled out three teaspoons.

Julianne poured cream into a pitcher and set a few cookies she'd made yesterday on a china plate.

Moments later Carl carried the tray to the parlor. After she poured and they all sat down, he grinned. "We are quite the team now, aren't we?"

"I should say so." After she took a fortifying sip of hot tea, Julianne smiled too. "Why is it that something made by someone else always tastes better?"

"I couldn't say, but I will agree that it is true."

When she set down her cup, Abby clasped her hands primly on her lap. "Now that we've determined that for now, at least, you cannot follow the captain, we need to work on your belief in him."

"I'm afraid it isn't as simple as that."

"Of course it is," she said earnestly. "It's like faith, don't you see?"

"No, I don't."

"Remember the parable about Jesus and the mustard seed?" she said quietly. "How Jesus chastised his followers, saying one only needed the smallest amount of faith to believe?"

Feeling a little helpless, as though they were talking about two different things at the same time, Julianne sputtered, "Of course. But—"

"You need to have faith, Julianne."

"I do have faith in God."

"No, not just in God. You need to have faith in the captain too. Because they aren't two different things. The Lord wants you to have faith in him, and in how he is guiding your life. And I feel if you keep that faith, and you let Captain Monroe know how much you believe in him, in the two of you, well . . . everything will work out like it is supposed to."

Julianne frowned. This young girl, with her sprite-like mannerisms and perpetual optimism, made it sound so easy.

But it wasn't. Was it?

Or . . . maybe it was? Maybe that's what it took to understand how things worked, she realized. Life was hard. But love and faith? Perhaps they didn't need to be.

"I am beginning to believe your fiancé has found himself a perfect partner."

Eyes sparkling, Abby raised her chin. "Of course he did," she replied with a cheeky grin. "He asked for my hand in marriage, didn't he?"

Her brother grunted. "As you can see, the Lord has much to work on with my little sister. On her humility, for example. That's obvious."

"Not at all," Abby retorted. "I am well aware I have many flaws."

"And a lack of humility is a big one."

Julianne giggled. "I'm glad you two came over. You've done wonders for my mood."

Carl leaned forward, about to reply, when a noise outside caught his attention. Getting to his feet, he looked out the window. "Are you expecting more company?"

"No." Walking across the room, she looked out the window. Then felt her stomach drop. He'd come back. "Oh no," she whispered.

Abby joined them. "Do you know this gentleman?"

It took everything she had to keep from saying her visitor was most definitely not a gentleman. Instead, she merely nodded. "I know him."

"What is his purpose? Why is he simply standing on your walkway?"

"He knows he's not welcome inside."

Carl's expression hardened. "Has he been giving you trouble? Would you like me to ask him to leave?"

The very last thing she wanted was for these young people—so fresh, so innocent—to be tainted by Daniel Bushnell. "I think it would be best if you stayed inside with Abby while I go outside to speak with him."

"Of course you cannot do that."

"He is rather unsavory." A knot filled her throat as she struggled with how to continue. How could she tell them this was the man for whom she'd been a mistress? And Devin had told her not to open the door to him, but she was afraid he'd create a scene—threaten Abby and Carl.

Looking out the window again, she felt Daniel's gaze right into her heart. He was standing there, taunting her. And there was a new expression on his face. He looked triumphant.

But why?

What had he done?

Feeling as though she were about to enter a deep, dark hole, she rushed to the door.

"Julianne!" Abby called out. "What is wrong?"

Suddenly, she felt even more unkempt than she had before the pair arrived. Brushing back a strand of hair that had fallen onto her face, she realized she was going to have to confess all. "That man is Daniel Bushnell. I was his mistress during the war. He . . . he is everything you don't want to know, Abby."

"But I thought you were done with him," Abby protested.

"I thought I was too." She opened the door, stepped outside, and closed the door. All she could do was hope and pray neither of her guests decided to follow. She would really like to shield them. "Daniel," she said. "What do you want?"

A slow, knowing smile lit his face. "It seems pigs do fly. At last, you are speaking to me again."

"What are you doing here?"

He folded his hands across his chest. "I wanted to see your face when I told you your new protector will no longer come to your aid."

All the trepidation that had engulfed her fell away. And though everything inside her ached to simply turn her back on him and go back inside, she couldn't ignore his words. "Why not?"

All traces of amusement faded from his gaze as he stared at her. Hard. "Because I went after him, Julianne."

"After Devin?" She could hardly get the words out.

"Of course, Devin. I followed him out of town yesterday. Then I shot him."

She gasped.

"For what? For *calling* on me?"

"He threatened me with that false story about me giving away secrets during the war. But mostly because you are mine, Julianne. I wanted you when no one else did. I took care of you when no one else would. Did you really think I was going to stand aside and let a man like Devin Monroe have you? Touch you?"

She could barely hear his words. Could barely understand them. "Is he dead?"

"I shot him in the back. I doubt he made it another hundred yards before falling from his horse."

"So you don't know for sure? He could be suffering on the ground somewhere, all alone?"

Daniel narrowed his eyes. "That is extremely doubtful. You forget that I shot my fair share of men during the war. I know how to shoot to kill." While she gaped at him, he continued on, his voice gaining confidence with each word. "I don't know why you are concerned about him, anyway. He is of no consequence."

"If you killed Devin, you will rue the day."

"I'm sure I shall." He raised his eyebrows. "But perhaps the two of us will rue the days together, no? Because one day soon I'll be back. And since you'll have no one else . . . Well, I'm sure I'll have you again. It will be just like old times."

"Never," she countered as he turned and walked away.

"Of course I will. You're my property, after all," he said over his shoulder. "I bought and paid for you long ago." Then he mounted his horse and rode out.

Julianne felt frozen. She wrapped her arms around her middle again, trying in a futile attempt to keep herself together when all she really wanted to do was fall in a heap on the ground.

"You don't know he's dead. He could have made it to San Antonio. You've got to find him," Abby said from behind her. "You need to get packed and let Carl help you get on the next stage."

Feeling as if she was still in a daze, Julianne turned. Abby was standing next to her brother. Close enough to have heard every ugly word Daniel had just uttered. The way they were both staring at her in concern confirmed that guess.

She hated that she'd tainted their innocence this way. "I am sorry you had—"

"Forgive me, but I think we're done with apologies, don't you?" Carl said crisply. "Now, please, stop arguing and do what we say. Listen to Abby. If this man you care for made it to his friend in San Antonio, he's going to need you as soon as possible. I mean, you aren't simply going to step inside and assume Captain Monroe didn't survive, are you? Or hope some old major was able to adequately help him?"

Eyes swimming with tears, Julianne bit her lip.

Carl was right. So was Abby. She needed to stop waiting. Stop degrading herself. Stop worrying about her past. Stop being afraid Devin could have changed his mind about her.

"You're right, Carl." And with that, she walked through the front door, pulled a carpetbag from a hall closet, and walked to her bedroom. "I'll be out presently."

Abby called after her. "I'll stay here with Ginger until Bula returns and explain she'll need to take care of everything here. Carl can come back for me once you're on the stage. And I'll clean up the tea service too."

Julianne almost laughed. She'd completely forgotten about the tea.

All she did know was that Carl and Abby were right. She needed faith in the Lord and faith in Devin.

She also needed to embrace her reality. She cared for Devin Monroe, and she needed to get on the next stage to San Antonio.

There would be plenty of time to think about her future when she was sitting at Devin's side.

If she made it in time.

19

Johnson's Island, Ohio
Confederate States of America
Officers' POW Camp

Ethan could practically feel Thomas Baker's intense gaze. Stretching his legs out on his cot, Ethan tried to ignore the younger man's fixation on the letter he held in his hand. After all, this wasn't anything new. Thomas was alone in the world and had yet to receive a letter from a loved one. Consequently, he ate up everyone else's news from home like a starving man being given a Virginia ham.

But that didn't mean Ethan was always in favor of sharing his mail with him. Some news was meant to be private. Such as letters like this. Letters from Faye.

Wanting to draw out the anticipation of it, he ran a finger along Faye's perfect handwriting. One day she was going to be Mrs. Ethan Kelly. One day he wouldn't have to wait months and months to talk to her. He'd simply be able to roll over and pull her into his arms.

Thomas groaned. "You've been staring at that envelope for fifteen minutes, Ethan. When are you ever going to open it?"

Tearing his gaze from the letter, he glared over his shoulder at Thomas. "Whenever I feel like it. No offense, but it has my name on the envelope. Not yours."

A flash of pain appeared in Thomas's eyes before he spoke. "Yeah, all right. But at least answer me this. What are you waiting for?"

"I don't know."

"Oh."

Two cots over, Phillip Markham chuckled softly. "Guess he's in a selfish mood today, Baker. Want me to read you part of my letter from Miranda? They had a fierce storm in Galveston last month. She described it in detail."

"Thanks, but I'll pass, Lieutenant. While I'm sure Mrs. Markham's account is real exciting, we had our own storm here yesterday."

Phillip laughed. "You have a point there."

"I'll read you part of my letter, Baker," Devin said. "My cousin has a new baby."

"Thanks, Cap."

Behind him, Ethan could hear Thomas walk over to Devin's side. Seconds later, Devin was reading him a passage of his letter. It was obvious most of the men were listening too.

And that gave him the small amount of privacy he craved so badly.

Smoothing the envelope again, Ethan forced himself to wait another two minutes. Faye didn't write all that often. It was likely he wouldn't receive another letter from her for several weeks. He hated to rush it.

Which privately embarrassed him. Never would he have thought he'd be the type of man who put so much emphasis on a single letter.

Though it wasn't especially constructive, sometimes he couldn't help but reflect on where he'd been. He'd grown up a gentleman of privilege. His family had gained thousands of acres of land back when Texas was still a republic. His ancestors had nurtured their investment and tripled their wealth.

Consequently, before Texas entered the War of Northern Aggression, he'd lived a rather narrow and spoiled life. He'd had more servants than he could count to see to his every need. He'd been surrounded by beauty and comfort and had eaten well. His family, both his parents and his two siblings, had been affectionate and agreeable. Even his time at West Point had been successful. He'd distinguished himself by having an affinity for strategy. He'd also been able to get along with most everyone and been popular with both the instructors and his fellow plebes. For the most part, he'd lived a charmed life.

Then he entered the war. He'd fought with honor. He'd fought with valor. He discovered he was capable of not only guiding troops but devising strategies for battle. Truly, he'd felt at home being an officer.

But then, while on a scouting mission, he, Monroe, Truax, and Markham had been taken prisoner and put on a train north. Now he was living in circumstances that were unfamiliar and difficult. He was doing menial tasks, and growing hungry, and seeing good men die all around him.

All of this was hard.

But the worst was that he was no longer ever alone. Ever. He was sure it was a fact that man needed time and space. It was a necessity.

Feeling he'd waited long enough, he carefully opened the letter's seal and pulled out Faye's letter. He frowned when he realized it was only one page in length.

And only written on one side of the paper.

Dread filled his insides as he smoothed the fine stationery and began to read.

Dear Ethan,

As much as it pains me to tell you this, I fear I can no longer put it off. You see, I got married two weeks ago.

Ethan blinked, sure he had read Faye's words wrong. Hands now shaking, he turned the paper over and opened up the envelope, looking for another sheet of paper. Maybe he'd missed something?

There was nothing.
He turned back to the letter.

I am sure you understand how hard life have been for me here, what with you being taken prisoner and all. People have told me stories about the atrocities that happen in those camps. Thinking about you in such a situation has been hard for me.

He didn't. He didn't understand at all.
But maybe the opposite was true?
Maybe he understood too much. Faye was certain he was either being tortured or starved—if he was not already dead. She had decided he wasn't worth her loyalty or love. He'd become a burden she didn't want to shoulder.
It took every ounce of willpower to read the remainder of the letter.

I recently met a very nice lieutenant who was discharged because of an injured leg. Luckily, he healed well and won't even carry a limp. I didn't expect him to ask for my hand so quickly, but he claimed he could not wait to make me his.
If you do get this letter, I hope you will understand my decision. Please know,

too, that I'll keep you in my prayers, just like I pray for all our brave men.

Mrs. James Chubb

She'd married another. A Lieutenant James Chubb, who was whole and present while he was not. Who was eager to place her in his marriage bed and willing to ensure Faye would not be shackled to an imprisoned soldier with an uncertain future.

Well, he guessed he now knew what Faye had wanted. He blinked, realizing tears had filled his eyes. It seemed rejection was as painful for him as anyone else.

Unable to stare at her words any longer, Ethan crumpled the thin sheet of paper in his hand, then tossed it on the floor beside his cot.

His movements didn't go unnoticed.

"Major, are you all right?" Thomas asked. He'd come to stand by his side. "Is something wrong at home? Was that from your mother?"

His mother wrote long, involved letters about nothing. Nothing besides her shopping, her gardening, and what minor inconveniences she'd been forced to endure because of the war. For some reason, Thomas found her letters to be his favorites.

"No. It was from Faye."

Gesturing at the wad of paper, Thomas cleared

his throat. "I'm guessing she didn't send you any good news."

"She did not."

"Do . . . do you want to talk about it?"

"Baker, you would try the patience of a saint."

Thomas stepped away. "Sorry, Major."

"Don't be so hard on him, Ethan," Markham called out. "You know Thomas meant no harm. He was just asking what the rest of us were wondering. Besides, we've been stuck inside these bare walls for three days now. You can't blame a man for being curious about the contents of a letter you just crumpled in a ball and tossed on the floor. What did she say?"

He wanted to ignore them all. To tell Thomas his pain wasn't any of his business. To tell Phillip Markham Faye's letter was too personal to share. But Markham received regular missives from his beauty of a wife and read aloud much of what she'd said . . . all except the really private parts, where she supposedly professed her love in nauseatingly glowing ways.

Feeling as though he had no choice, he bent down, smoothed out the paper, and read aloud Faye's letter from start to finish.

Feeling helpless, he glanced at the other men.

As a whole they were motionless. Some of the men were staring at him. Others had their heads bent down, as though they were afraid to meet his eye. The barracks were completely silent.

Only the sound of sleet hitting the walls and roof and sliding through the chinks in the mud cement could be heard.

The silence was so desperate, so out of sorts, that Ethan realized he had not misunderstood anything. Faye had found someone else and didn't even sound terribly regretful about breaking his heart.

He tossed the letter on the floor again. "So that is what was inside, gentlemen. A not-too-gentle dismissal of my love and my future, all wrapped in a dozen sentences."

"It's good you're rid of her," Thomas said. "I've known a lot of women and men who take what they can and when they can. They're a smarmy lot. She would have made you miserable in the long run."

"Would she? I'm not so sure about that."

As Thomas retreated to his cot, Ethan hung his head. He hated these barracks. Hated this situation. Why had the Lord placed him here? Why could he not even have a few minutes of privacy when his heart was breaking?

Needing to get out of the room before he broke down or broke something, he stood up. "I can't sit in here any longer. I'm going to take a walk."

"You think that's wise in this sleet?" Phillip asked.

"Does it really matter? I've already been

assumed dead or worthless. I've already been tossed over for a Lieutenant Chubb. He's whole, you see. And hasn't had to live through the vulgarity of a prison camp." After throwing on his tattered jacket, he grabbed a blanket, threw it over his shoulders, and headed out into the elements.

When the freezing sleet brushed against his face, stinging his skin, he welcomed the pain. And when he got back inside, no one would realize he'd been crying.

Then, to his surprise, the door to the barracks opened again. Out came four of his friends, wrapped in blankets like he was.

"Couldn't let you have all the fun," Devin Monroe said. "Besides, after everything we've been through? Well, we figured a little bit of sleet and ice wasn't going to hurt us none."

"We're made of tougher skin than that," Markham added.

When Thomas started whistling and walking ahead, Ethan, Truax, and the other two men followed. And that was when he knew Markham hadn't been exaggerating. They were war hardened and mentally and physically tough. A little bit of bad weather wasn't going to faze them. It seemed only letters like Faye's could.

Receiving a letter like that? It cut like a knife.

20

She'd lived within a three hours' ride to San Antonio all her life, yet Julianne had never ventured close to it except that one time when she'd met Bushnell at the officers' ball.

When she was younger, there had been no reason. Like children so often do, she'd been comfortable in her surroundings. She'd mistakenly assumed everything she saw and experienced was all there was in the world.

Then as a young woman, she realized there was far more to see than what was in Boerne, Texas. But she had been afraid to leave the security of home. She'd become aware that she'd been blessed with good looks but little money and no prestige.

And that, she'd come to realize, was a dire recipe for a successful match. She'd been afraid to go to any of the large assemblies in her town, fearful that her grand dreams of fitting in and being courted would be easily put to shame.

Then, when the war had come? Well, she'd ventured all the way to San Antonio—and circumstances had conspired against her.

When Devin Monroe approached her at the mercantile, Julianne dared to wonder if he was the answer to years of hopes and prayers. During the war she'd seen her world grow dim, and what she'd thought to be true had been turned on its ear. She'd lost hope in both herself and that anything could be different.

But from that first conversation, Devin had brought a good amount of light into her world. And by the time he told her he wanted to marry her someday? Well, her life had changed again. He'd restored her belief in humanity and the future.

But that didn't mean she had been willing to do anything but wait for him to make the next move, to come back as he promised. As hard as it was, she'd been willing herself to sit home and dream and wait. To hope.

The truth was, until Abby and Carl had encouraged her that morning, a part of her had been resigned to being alone for the rest of her life. It was too hard to believe a man like Devin Monroe would want to risk everything by taking her for his wife one day.

Until Daniel told her what he'd done.

Then everything in her world changed again. The moment she learned Devin had been shot, and wanted to believe he was still alive, she knew it was time to do whatever was necessary to be by his side. She owed it to them both to be stronger than she was. That was what love was, she guessed.

With Carl's help, she'd purchased a ticket

for the stage to San Antonio. And now it had deposited her at the entrance to the Menger. She'd hardly had time to gaze at the sprawling brick building before she was greeted by two bellmen. In no time at all, they'd taken her small carpetbag in hand and were escorting her inside.

They were treating her with respect. Like a lady. As though she were a woman of means. Like she used to dream she would one day be treated. But that wasn't important to her now. Learning of Devin's fate was.

"Did you have a good trip, miss?" the youngest bellman asked, his expression filled with appreciation as he helped her walk up a small flight of stairs.

She forced herself to smile as she hurried. "Yes, I did. It was uneventful, which is always good, I think."

He smiled. "My ma says the same thing." Blushing slightly, he tipped his hat and nodded toward the reception desk. "Well, here you go. Mr. Howard, the manager, will get you set up in your room."

"Thank you for your help." Despite her urgent quest, she remembered she should give him something for his efforts. She pulled out a bit and pressed it into his palm. He blushed again before turning away.

"May I help you?" Mr. Howard was a rather haughty-looking man.

"Yes. I believe Captain Devin Monroe is here. I just learned he was injured while on his way here. I believe he would have come to one of your guests—a Major Kelly."

"And you are . . . ?"

"I am Miss Julianne Van Fleet, a friend. Please answer my question. I must know."

Howard looked reluctant, but he answered. "You are correct. Captain Monroe is here, with Major Kelly in charge of his care."

She lowered her head for a moment in relief before gathering herself again. "Thank you, sir." She was eager to go straight to Devin's side, but she knew she needed to wash off the worst of her travel dust. "Now, may I please have a room."

He lifted his chin and looked just beyond her, as if he was looking for someone important. When he directed his stare back at her, his voice was even cooler. "Do you have an escort?"

"Pardon me?"

"A chaperone?" he added with obvious impatience. "We only accept ladies here."

"I arrived on my own."

"If you are traveling by yourself, it would be best if you moved to a different hotel. This is the Menger, you see. We have a reputation to uphold."

They had a reputation to uphold? Well, so did she! And she wasn't leaving Devin.

Staring at the supercilious man, Julianne

realized she'd had enough. She had had enough of men telling her what to do and where to go. She'd just survived several hours in a cramped and hot stagecoach next to a pair of men who had obviously not bathed in weeks and a pair of elderly women who insisted on talking about nothing the entire journey. Her head hurt, her body ached, and she was afraid for Devin Monroe.

She needed to see him, and as soon as possible.

She drew herself up to her full height and dared to look at the manager in the eye. "It would suit me best if you gave me a guest room, helped me with my baggage, and then directed me to where Captain Monroe is recuperating."

When the man gaped at her, she raised her voice. "Perhaps I need to speak more clearly. I demand that I be taken care of immediately."

His eyes darted behind her, glancing around the lobby warily. She, too, was aware their discussion was being overheard, and no doubt gossiped about.

Though she wished it wasn't the case, she had no choice in the matter. She had lived for years with a tainted reputation. She wished the same thing wasn't happening here, but Julianne knew she could handle it.

Keeping her voice firm, she held out a hand. "Mr. Howard? My room key, if you please?"

Looking resigned, he drew out his guest book,

spoke to the gentleman behind the counter, and pulled out a key. "Here is your key, miss."

"Thank you. And now may I please have Captain Monroe's room number?"

"We don't announce guests' room numbers. When you are ready, Jim here will escort you," he said with pure ice in his tone. "He will assist you with your bag as well."

She was so relieved—not only because the man had acquiesced but at the confirmation that Devin was alive—she felt like crying. Holding on to the last of her composure, she turned to Jim, who was of African descent, and was also standing as tall and strong as a redwood. "Thank you, Jim. If you could accompany me now, I would be appreciative."

He nodded. "Miss," his deep voice lumbered.

Aware of the many curious glances, she followed Jim, taking care not to look either left or right.

"Your room is on the second floor, miss."

She climbed the stairs, her feet feeling like lead as she maneuvered her skirts. Then they walked silently down a long hallway. Both the hallway and the doors were painted a cream color. Brass gas fixtures cast a faint glow on the carpet and walls, making the hallway seem warmer and more inviting than her greeting in the hotel's lobby.

When they stopped at her door, Jim unlocked

it for her, opened it wide, and then stood to the side. "I'll wait here for you, miss."

Eager to see Devin, she nodded. "I'll be back out in no time, Jim."

He shrugged. "Don't make no difference to me, miss. Take your time."

Smiling softly, she said, "All the same, I won't be long."

When she closed the door, she exhaled. She had done it. She had poked and prodded her way into San Antonio, and into the Menger Hotel. Now all she had to do was hope and pray Devin would be pleased that she had come.

If he wasn't? Well, it wouldn't be the worst thing that had ever happened to her. Not by a longshot. She was a survivor, and no matter what happened, she would survive again.

Julianne felt all her bravado fade twenty minutes later when she was following Jim again. It didn't seem to matter that she'd donned a rust-colored taffeta gown with jet buttons and an attractive curve to the bodice and sleeves.

She might look her best, but she knew even when armed with a whalebone corset and a well-fitting garment, nerves could get the best of her.

Without a word, Jim escorted her back down the stairs, down yet another glowing hallway, then eventually to a large, ornately carved oak door.

"Where are we?"

"This here is where we put guests who don't want to be found, miss."

"And that is where Captain Monroe is?"

Jim shrugged again. "Seems that way."

"Is he a frequent visitor here, then?"

He looked down at her, his expression carefully blank. "Don't believe so, miss. To my knowledge, this is his first visit—at least as a guest."

"I'm told Major Kelly is with him. Is that correct?"

Jim didn't look as though he wanted to answer. After a small pause, he nodded. "Yes'm. I heard the major was watching out for him right now."

Realizing just how little she knew about Devin, she swallowed. "It's good to know he has a friend here."

Jim looked as though he was tempted to say something about that, but merely nodded. "Yes, miss."

He guided Julianne into a far dimmer hallway, then stopped at a closed door just off to their right. "This is it," he said, then turned before she could thank him for his assistance.

Seconds later, she was alone in the hallway and staring at the door. She hesitated, listening for voices on the other side. She heard nothing. But it was time. Drumming up her courage, she twice rapped her knuckles on the plain, nondescript door.

It swung open abruptly.

To her surprise, a tall, lean man filled the threshold instead of the older man she'd been expecting. Leaving her to face an attractive man about Devin's age with brown eyes, light-brown hair, and a forceful presence. "Yes?" He spoke in a low voice, and she followed suit.

"Are you Major Kelly?"

"I am Ethan Kelly, yes."

Feeling more assured, Julianne looked him in the eye. "My name is Julianne Van Fleet. I have come to see Devin Monroe. I believe he is in here?"

The man's expression hardened. "How did you know he was here in this room?"

"From Mr. Howard."

His eyes narrowed. "Howard simply came out and told you?"

"Well, I had to do a bit of persuading. And to be fair, he never did tell me the location or the room number. Instead, he had Jim escort me here."

"Jim."

"Yes. He's, um, he's a servant here, I believe. He walked me to my room, then here. He was very nice."

"Miss, perhaps I should rephrase my question. How did you know Captain Monroe was in residence at the Menger?"

"Someone told me he'd been hurt, and I knew he'd been on his way to see you." Feeling his intense gaze practically sear her insides, she swallowed.

"Who told you?"

Though she knew he deserved an answer because he was only trying to help Devin, Julianne didn't want to admit to learning about Devin's injury from the man who'd shot him.

Remembering that speaking forcefully had gotten her a room key, she adopted the same tone again. "Sir, may I please enter now? I've traveled some distance to get here, you see."

But still, he didn't budge. "Beg your pardon, but your needs do not interest me in the slightest."

His words were a shock. On the outside, he looked just as gallant as Devin appeared to be capable and forthright. At first glance, one might even assume they were polar opposites. But now she saw the similarities. They were both hard on the inside.

This man, this Major Kelly, seemed just as solid and steady in his views and viewpoints as Captain Monroe was. He did not waver. Ironically, instead of causing her worry, it made Julianne feel more secure in his company. She could handle anyone who was honest. It was the liars and the charlatans that gave her pause.

"Perhaps I should have given you more information when I introduced myself," she said slowly. "I know Captain Monroe is here because he told me he was coming to you. And I know he suffered a bullet wound on his way. And I know this because I also know the man who shot him."

"And how do you know that man?"

"Because I used to be Daniel Bushnell's mistress. When I scorned his latest attempts at my home yesterday, Devin was there. He threatened him, and he shot Devin in retaliation."

Something flickered in the major's expression. Because of the dim lighting, Julianne wasn't exactly sure what it was. Disapproval? Shock? A vague sense of humor about how small and insular their world had become?

Whatever the reason, he seemed to have at last come to a decision. And with that, he opened the door wider, stepped backward, and bowed. "After you, Miss Van Fleet."

Putting her extensive experience of looking composed to good use yet again, she walked through the doorway.

Then she saw Devin Monroe lying in bed, his chest and shoulder bandaged, his skin a deathly white.

She was going to lose him. Before she'd ever had Devin, she was going to lose him.

And the knowledge was so dark, so tinged with despair, Julianne burst into tears.

Uncaring of her lovely dress, uncaring of her audience, she went to the bed and sank to the floor by his side. Clasping Devin's hand, she pressed his knuckles to her lips and cried.

21

Even if the open doorway hadn't brought a chill into the room, Lizbeth was certain Ethan's frosty demeanor would have. From her position, where she sat on a small wooden chair next to Captain Monroe, it seemed as if Ethan had brought in a cold wave of anger.

That was surprising. What was more surprising, however, was the anger and irritation that had emanated from him as he let one of the most beautiful women she'd ever seen into the suite.

Concern mixed with a thick dose of jealousy hit her hard as she watched him close the door behind the woman. Where had she come from? And why had he let her into this sanctuary?

But although she had many unanswered questions about Ethan, she couldn't help but stare at the woman. After all, how could she not? It was dark in the room. Lizbeth thought for a moment that it should have made the woman's hair look faded or even dark. Instead, the rich auburn color fairly burned brightly. As did her blue eyes. Her striking looks, combined with the rustle of her well-made gown, made Lizbeth feel much like the country mouse in the big, bright city.

Lizbeth wondered if the woman even realized

she was in the room. Because the moment she walked near the bed, she stilled. Her hand lifted. Pressed against her mouth.

And then, without warning, she sank to the floor and burst into tears.

Stunned, Lizbeth jumped to her feet and crossed the room. Eager to help, she glanced at Ethan to see if he wanted to give her direction.

He appeared just as taken aback as she was. Actually, he looked rather frozen in place, as if he had no idea how to deal with this. Then something clicked and he stepped closer. Bending at the waist, he reached for the woman's arm. "Miss, allow me to help you to a chair."

But the woman didn't acknowledge him.

Lizbeth didn't think she heard Ethan. After a small sigh, she pressed her lips to the captain's hand again. "I'm so sorry, Devin. So very sorry."

Her devastation and obvious love for Ethan's friend was both beautiful and heartbreaking. Lizbeth felt herself choke up.

After several more minutes, the woman whispered something in his ear. Then, with softly murmured thanks, she accepted Ethan's help and rose to her feet, looking bereft and alone, staring down at Captain Monroe with such longing in her eyes that Lizbeth felt like an intruder.

Ethan must have felt the same way, because he stood motionless as well. When he darted a look in her direction, Lizbeth knew she had to ease the situation. It seemed all her experience with tears was going to come in handy.

"Miss?" she asked.

Obviously startled, the woman turned to her. "Oh! Hello. I do beg your pardon," she said in a voice as smooth as fine cream. "I'm afraid I didn't realize you were here."

Lizbeth certainly didn't care about that. "Miss . . . uh, would you care for anything?"

"It's Van Fleet," the woman supplied.

She smiled at her. "Miss Van Fleet? Please, do sit down."

"Thank you." With a wan smile, she took the chair Ethan had provided for her. "Please forgive my behavior. It's just that it is difficult to see him in this state. Every other time I've seen him, I felt as if he was invincible." Her gloved hand shook. "I know it makes little sense, of course. I mean, I know he suffered injuries. I just . . . well . . ."

"Seeing the reality can be far more difficult."

"Yes." Looking frustrated with herself, Miss Van Fleet carefully unfastened the small buttons at the base of one glove, then pulled it off. After looking about her person in confusion, she simply swiped at her tears with two slim fingers.

"Miss Van Fleet, allow me," Ethan said as he handed her a white handkerchief.

"Thank you." Though she still kept her eyes on the captain, she murmured to Lizbeth, "My name is Julianne. Miss, are you another friend of his?"

Lizbeth caught the curious tone, laced with, perhaps, a touch of jealousy. "No, I'm afraid not. I've never met him. I used to be a maid here."

"This is Miss Elizabeth Barclay. She is a friend of mine," Ethan said, directing a warm look her way.

His warm reassurance made her heart lift. Maybe she and the major actually were on the road to a real relationship. "Please, call me Lizbeth."

"I am pleased to make your acquaintance. Lizbeth, Major Kelly, what is the prognosis?"

Ethan answered. "Devin was shot in his upper back, almost at his shoulder. Miraculously, the bullet didn't hit his lungs or heart, but he did lose quite a bit of blood. The physician cleaned his wound and sewed it up as best he could. Now we can only sit and wait, I'm afraid."

Miss Van Fleet's bottom lip trembled. "Does he have a fever?"

Lizbeth shook her head. "Not yet. He's been either unconscious or asleep almost the whole time since he arrived."

"I see. Well, I came to help. How may I assist you?"

Lizbeth looked at the beautiful gown. Her polished demeanor. "Perhaps you could simply sit here with him?"

Miss Van Fleet looked at the cloths and the pitchers of water. And maybe she noticed how rumpled Lizbeth looked as well. "I put on my best gown, Lizbeth, but that doesn't mean I am a stranger to hard work. I am happy to attend to Devin as best I can."

The woman's matter-of-fact tone was a welcome relief. Maybe she could help her and Ethan after all. "Perhaps we could help each other how each one sees fit?"

"Thank you," she said hesitantly. "I'd like that."

To her surprise, Ethan came to her side and curved his hand possessively around her elbow. "Lizbeth, now that we have some help, why don't you take a break and rest?"

"I got some sleep last night."

"You slept on the chair. Go back to Mrs. Harrison's for a while. Get something to eat. I'll stay here with Devin and Miss Van Fleet."

The twinge of jealousy she'd been fighting grew. Lizbeth hated that she was thinking about herself when she should be thinking only about the captain's health, but she wasn't sure how to push it aside. "I really don't mind staying. Besides, Miss Van Fleet only just arrived."

"I rode in on the stage today to help Devin," she said. "I don't want to be anywhere else."

It seemed she had no choice. "All right, then." When she started toward the door, Ethan stopped her.

"Not so fast," he murmured, cupping his hands around her shoulders. "Promise me you'll get some rest. And that you'll think about my offer some more."

His offer? To her surprise, she'd forgotten all about his proposal of marriage! Feeling far lighter of spirit, she felt much of her jealousy drift away. In its place was something new and warm and comforting. "I'll do some thinking, but I don't believe my answer will change."

He leaned closer. "Then I guess I'll have to find a way to change your mind, won't I?"

She gasped. His words, his touch, the feel of his breath on her neck, it was suddenly all too much to take in. After clumsily saying her good-byes, she darted out of the room.

Ethan's words rang in her ears as Lizbeth walked to the lobby. Looking around the space, she scanned the few coat hooks near the main entrance. She'd somehow lost her cloak in all the commotion surrounding Captain Monroe's arrival.

Not immediately spying it, Lizbeth decided to walk the perimeter. Her cloak had to be somewhere out in the open. She didn't mind the search. It gave her a few precious moments to reflect on what had just happened . . . and the way Ethan had spoken to her. For the first time in her life, she wished she had more experience with men.

She didn't understand his repartee or his

statements laced with hidden meanings. He made her feel uneasy and at a disadvantage. That conversation, together with the captain's injury and Miss Van Fleet's arrival, had been a lot to take in. Aching for the quiet of her room, she increased her pace. With luck, she could be back at Mrs. Harrison's house in fifteen minutes. Then she'd be able to review everything that had occurred in her mind, pray for guidance, and try to make some sense of it all.

Finally, in a darker corner of the lobby, Lizbeth found her cloak tossed over the arm of a rather uncomfortable horsehair chair. Relieved to have located it at last, she quickly fastened it, then headed toward the front door. Lost in thought, she almost walked right past her cousin. But because she didn't, Lizbeth forced herself to stop and say hello.

Aileen looked just as surprised to see her. "You're still here?"

"I never left. I've been in the back rooms with Major Kelly and . . . his injured friend." She thought Ethan would rather she not mention his name, although she had a feeling Aileen knew it anyway.

"Oh. Well, where are you living now?"

"I'm at Mrs. Harrison's down the street."

"She allowed you to live there?"

"Why are you surprised, Aileen? Did you want me to be homeless?"

"No. Of course not." Her expression turned pained. "May I talk with you?"

"Are you sure your reputation will survive?"

She flushed. "I know I deserved that. I promise, this won't take long."

Lizbeth nodded. Talking with Aileen about her reputation was the last thing she wanted to do. But Lizbeth also had a feeling her cousin was being sincere.

"Thank you. We can walk outside. Let me go tell Dallas where I'm going and I'll get my cloak."

Lizbeth nodded and then tried not to feel conspicuous as she waited by the entrance for her cousin to return. Several workers looked at her curiously, but didn't say a word. It was obvious they were being observed by Dallas Howard.

Luckily, Aileen appeared mere minutes later. "Thank you for waiting," she said, glancing at her husband before they went out the door.

"What did you want to say?" Lizbeth asked once they were outside.

"That . . . well, that I am sorry about how things have been going between us."

As far as apologies went, Lizbeth figured this was one of the worst. "You are sorry for the way things have been going?" she sputtered. "You sided with that . . . *that man* instead of me. You said my reputation interfered with the hotel's and you asked me to leave. Dallas barely gave me my full payment. That is how things have been going between us."

"All of that is true. I really am sorry."

"You know, what I don't understand is how you could treat a member of your family like that."

"I guess a part of me always resented you." She closed her eyes. "It wasn't until you left last week that I realized just how badly I've behaved."

Lizbeth couldn't let her off that easily. "You have tried your hardest to make me pay for things that were never my fault, Aileen. I never wanted my mother to treat you badly. I never wanted the two of us to be in competition with each other."

"I realize that now."

"I wish you would have realized that before. You know it was hard to ask you for a job, but I did. And you know what I went through too— alone in that house during the war."

"Again, everything you have said is true. I don't have an excuse, other than I was so eager to start over. I was eager to push away everything from my past . . ." Her voice drifted off. "I guess that doesn't make sense, but in time, maybe you will one day be able to forgive me."

Aileen's statement struck a chord. Lizbeth actually did know how it felt to want to start over. To push away the past and pretend it never occurred. "You don't need to wait for one day, Aileen," she said quietly. "I forgive you now."

"I appreciate that. Thank you. What are you

going to do now? I mean . . . do you want me to talk to Dallas about getting your job back?"

If there was a silver lining in all that had happened, it was that Aileen's harsh treatment had pushed Lizbeth out of her self-inflicted prison. No matter what God had in her future, she was certain she couldn't go back to the way things had been. "I don't know what my future holds," she said lightly. "I was thinking maybe I would move."

"Really? What about the major? You two seem close."

Lizbeth almost smiled. They had seemed to be getting close. So close he'd even proposed to her the day before! "We are becoming friends," she said.

"Maybe there will be something there, then."

"I don't know what will happen. Only God does." Suddenly feeling exhausted, she stifled a yawn. "Aileen, I'm sorry, but I must go. I fear I must get some rest."

"Yes. Of course. Take care of yourself, cousin. I mean that sincerely."

"And you too, Aileen," she said, surprising herself.

When she finally got to her room at Harrison House and lay down on her bed, Lizbeth's mind spun. She wasn't sure what was going on, but it had been an exceptionally tumultuous couple of days.

She could only hope the rest of this day was far quieter. She rather doubted that would be the case, however. After all, it was only a little after two.

22

"Feel free to get some rest, Major," Miss Van Fleet said after the two of them had been sitting in silence for the last half hour. "If you would let me know how to send word to you, I promise to notify you the moment Devin's condition changes."

With a start, Ethan realized he'd been standing against the wall, lost in thought. He'd also been staring at her. That had been rather rude. Abruptly, he sat down in the chair next to the small writing desk. "Thank you, but I will stay here as well."

"There's really no need for you to do that."

"Actually, I think there's every need."

She turned to face him. "Are you staying because you don't trust me? I promise I won't leave his side."

It was true, he didn't trust her. But it was more than that. "Devin Monroe is one of my closest friends on this earth. I have no wish to be anywhere else."

Her expression softened. "I understand." Then, with a rustle of taffeta, she turned back to Devin.

He watched as she leaned closer to him. Pressed her hand to his cheek and forehead, obviously checking for fever. He hadn't thought to do that.

Feeling awkward, he got to his feet again. "How does he seem? Is he running a fever?"

"There's no change. Not that I can discern, at least." She sighed. "He does seem to be sleeping peacefully. That's something, at least."

"I agree. Rest is what he needs." He started to bring up his experience when recovering from a gunshot wound, but stopped himself in time. Stories about war wounds were not acceptable conversational topics. The timing couldn't be worse either. After all, what could he say? That he'd felt blessed not to have died like the other men in the surgical tent had?

Her attention still focused on Devin, Miss Van Fleet nodded. He wondered if she had even heard what he said.

Though he knew he should probably sit back down again, he resumed his position against the wall. He watched her watch Devin.

Each minute passed more slowly than the next.

Miss Van Fleet was right. There was no reason for them both to keep vigil. But he could no more leave than heal Devin. Only God and time could heal his friend.

Bored, and feeling a bit at loose ends, he studied Miss Van Fleet. *Julianne*. Maybe it was her auburn hair, maybe it was the curve of her jaw and neck, but he found himself gazing at her in appreciation—much like one might stare at a painting or a particularly beautiful flower.

She was striking. He could see how she would have caught Devin's attention.

"You are very beautiful," he murmured.

Obviously startled, she turned her head, capturing him with her blue eyes. They looked wary, as if she didn't know how to respond.

He didn't blame her; his comment had been too blunt. Maybe too honest.

"Thank you," she said after another moment. After his nod, she turned away and went back to holding Devin's hand.

Ethan folded his arms across his chest and continued his bold perusal. In all the time he'd known Devin, the man had never displayed more than a passing interest in any female. How had this one come to mean so much to his friend so quickly?

"Is that what caught Devin's attention?" he blurted. "Your beauty?"

"I couldn't say. You'll have to ask him when he wakes up."

Her modest answer was everything proper. He appreciated that. But he couldn't help but wonder if his old friend—who was so capable and forthright among men but inexperienced with women—might have been taken advantage of by this beautiful woman. He'd watched his sister and mother use their looks to their advantage any number of times. "I guess you are accustomed to using your looks to get what you want."

She turned to face him again. "Not necessarily," she said, her voice noticeably cooler.

And why wouldn't it be? He was jabbing and prodding at her like a child might bother a stray animal. Practically goading her to retaliate.

This wasn't like him. Far from it! But part of him was glad he was goading her. If she broke her composure and admitted to manipulating Devin, he could have a reason to make her leave.

Then he would finally be able to do something of worth. To take care of something, even if it was to get this woman who was so unsuitable for his friend out of his life.

Returning his attention to her reply, he pushed some more. "No? Not many women can say they survived the war as well as you did."

"I imagine that is true." Her chin lifted.

That chin lift told him much. He wondered, if the room hadn't been so dark, would he have been able to see more of a reaction than she was showing now? Would he have spied pain in her eyes? Regret?

"Is that how Bushnell acquired you?"

She visibly flinched. It brought him the reaction he'd been searching for . . . and made him feel ashamed. "I beg your pardon, Miss Van Fleet. That was beyond the pale." His mother would have been ashamed too. Oh, who was he kidding? Lizbeth would be upset with him too.

To his surprise, she stood up and walked

toward him. "Oh, no, Major Kelly. Let us not start begging each other's forgiveness, especially since we both know you don't regret your words."

Her words stung . . . and brought his worst thoughts back. "All right, then, perhaps you could tell me how you became the paramour of such a miserable man."

She cocked her head, stepping closer. The faint scent of rose, laced with an undertone of spice, wafted toward him. He hated that he noticed it.

"I don't owe you an explanation, sir. But if it will help you understand that I am not about to hurt Devin, I'll attempt to explain myself." She sighed. "By the time the war had been going on eight months, my grandmother and I were starving."

His mouth went dry. "Starving."

"Although my father maintained a nice enough home for us in Boerne, my family was by no means well off before the war began. Then, as you might imagine, after Texas joined the Confederacy and the fighting continued for months and months, our situation grew worse." After a pause, she continued, her voice thick with emotion. "My father had been killed, my mother left to live with my sister elsewhere—and sent no funds to help us—and my grandmother was ailing. I didn't know what to do. When I heard about an officer's cotillion in San Antonio,

I decided to go. Women talked about how some men were eager to leave a wife behind when they were off fighting. Some were so eager, they weren't too particular about who said yes. So I put on my best gown and decided to find myself a husband."

"You went to make a match."

She laughed softly. "Yes. But I soon realized that was a fool's quest. Gentlemen officers like you were not so desperate as to marry a woman who was not only awkward and shy but also had no money to speak of. Then, out of the blue, one man did show interest in me."

"Bushnell."

"Yes. He said things, things to make me believe he cared for me. He called on me at my home, acted as though he was about to make me an offer of marriage." She swallowed, clearly in no hurry to share more of her story with him. "Suffice to say I misinterpreted his regard and soon had no options left but the one he did offer."

"So you sold yourself."

"I did what I had to do. Daniel Bushnell was, in many ways, the answer to a prayer."

He scoffed. "I find it something of a stretch to categorize Bushnell in those terms. He's as far from angelic as a man can get. Truly, he is a scoundrel of the worst sort."

"It was because he is a scoundrel that I was able to take care of my grandmother."

"And yourself," he pointed out.

"Yes, sir. And myself." She stared at him intently. "I'm curious as to why you are judging me so harshly, Major Kelly. You fought on battlefields. Instead of dying, you lived. I know from Devin that you also survived a lengthy imprisonment in enemy territory. I would think you would have seen far worse than a desperate woman choosing to survive."

"You risked your reputation."

"I did. And I lost it as well. It was a gamble I had to take." She tilted her head to one side. "I must confess your disdain for my actions surprises me. Aren't you a gambler now?"

Her point, because it was valid, stung. And he wondered just how much Devin had told her about his friends. "My current occupation has nothing to do with this discussion."

"I beg to differ. We're discussing weighing probabilities of life and death."

"We are not. We are discussing your less-than-illustrious past."

"I'm not going to apologize to you for the choices I've made."

He shifted. She was right—to an extent. But she was also very wrong. Maybe she'd been alone so long that she'd forgotten what it meant to have close friends who looked out for each other.

Or maybe she'd been so self-serving that she forgot the rest of the world would judge Devin

Monroe for courting a woman of her reputation. Devin had not let on that his acquaintance with her had come to that when he'd seen him days ago, but an understanding between him and this woman seemed obvious now.

"Bushnell used to talk about you," he blurted. "He talked about his ladybird." He'd used far coarser words, actually.

To his surprise, instead of being shocked, a faint glimmer of amusement entered her eyes. "I imagine Daniel did talk about me. He saw me as ornamental, you see. Having me made him feel important."

In contrast to the gleam in her eyes, her voice sounded empty. Almost hollow. "And you didn't find that distasteful?"

"Not enough to give up eating or having a roof over my head. Not enough to sacrifice my grandmother for misplaced honor."

"Is she still alive?"

"No. She died not long after my arrangement with Bushnell began."

"So you could have ended it."

"Not easily. The colonel and I had a business agreement. As you've just pointed out, it was very far from a love affair."

"Did you even try to break things off?"

"What, exactly, are you doing, Major Kelly? Are you attempting to understand why I did what I did? Or hoping to devise a way to make sure Devin distances himself from me as far as possible when he awakens?"

Her questions hit the mark.

She was smart. Smart and quick and proud. It was obvious why Bushnell had been so proud to call her his. She was beautiful, strong, and had gumption.

But she was also very far from the type of woman Devin deserved. He needed someone sweet. Innocent. A woman worthy of his honor and reputation. "Maybe I'm doing both," he admitted.

"Why? Do you imagine that I would have kept my past from Devin?"

Devin had told him what she was. And why. Still . . .

"Devin Monroe is a great many things, but wise to the ways of women is not one of them. How much did you admit to him about what you did?"

"What I did?" she scoffed. "Do you desire details, Major?" she asked, her voice thick with sarcasm. "Do you want to know what Daniel made me do when he visited my house when he was on leave? Is that the kind of thing you enjoy hearing?"

Her implication was shocking. So much so, he didn't even try to read the sarcasm in her expression or attempt to match her tone. "No," he bit out. "Of course not."

Her voice turned even more brittle. "Then what do you want from me?"

He knew in his heart that she was playing a role. She had put on a shield, acting in a way she must have perfected when so many people looked down on her.

But he, however, was not acting. His only concern was Devin, and Lizbeth. He didn't want this woman near either of them. Lizbeth was too fragile and Devin was too weak. "I want you to leave," he said, not feeling a trace of remorse. "I want you to walk away from Devin and give him space. Allow him to find a woman who is more worthy to stand by his side."

Even in the dim light, he could tell his barb had met its mark. He'd wounded her.

Though he knew she wouldn't believe it, he was sorry. He wasn't cruel by nature. But like a parent disciplining a child out of love, he felt he had no choice. "Miss Van Fleet, I'm sorry to speak so severely, but you mustn't be surprised. I've gone to hell and back with Devin, and I'd do it again to keep him safe from harm."

He was so focused on her face, on her tense expression, that the words he heard caught him off guard.

"Ethan Kelly, if I didn't have a hole in my back, I would beat you bloody," Devin rasped. "Apologize right now."

Julianne gasped and rushed to his side.

"Devin!" she exclaimed as she fell to her knees next to him. "Look at you! You're awake. Oh, thank the Lord!"

Ethan didn't seem able to move. He stood frozen while Julianne kneeled next to Devin, her hands reaching for his, tears already running down her face.

Slowly, the captain's fingers curled around hers. Gently.

But he was still staring at Ethan as if he were an enemy.

His spine prickled in unease. "You know I was only trying to help you."

"Let us not play games. I am not an innocent woman susceptible to your verbal innuendos."

Julianne ran a hand along Devin's jaw. "Devin, I'm fine. Please, don't worry yourself."

"What I heard was not fine," he said softly before staring at Ethan again. "You were being deliberately cruel. Disrespectful. After she's come all this way. You were taking advantage of the fact that I was lying here, unaware."

Each word was harshly stated. Each word was punctuated by scorn. Seen from Devin's perspective, maybe Ethan deserved his friend's contempt. But surely he wasn't so naïve as to think people who cared about him wouldn't hesitate to protect him. "If I overstepped my bounds, please accept my apology."

"That is not good enough," Devin rasped, his

tone still cold. "You are apologizing to the wrong person."

Taking a deep breath, he continued. "Miss Van Fleet, I am sorry for the way I spoke to you. It . . . it was uncalled for and undeserved. Please accept my apology."

His mouth was dry. He wasn't surprised. He felt as if each word had been pulled from his insides. But Julianne didn't even turn to look at him. She didn't do anything but bend her face over Devin's hand. "I've been so worried, Devin," she murmured. "I prayed so much, I doubt there's an angel in heaven who didn't hear my prayers."

Ethan listened, dumbstruck. It was as if he didn't exist for her.

It seemed only Devin did.

Devin whispered something to her before glancing at Ethan once again. No emotion flickered in his gaze. It was as if they were strangers. Definitely not friends.

Ethan felt that loss. His fists loosened as he racked his brain, wondering how to fix what was beginning to seem unfixable. "Devin, if I may—"

"Leave us."

He stepped forward. Ready to argue. To press his point. "But—"

Devin cut him off again. "Allow me to make myself perfectly clear," he rasped, his light-blue eyes glinting like shards of ice. "Get out, Major Kelly."

His voice was sharp. Hard. And his glare? Well, Ethan never would have imagined it would be directed at him. Not only because of Ethan's rank, but because of all they'd been through together.

Appalled at the situation, Ethan turned and strode from the room. Neither Devin nor Julianne acknowledged his departure.

When he was out in the hall, Ethan rested his head against the wall and closed his eyes. He felt sick. Obviously, he had gone too far.

"Sir?" a young maid asked as she walked down the hallway. She was the one who had helped Lizbeth with supplies when they first brought Devin to this suite. He was surprised to remember her name. It was Cassie. "Sir, are you all right? Do you need something?"

He laughed grimly. "There's nothing you can do for me, miss. Not a single thing in the world."

When she scurried away, he straightened and walked down the hall. Lizbeth had refused him; Devin had almost died. And he'd just gone out of his way to offend a perfectly decent woman.

It was time to pray and make plans . . . before the day got any worse.

23

Devin found it hard to believe Julianne was kneeling by his side. When he'd awoken in the strange room, at first all he could surmise was that his shoulder burned as though it were on fire, but he was alive.

Then, little by little, he'd come to the realization he wasn't back on the battlefield. He wasn't recuperating in a field hospital on a make-shift cot with a score of men surrounding him in worst straits than he was. Instead, he slowly became aware of the tangy scent of lemon oil in the air and a soothing warmth emitting from the fireplace across the room.

Then, as if he'd conjured it, he'd inhaled a familiar rose scent. It was one he knew he would always associate with Julianne Van Fleet. He'd been stunned, especially since he was in San Antonio, not Boerne. She would have traveled to get to his side.

And then the fogginess in his brain subsided and he comprehended what Ethan was saying.

That was when he'd felt an anger the likes of which he'd never experienced surge through him. It was as unexpected as it was explosive and hot. If he could have stood on his own two feet, Devin was fairly sure he would have slugged Ethan.

Thank goodness he'd only had the strength to demand he leave.

Now he was alone with Julianne and at a loss for how to soothe the pain she must feel after Ethan's words.

"I'm so sorry," Devin said when he felt he could speak in a coherent manner. "I don't know what got into Ethan. He usually is everything kind and gracious."

As Julianne rose to sit beside him in a chair, she raised one shoulder in a gesture that said so much. She was hurt but hadn't expected much else. "He cares about you."

"That was no excuse. His accusations were uncalled for." Glad her hand was still in his, he ran a finger along the delicate skin on the back, feeling the faint outline of the bones and veins underneath. "I don't agree with anything he said. I hope you know that."

"He wasn't exactly wrong, Devin. You are a celebrated officer. Everyone who admires you would no doubt hope to see you with a woman who is your equal."

"Of course you are that."

She looked down at her lap. "Let's just say a woman of better reputation."

"I don't want to discuss our pasts or reputations anymore. They don't matter. Times have changed."

Lifting her head, she cast him a doubtful look.

"Not that much. People are more accepting, but not of a woman's reputation."

"It doesn't matter to me."

"But it will to other people," she said haltingly. "We can't live in a cave, Devin."

"No, we can't. But we can't live filled with apologies and regrets either. What matters is that I've found you." He slid his hand over hers, linking their fingers together. Maybe his grip was too tight, but he was willing to risk it. She needed to know he wanted never to let her go.

She blinked before gifting him with a tremulous smile. "I didn't know you were such a romantic, Captain."

"I'm not. I guess you're bringing that out in me." Realizing he was a new recruit to relationships, he added, "Is it too much?"

Julianne chuckled. "No. I seem to like it."

"Good."

"I never thought I was especially romantic either. But it seems we've been waiting for the right time, haven't we?"

He smiled. "I'd ask you to lean down and kiss me, but I don't think my heart could take it." He no doubt smelled to high heaven too.

"I guess I'll just wait in anticipation, then." Lines around her eyes formed as she smiled again. "Now, though, we need to see if we can make you better." Getting to her feet, she leaned over him, gently curving her hands around his uninjured shoulder and under his opposite side. "Sit up, sir, and I'll straighten your bedding and get you some water."

It hurt, but he bit back his moan of pain and let her move him about. Her hands were soft and cool, and her touch was gentle. So different from the way he'd been treated the last time he'd sustained a bullet wound.

"Are you all right? Am I being too rough?"

"Not at all. I was just thinking about the last time I was injured."

"During the war?"

"Yes. I was in a hospital tent, being treated by a medic and a volunteer nurse who was burlier than me."

As he'd hoped, she laughed. "I bet you were afraid of her."

"I was afraid to cross her." Remembering the woman, he said, "We were all a little afraid of her. I was as obedient toward her as I've been to anyone. Probably even more so than toward Lee himself!"

"She sounds impressive. And frightening."

"She was indeed. She probably saved more lives than anyone realizes."

After she helped him take a few sips of water, she looked at him in a worried way. "I could use another nurse at the moment. I want to give you some beef broth, but I don't want to leave you alone."

"Don't worry. Ethan will come back eventually."

"I'm not so sure about that. You told him to leave."

"I did. But he knows I need him."

"Another woman was here when I arrived. Maybe she'll return."

Devin didn't care about broth. "Tell me how you got here. What happened, Julianne?"

"Daniel returned to my house. He told me he shot you. Bold as brass, he was."

"I can't believe he had the nerve to do that." The ire that had settled after Ethan left slowly burned hot again. Hating that he was lying in bed so helplessly, he looked her over. "Are you all right? Did he hurt you?"

"I'm all right. I was actually talking to two . . . well, friends of mine. A young man and his sister have adopted me, of sorts."

"Is that right?"

"There's a story there, of course. But what matters is that the three of us were having tea when Daniel arrived. He was full of bluster, saying he took care of you."

"Thankfully, not yet."

"He said he'd be back."

"And?"

She bit her lip before continuing. "I think he wants what you might expect, Devin," she said softly. "He wants me to welcome him back into my life with open arms. He said he owns me."

"Over my dead body." When she flinched, he cursed his choice of words. "I do beg your pardon."

Her expression softened. "No worries. I knew what you meant. But it doesn't matter anyway. I sent him on his way."

Staring at her, watching the array of emotions run across her face, he was sure much more had happened than that. Knowing Bushnell as he did, knowing her as he was beginning to, he worried he had threatened or hurt her and that she was keeping it from him. "Julianne, don't shield me from the truth. I want to know what he did." So he could give those reasons to Bushnell when he beat him to a bloody pulp.

"Nothing you need to worry about, Devin. I handled things myself."

His eyes lit with admiration. "Good for you."

"To be honest, I don't know who was more shocked by my gumption!"

"I know I'm proud of you." He *was* proud of her and glad she'd stood up to the man. But that didn't mean he wasn't going to go after him the first chance he got. But for now? He was suddenly exhausted. "Julianne, if I lie still, could you rest next to me?"

"Certainly not."

"I'm under the covers. You could lie on top of

them," he coaxed. "You could just stay for a few minutes."

"I don't want to hurt you."

"You won't. You'll make me feel better."

"Devin, now is not the time," she protested, but not very strongly. Her voice was warm. Her gaze was too.

"You can see my scars, Julianne. This is not the first time my body has been injured. I have spent my fair share of hours in hospital tents. When I close my eyes, those memories come back."

"I'll stay by you."

"They'll dissipate if you lie down next to me. And if you rest on my good side, I'm sure I'll hardly be aware of anything except your perfume." And the way she felt against him. And the way it felt not to be alone.

"Devin . . ."

Ah. She was wavering. "Come now. I know you must be tired too. No one is here, and they are unlikely to return anytime soon. Your reputation wouldn't suffer."

"If your friend discovers me there, it will discount everything I tried to prove to him."

"You have nothing to prove to him. But no worries anyway. He's not going to step in here for hours. After all, as you said, I was very firm with Ethan."

"I suppose that is true."

"Good." He patted the mattress. "Now, have

pity on me, Julianne. I'm injured and exhausted. Come rest next to me. I'm not hungry now. Help me sleep."

"I'm beginning to think you survived by your wiliness instead of your expertise in the battlefield."

"I'd comment on that, but you'd realize I have no modesty."

She smiled. "I suppose I'm going to have to let you have your way. I don't seem to be able to resist you."

He might be lying in the bed, but her words made him feel as though he were a hero. He made sure not to look too pleased, though. "I think I should apologize in advance. I fear I won't be able to keep awake much longer."

Looking as if she were half afraid a bunch of scandalized women were about to step out from behind the curtains, Julianne crossed to the other side of the double bed and lay down beside him.

"You should take off your shoes."

"Certainly not."

"Whatever you wish, miss."

"Oh, hush, Devin."

He closed his eyes, smelled that faint rose scent, felt her softness curve beside him. And even though he'd been shot by an arch enemy, he was angry with his best friend in the world, and his shoulder burned, he found himself smiling.

Few moments had ever felt so perfect.

24

When Lizbeth returned to the Menger the next morning, she discovered Ethan lounging on one of the formal settees in the lobby of the hotel. Everyone who walked by was giving him a wide berth. Lizbeth wasn't surprised about that, given the way he was glaring at the closed door leading into the secret hall.

She was surprised by his appearance, however. His suit looked rumpled and his expression was haggard. He looked as though he hadn't slept at all. He looked the exact opposite of his usual, perfectly tailored self.

When he spied her, he got to his feet. "Lizbeth."

"Good morning, Ethan," she said simply.

He ran a careless hand through his hair. "Huh. I guess it is morning already."

"You look like you've been lounging here all night. Is everything all right?"

"I have. And no, it is not."

His voice had an unfamiliar rasp. He was upset. "What happened?" she asked as she sat down on one of the padded chairs nearby. "Is the captain worse?"

"I don't know," he said as he sat back down with a grateful sigh. "I haven't been in his room since yesterday afternoon—although I made sure he let in the doctor when he came. And the maids in with some food and fresh water."

"But otherwise he's been alone?" She was shocked—and worried. The captain's wound had been angry, and he'd lost a lot of blood. He needed constant monitoring and was too weak to fend for himself.

"No. Miss Van Fleet stayed with him."

"Why didn't you join them?"

"Devin asked me to leave."

Her eyes widened as she tried not to let on how very shocked she was. But of course it was impossible to hide the fierce blush that was no doubt staining her cheeks.

Ethan did notice. "It wasn't like that, Lizbeth," he said, a touch of amusement lightening his tone. "I . . . well, I offended Miss Van Fleet. Devin heard and was furious."

Belatedly, she realized what that meant. "So Captain Monroe awoke when—"

"He did. Then ordered me from his room." He leaned back against the sofa's cushions and stretched out his arms along its length. When a lady tittered at his position, he glared at her.

Feeling sorrier for him by the second, she said, "That wasn't very kind of Captain Monroe. You went to so much trouble to care for him."

"It was no less than I deserved, I'm afraid." Staring at the closed door again, he shook his head. "What I said was cruel and crossed the boundaries of acceptable behavior. I do not fault Devin for sending me out. Only his injury kept him from hitting me. I would have."

"But you didn't want to leave, did you?"

He shook his head. "I decided to stand vigil out here, in case Miss Van Fleet came out and needed something beyond what the doctor and maids provided. However, she has not."

"It's morning now. Maybe the captain's temper has cooled." Touching his arm stretched out closest to her, she added, "Let's go see him. Maybe we can take them both some coffee and pastries. That usually brightens any mood."

He got to his feet. "I think you're right."

"I'll go to the kitchens. One of the cooks is my friend. I'm sure she'll help me get a tray together." When he made a motion to accompany her, she shook her head. "You had better not wander around the servants' quarters, Ethan. You'd likely send the staff into a fit of vapors. Just wait for me here."

"Thank you. Once again, you've proven to me that while I hope to help you, you seem to be better at helping me."

His words settled in her heart as she walked to one of the servants' staircases and headed to the kitchens. She wasn't immune to his charm, it seemed. Even when he wasn't trying to be particularly charming.

When she opened the door, a blast of warm

air and the low rumble of conversation greeted her. Though she didn't miss many things about working at the Menger, she did miss this place. The kitchens were made up of four large rooms, housing everything from china, glassware, cutlery, linens, and serving platters and trays to a walk-in pantry and an ice room, a washing station, and a huge stove.

Her appearance drew a couple of pointed stares, but then she spied Meg, who was rolling out pastry dough along a marble surface.

"Well, look who's here. It's Elizabeth Barclay!" she called out. "What brings you back to our world? Did Mrs. Howard hire you back on?"

Lizbeth had no desire to discuss her relationship with her cousin. "I'm actually on a mission for rolls and coffee."

Meg grinned. "I heard you're at Harrison House. You entertaining over there?"

"No, of course not. I offered to help Major Kelly. It's for him and a guest of his. Would you help me out?"

"I can. But does Mrs. Howard know you're asking?"

She shook her head. "Does it matter?"

Bertha, the dining room's head cook, strode forward. "Of course it doesn't, Lizzy. If the major wants something, he gets it immediately." She tossed Meg a chiding look. "Everyone here knows that."

Lizbeth hid a smile. It seemed her major had wrapped even their querulous cook around his little finger. "Thank you."

"Of course." Reaching out, she squeezed Lizbeth's shoulder. "But I should tell you that we'd do it for you too. We miss you around here."

"It's been far quieter ever since you left," Meg added. "No one else on staff is as well liked as you."

Lizbeth felt her cheeks heat. The women's kind words meant the world to her. She needed to remember she did have friends here at the Menger. "I'd best get these things together," she said. "The major is waiting."

"Did you say you wanted coffee and pastries?"

"Yes. For four, if you please," she said, figuring she might as well treat herself too.

Bertha pointed to one of the larger silver-plated containers. "Go grab one of those and a couple of cloths. The rest of us will set everything up."

"Thank you, Bertha."

"No thanks needed. You were one of ours. We'll keep claiming you too. As long as you'd like us to, anyway."

Ten minutes later, Lizbeth carried a silver tray toward Ethan. On it was a full coffee service, four china cups, four china plates, and a large silver container of pastries and muffins.

Ethan raised his eyebrows. "I was starting to wonder what was taking so long. Now I realize

I should have been asking you to take care of my meals all along. That's quite a spread."

"I have connections in the kitchen," she teased. Thinking it was time for her to be the person who pushed things along, she said, "We should head right down to the captain's room, Ethan. The coffee is hot."

Steeling his nerve, he nodded and took the heavy tray. "It can't get any worse, right?"

She didn't dare comment on that. After all, she'd learned time and again that things could always get worse.

He hated this. Hated the feeling inside of him clamoring for acceptance and release. "I should probably let you know Devin might refuse us entrance."

"I understand."

With a sense of foreboding, he rapped on the door. "Devin, it is I and Lizbeth," he called out. "We brought you coffee and pastries."

They heard shuffling, then Julianne answered the door. She, too, was wearing the same clothes as the day before. He noticed she also looked rumpled. "Major Kelly, good morning."

"Miss. I trust you remember Miss Barclay?"

Her expression was somber as she nodded. "Indeed. Good morning, Lizbeth. Thank you for this."

"I'm happy to help," Lizbeth said with a smile.

Afraid she was going to shut the door in his face, Ethan managed to grip its side with one hand while balancing the tray with his other. "May we come in? Both of us?"

Julianne looked behind her, and then after she'd obviously gained permission she stepped backward.

Ethan placed the tray on the coffee table. Immediately, his gaze strayed to the bed, but it was empty. The covers had been straightened and the pillows fluffed. It looked as if a maid had already come and tended to the room.

Devin was sitting in one of the chairs next to the fireplace. Julianne had placed a blanket over his lap for warmth. "Ethan," he said by way of greeting.

Well, it wasn't much, but it was better than being refused admittance. "We've brought sustenance," he joked. "And Miss Barclay— Lizbeth—please meet Captain Devin Monroe."

She bobbed a curtsy. "Captain. I am glad to see you awake this morning."

"I'm told much of my recovery is because of your earlier assistance. Thank you."

"I didn't do too much. But you are welcome." Smiling at Ethan, she said, "I was told on good authority that you had a life worth saving."

Meeting Ethan's gaze, Devin said, "That's the benefit of a long friendship, I think. Even when things are not easy, they are appreciated."

It was an apology of a sort. Ethan hadn't expected to hear those words. Or to be let off so easily. Emotion gripped his throat. He knew what he needed to do. Turning to Julianne, he bowed again. "Miss Van Fleet, may I offer you something to eat or drink?"

She smiled as she sat down in the chair next to Devin. "If coffee is in that china pot, I will be forever grateful."

Ethan relaxed slightly. Things might not be good between them, but at least they'd gotten this far. That was something, he supposed. "Lizbeth, I fear I'm all thumbs when it comes to china pots. Would you please do the honors?"

"Of course." She competently poured a cup of coffee. "Miss Van Fleet, how do you take yours?"

"With both cream and sugar, if you please."

"I'll have mine black, miss," Devin said.

After preparing Julianne's cup, Lizbeth handed Devin his. "Here you are, sir."

"Thank you."

While Lizbeth continued the coffee service, Ethan handed out the pastries. Then he sat down by Lizbeth's side on the sitting area's settee.

After an awkward moment, they all began eating.

"Let us not waste any more time," Ethan said after swallowing his first bite. "Devin, you can give me details about your encounter with Bushnell at Julianne's home later, but I got the gist of what happened from her when she arrived. Now, assuming he gave you no clue about where we can find him, what do we need to do? He can't get away with this."

Devin looked at Lizbeth warily. "Perhaps we should wait to talk about this at a later time. I fear our plans might shock Miss Barclay here."

Before Ethan could say anything, Lizbeth spoke. "I am afraid I am not without my own concerns about Colonel Bushnell."

When Julianne suddenly looked up, Ethan knew he needed to explain what Devin already knew. "He attempted to force his attentions on her when she worked here," Ethan said quietly. "Just last week."

Lizbeth paled, and he reached out to her, glad he'd never told her about confronting Bushnell. He was still afraid Bushnell would retaliate by hurting her further, and he didn't want her to come to the same conclusion. "I know this makes you uneasy, but I promise, you are among friends. We can speak freely."

But instead of looking relieved, she seemed to become even more distressed. "I'm afraid I have more reasons to hate him than that, Ethan."

Forgetting they weren't alone, Ethan gripped her hand. "Has he accosted you here another time?"

"No. He, uh—" She stopped abruptly, cutting herself off as though she were slicing a knife through her thoughts. Ethan watched her closely, caught on her words. Bushnell had done what? A dozen scenarios crossed his mind, each more far-fetched and disturbing than the last.

As the silence pulled longer, and Lizbeth so obviously tried to gather her thoughts, he willed himself to wait impassively. During the war, he'd learned the value of patience, but never before had it been so difficult to put into practice.

He felt rather than witnessed Devin react the same way.

Looking apologetic, Lizbeth swallowed. "I'm sorry," she said. She smiled weakly, but at Julianne, not him. He realized it was easier for her to look at Julianne than at him.

A relative stranger.

At last, she lifted her chin and pushed a thick lock of her dark hair away from her face. His eyes traced the patch of skin that had been uncovered. Her skin looked pale and smooth. Her perfect cheekbones as finely sculpted as ever. And yes, even the red line of her scar looked as it always did. A faint mark emphasizing her other features' perfection.

"He is the one who gave me this scar," she said in a rush.

It took a moment for the words to register. With effort, he pushed away the memory of what her scar had looked like when he first saw it. When he, Thomas, and the rest of the men had come on her property. The mark had still been bright red and thick on her forehead. Freshly healed.

Her hand shook as she loosened the stray curl she'd tucked behind her ear. As if it had been happy to be sprung, it curled back into place. Almost covering up the mark. "I got this during the war," she said. "I received it when Bushnell and his men raided my home."

He'd always known men had arrived before they had, and assumed one of them had harmed her. But Bushnell?

Ethan was vaguely aware of Julianne making a pained sound and of Devin cursing under his breath. Ethan felt chilled to the bone. How could such a coincidence exist? "What are you saying?"

"I'm saying Colonel Bushnell came to my house during the war."

It was too much to come to terms with. "Many men in uniform look the same at first glance . . ."

Lines of strain formed, settled in faint lines around her lips. She looked at him. "I wouldn't forget him, Ethan. He haunts my dreams almost every night."

"Of course. Forgive me for doubting you." Staring at her face intently, he said, "So Bushnell was the man who cut your face."

"Oh, he did far more than that," she said, her expression vacant. "He had his men take nearly everything of value—everything they could find. But then as they waited outside, he forced himself into my house, pressed a knife to my skin, and cut me." Her voice lowered, but her gaze did not. She kept her eyes directly on his own. "And then he raped me."

When a china cup crashed to the floor, Ethan wasn't sure if it was his own or someone else's.

He supposed it didn't really matter. He felt broken inside.

25

Johnson's Island, Ohio
Confederate States of America
Officers' POW Camp

"Never thought I'd be playing nursemaid to you, Captain," Ethan Kelly said as he rinsed out the cloth he'd been using to sop up the blood that didn't seem in any hurry to dissipate.

As Devin examined the jagged cut that ran most of the length of his forearm, he tried to bluff the sting away. "I never thought I was going to get my worst injury in the war from gardening. It's embarrassing."

After folding the cloth into a thick rectangle, Ethan pressed it on Devin's arm. The pressure hurt like the devil. "Easy, now."

Instantly, his pressure lightened. "Sorry. You hold it in place." When Devin complied, Ethan sat down on the side of one of the cots and started threading the needle in his hand. "It's not embarrassing. The blade on that hoe is sharp."

Indeed, it was. Razor sharp. "This is proof of that." Thinking of how he'd gone and tripped on the pile of rubble Truax had left out, Devin grimaced. "Still, it was a foolish mistake."

"The blame goes to Truax. Not you."

It was a childish maneuver to pass the blame. It wasn't like him not to accept responsibility for his actions either. However, he was in enough pain to make an exception. "I'll take that. Where is Robert, anyway?"

"I heard he's over at the cemetery," Thomas Baker said from where he was lounging two cots over.

Momentarily forgetting his injury, Devin turned to Baker. "Why? Did something happen?"

"No, sir. He, uh, well, he likes to pull the weeds around the markers."

"That sounds like Robert Truax," Ethan said as he lifted the cloth covering Devin's wound. "Still bleeding," he pronounced. As if Devin couldn't see that for himself.

Feeling a little lightheaded, Devin focused on the conversation, such as it was. "Hold on. Why does visiting the dead sound like Robert?"

"He has a soft spot for things like that," Ethan said. "I thought you knew."

Robert Truax was a lot of things. He was forthright, a good fighter, and extremely patient. He was also hard as stone. He had no family, born as he was on the streets. He looked after himself. That was it.

"No, I guess I didn't know that."

Baker got to his feet. "Do you need something, Cap? 'Cause I can go get him for ya."

"No."

"I need you, Baker," Ethan said. "Get over here and hold the captain's arm steady while I stitch."

"All right."

Baker was the biggest of all of them. The roughest too. No doubt his grip was going to be as painful as Ethan's stitching. "No need for you, Baker. I'm not going to need anyone to hold me down."

"It might come as a bit of a surprise, but I have no experience stitching skin," Ethan said in that lofty way he adopted when his pride was stung. "I doubt I will have a tender touch. You're going to move. Baker will help you stay put."

Devin pulled his arm away and slapped the soiled cloth back on his arm. "Hold on. You've never given a man stitches before?"

"Of course not. Have you?"

"Once." Remembering what a mess he'd made of it, he frowned. His only saving grace had been that the soldier he'd been stitching passed out. He, on the other hand, was currently wide-awake. Eyeing the needle and thread in Ethan's hand, he said, "Where did you get the needle and thread? I thought it was in your kit."

"I got it from Thomas."

"You?"

Thomas shrugged. "I thought it might come in useful. And it did."

Devin noticed then that Thomas was eyeing

Ethan with more than a little bit of wariness. "Baker, have you ever stitched a man?"

He nodded. "I have."

"More than once?"

"Yes, sir. Many a time." Darting a sidelong glance his way, Thomas continued. "There weren't a lot of physicians wandering around the slums sewing up nicks and scrapes. We took care of our own."

Ethan looked affronted. "It isn't my fault I grew up in different circumstances."

"Of course not, sir," Thomas said.

Devin made a sudden decision. "Baker, I want you to sew up my arm."

While the sergeant nodded, not looking the least bit intimidated by the length of the jagged cut, Ethan threw up his hands.

He was offended. "Do you not trust me?"

"In a word? No."

Devin shifted, holding his arm in a stiff way. "I'd be obliged if we could simply get this over with, Baker. We can discuss your experience at a later time."

"Yes, sir." Holding out a hand to Ethan, Baker said, "I'll take a thread. And light a candle for me, if you please."

"Why?" Ethan asked suspiciously.

"I need to put the needle through a flame first."

"Why?"

"Just do it, Kelly," Devin said through clenched

teeth. His arm really was starting to burn. And the anticipation? He had never imagined himself to be nervous about anything involving an injury, but the men's bickering was beginning to take its toll.

As if Kelly had come to the same conclusion, he handed the needle and thread to Thomas, lit one of their precious candles, and held it steady while the sergeant held the needle over the flame.

A moment later, Baker sat down next to him, gestured for his arm, and lifted the bloody rag. The wound was still oozing, though the edges of the cut looked a little less fragile.

After examining the wound and the amount of thread on the needle, Thomas spoke. "I think I'm going to start in the center, sir. There's a sizable hole there, you see."

Devin was starting to feel he had no desire to discuss the wound another second. "No need to describe what I can already feel, Sergeant. Just begin, if you please."

"Yes, sir." And then, without another second's hesitation, Thomas pinched the aforementioned gaping section together and inserted the needle.

It stung. Stung like a mess of fire ants had descended on his arm. He clenched his teeth to prevent his body from flinching as the needle continued through his skin. There was no way he wanted Ethan to start holding down his arm.

"Huh," Kelly said. "You really do know what you're doing."

"Weren't no reason to lie," Baker said easily as he continued his work.

Devin held still as the door opened and more men entered. Seeing what was happening, they all walked over, peering at Devin's arm and admiring Baker's work.

"Looks like we can set you up your own dress shop when we get out of here," General McCoy said to Baker. "Those are some impressive stitches. I reckon that wound is going to heal real nicely. One day it will hardly have more than a fine line visible."

"Thank you, sir," Baker said as he did something painful. Devin turned his head to see Baker slice the thread with the tip of a knife someone held out for him.

"We done?" Devin said.

McCoy laughed. "You sound a little peaked, Captain. The sight of blood bothering you?"

Since they'd all seen more blood on the battlefield than any of them had ever thought possible, Devin grinned. "I guess so. Or maybe I've been sitting here worrying about my scar. I've got to get a wife one day, you know. Don't want to scare her off."

"Women like their men scarred and marred," Ethan joked. "Makes them think we are invincible."

"I'm sure all the women I court are going to be real impressed with my gardening accident," Devin joked. "Makes me sound like a real hero."

"Don't worry yourself," Bushnell interjected from the back of the room. "Kelly is right. Men's scars don't matter. Only the women's do."

The statement was so outrageous, Devin looked over at the colonel, just to get a sense of how he looked. And there he was, standing tall and smug, full of blustery pride. "I'm afraid you've lost me, sir. What do you mean?"

"Nothing out of the ordinary, Captain," he replied, each word sounding like a lazy drawl. "Only that a man with a scar can still look attractive while a woman isn't so lucky. All she'll look is marked."

"Anyone who survives an injury is to be respected, no?" Ethan asked, his voice sounding frigid.

"Perhaps . . . unless the woman isn't the kind to be respected anyway."

A couple of the men surrounding him laughed nervously, but Devin stared up at Bushnell curiously. The comment was both in poor taste and rather odd.

Beside him, Baker pursed his lips as he ran the needle over the flame again. It was obvious that Thomas Baker knew what Bushnell was referring to and didn't approve.

"Colonel Bushnell, you sound knowledgeable on the subject. Do you know something in particular about women and scarring?" Kelly asked.

There was an edge to his voice. It also had a cadence to it Devin recognized as a warning. Whenever Kelly was particularly offended, his tone didn't just turn haughty. He started pulling out all his fancy vocabulary.

But Bushnell didn't look offended or caught off guard in the slightest. "Not especially. Only that their scars detract from their beauty."

"Because they had the misfortune to be cut?" General McCoy asked.

"I'm sorry if I've caused offense," Bushnell said. "I sometimes forget some of you are so fainthearted."

"That should do it, Captain," Baker said.

Looking down at his arm, Devin realized Thomas had, indeed, already finished. There on his arm were eighteen perfectly executed stitches. His flesh was neatly closed. He tested them, moving his arm this way and that. "You did a fine job, Thomas. Thank you."

"It was nothing, Cap." Looking bleak, he added, "As the colonel said, men seem to be able to handle cuts easier than women."

Of course, that wasn't exactly what the man had said.

But Devin had to agree with what Baker

said. Men were tougher. They were built and conditioned to stand pain.

But of course, his father had taught him to protect women. Look after them. Not comment upon the state of their scars.

26

The sound of the cup crashing to the floor should have spurred all of them to action, but Julianne couldn't seem to move a muscle. Devin, sitting next to her in an overstuffed chair, looked frozen.

That sweet little Lizbeth looked crushed, as if she regretted revealing a dark secret she had promised to take to her grave. Ethan Kelly looked even worse. Devastated.

Julianne understood how he felt. Even after enduring taunts and whispers for years, she'd never felt more unworthy or empty than she did at that very minute. After all, she'd allowed Daniel Bushnell to keep her in comfort even though she knew he was married. She'd allowed him into her bed even though she knew it was sinful. While she would never categorize those experiences as pleasant—he had certainly never raped her. He had beat her, but not this.

No, it seemed he had only done such things to innocent women when he raided their homes.

Feeling sick, bile rose in her throat. How long would it take before Ethan told Lizbeth about her being Bushnell's kept woman? And surely a gentleman like Devin Monroe would at last see the error of his ways and never associate with her again.

And Lizbeth? Well, that poor woman would probably go out of her way to avoid her at all costs. Julianne wouldn't blame her one bit.

"I beg your pardon for my clumsiness," Ethan said, breaking the strained silence. After reaching for a neatly folded cloth on the serving tray, he knelt on the floor and started picking up the shards. "I, uh . . . I fear I must be more tired than I thought."

Julianne knelt to help. Taking the cloth from his grip, she sopped up the coffee as he dropped the pieces of fine-bone china on a tray. Each one made a delicate *ping* as it landed on the silver, providing the only sound in the room.

After cleaning up as much of the coffee as she was able, Julianne reached for the tray. "I'll go see if I can get a maid to help me clean this up. I'll have her fetch you a fresh cup as well, Major."

"No, I can do that," Lizbeth said. "This . . . this was my fault, anyway."

"How can you say such a thing?" the major bit out.

"I shouldn't have shared what I did. Especially not right now. Captain Monroe is injured."

"You didn't offend me, miss."

But instead of looking reassured, Lizbeth appeared more agitated. "I'm sure I, uh, spoke out of turn. What happened is in the past. It's best forgotten."

"I, for one, am glad you spoke so freely," Devin said, his voice scratchy with suppressed emotion. "The truth is a far better ally than enemy."

Julianne had never heard that statement, but she supposed it was true—if one had nothing to hide. Not knowing where to look, she shifted uncomfortably.

Just as Lizbeth was making her way to the door, Devin's voice rang out. "Miss Barclay? I would be very grateful if you could fetch us another cup, and perhaps more coffee too. And, Julianne, if you wouldn't mind, please go with her."

"I don't mind at all." She knew what his request was. A thinly veiled plea for the two of them to vacate the room and give the men some privacy. She didn't care what the reasoning was behind it, however. She was grateful for the reprieve.

Lizbeth opened the door. "I'll inform the cook you'll need something with more sustenance as well, Captain," she said before departing.

When Julianne closed the heavy door behind them, she exhaled. "That was brave of you. Are you all right?"

Lizbeth lifted a shoulder. "I had never intended to tell anyone exactly how I got that scar. It just slipped out. My cousin knows a man cut me in the war, but nothing else."

"Maybe God decided it was time for your story to be told."

"Do you really think so? I wonder if that was

the case. I saw Ethan's, I mean *Major Kelly's* expression. He looked angry."

"Of course he was. No one wants to think of you being hurt." She hoped she sounded more convincing than she felt. She felt as if she were balancing on a shaky tightrope. Any minute she was certain to fall and either injure herself or someone else.

Luckily, Lizbeth didn't seem to notice anything untoward. "I suppose not." Leading the way down the hall, she said, "As I told you, I worked here as a maid—until last week when I had my last encounter with Bushnell. My cousin and her husband are the managers."

"It's nice that you have family nearby."

"To be honest, of late I haven't been sure if it was a blessing or a curse."

"Are they difficult?"

"Not like you might be imagining. It's just that my cousin knows how I used to be, you see. She can't seem to equate it with the person I am now."

Julianne smiled wryly. "Ah. Now I understand. But you shouldn't worry about that. What you are forgetting, I think, is that we all used to be different people. Time and experience change us. It can't be helped."

Opening a door partly hidden by a screen, Lizbeth said, "I'm going to try to keep that in mind right now. And keep you beside me, as well. Between the two of us, we should be able

302

to persuade Cook to make the captain a real breakfast."

"That should be no problem. I've persuaded a great number of people to do a great number of things. I'm rather good at it."

"I'll watch and learn then, Miss Van Fleet. I could stand to have a few more things come my way."

The moment the door closed, Devin motioned Ethan to his side. "Help me sit up better, would you? I feel like an invalid, lounging in this chair in front of the women."

Ethan didn't bother disputing the notion that he wasn't an invalid. He placed his arms under Devin's arms and pulled him up. "Better?"

"Yeah." After taking a sip of coffee, he met Ethan's gaze. "Did you have any inkling about this?"

"Of course not. I would have shot him in his chamber if I had." With effort, Ethan tamped down the dozen swear words and threats rumbling around in his head. His anger wouldn't serve any purpose, especially since he imagined Devin was no doubt thinking of some kind of retribution that didn't involve bloodshed.

After relating the details of his encounter with Bushnell at Julianne's home, Devin said, "I want to kill him."

Huh. It seemed he had been mistaken.

Weighing his next words carefully, Ethan said, "Any special way you want to go about doing that?"

Devin grunted. "You mean besides picking up my Colt, tracking him down, and firing two shots into his chest? No."

"Ah." This conversation was becoming increasingly full of surprises.

"What? And don't look at me that way, as though you are attempting to figure me out. Of course you must feel the same way."

"I do. But I'm wise enough not to act on it."

"We need to. Justice hasn't been served."

"First we need to figure out where he is," Ethan said. "I couldn't locate him when I returned from your place a few days ago. No one seems to know where he's gone. When you feel better, we should start combing other inns and hotels in the area. I think he preys on women who are alone or have no one to fight for them. That was certainly the case with Lizbeth."

"We can't conduct such a search on our own."

Ethan knew that, but he didn't want Devin to get too agitated either. "Don't worry. I'll figure out something."

"Ethan, go to the telegraph office and send for Truax and Baker. We need their help."

"I know we need help searching, but let's wait. I can handle Bushnell." Plus, it was his right. Bushnell had scarred Lizbeth. Violated her. For

304

that, the man would pay, and Ethan wanted to be sure he would be the one to make him.

"If it was a matter of you gunning down the man in cold blood, I would agree. But we need a plan to make sure no one discovers what we do."

An itch of foreboding flooded him. It was one thing to kill a man in battle. Or in self-defense. Maybe it was even understandable to seek vengeance when emotions were high and a man could be excused for letting his need to protect get the best of him. But to methodically seek vengeance in a cool and calculated way? Well, he didn't need to confer with a pastor to know that was a sin.

Devin was staring at him with those ice-blue eyes of his. "What's wrong?"

"I'm hesitant to get them involved."

"Why? Didn't we promise we'd help each other? Haven't we done that for them?"

"Yes. Of course. But Robert was fighting a nasty web of lies about Phillip Markham."

"He was also intent on making things right for Miranda."

"And Baker, well, he was fighting a gang of men threatening the woman who freed him from jail."

Ethan shook his head. "Make no mistake about his motives, Ethan. He wanted to help her not because she'd freed him. It was because he loved her."

Thinking about rough, jaded Thomas and how he'd gazed at Laurel with such tenderness, Ethan swallowed hard. Thomas Baker was easily the scrappiest of them all. He was rough around the edges and had a temper that could be ignited faster than a stick of dynamite. "Yes. That is true. However . . ."

"However what?"

"Is love involved now? I'm not sure."

"I am."

Devin was sure Ethan had fallen in love with Lizbeth?

"I don't know if I've fallen in love."

"Who said I was talking about you?"

Ethan wanted to ask if he was sure he understood what Devin meant . . . until he got up to answer a knock at the door and saw who was there.

Things might eventually get better. But not yet. Certainly not anytime soon.

27

Miss Van Fleet and Lizbeth stood in the back of the kitchens while Bertha, the cook, prepared a simple but substantial breakfast.

Lizbeth had asked for food for the men, but, as she always did, Bertha seemed to have a sixth sense about what was needed and set her staff to creating breakfast for four. She'd been grateful for the kindness, as well as the excuse to stand in the back of the noisy kitchens and pull herself together.

Of course, she didn't try to fool herself into thinking she was going to accomplish that goal anytime soon. She felt shattered inside. Embarrassed too. For some reason, admitting her most closely guarded secret had given her body permission to relive those terrible hours all over again. Though a part of her felt it had been bound to happen sooner or later, she would have given everything she had to relive Bushnell's abuse in the far future, preferably when she was alone.

It certainly would have helped the major, Captain Monroe, and Miss Van Fleet. They'd looked shocked and disturbed. Especially Julianne. Lizbeth couldn't blame her. She was soiled, at least to most people of good breeding and class, of which Julianne surely was.

It didn't matter that Lizbeth had been hurt by a soldier, that she was as much a victim of the war as the men littering the streets without limbs or disfigured from their injuries. Society had a different view of women who had been attacked and survived. They assumed they had allowed men liberties. That's why she'd never told anyone.

"Do you want to talk about it?" Miss Van Fleet whispered.

"I beg your pardon?"

Compassion warmed her gaze. "If you'd rather not talk about it, I understand, but I thought you might want to talk about it with another woman."

Talk about it? About how she'd been bleeding and hurt and alone for days . . . until yet another band of soldiers came through to take what few belongings she had left? About how they'd stared at the angry cut on her face and had known? *Surely they'd known.* But still they'd looted and grabbed until there hadn't been anything left.

A shiver ran through her. It seemed she was incapable of stopping her body from reacting to the memories. If she started talking about it now, in the middle of the kitchens? Chances were good she would collapse onto the floor.

"Thank you, but I don't think so."

Miss Van Fleet frowned at her stiff and formal tone. "Forgive me."

Her stomach sank. Somehow she'd managed to

make things worse. "It's kind of you to still be speaking to me, Miss Van Fleet," she said. "Many women of your class would now be pretending I didn't exist."

"Please, call me Julianne. I certainly am not one to pass judgment." Staring at the women bustling around the kitchen in front of them, she exhaled. "Sometimes I wonder if men will ever really stop to think about what their sisters and girlfriends and mothers endured when they left to fight." She shivered.

"Being left behind to worry and make do on our own was difficult, wasn't it?" Hearing her words, she flushed. Calling those years difficult was like calling Texas in July simply hot. But if Julianne found an issue with her statement, she didn't let on. She merely nodded and continued to watch the staff making preparations.

Minutes later, Meg approached with a tray in her hands. "Here you go, Lizbeth. Cook wants to know who to charge for the payment. The major or the captain?"

"I'm not sure. Maybe the major?" She looked to Julianne for advice.

Julianne nodded. "That's a good start. If the men find fault with that, they can clear it up later on their own."

Meg smiled. "Good enough." Before she turned away, she said, "I guess you are truly keeping company with the major now, aren't you?"

"He's been a good friend."

"I just bet he has." After smirking at her fellow workers, she said, "Don't mind us none. We're just a little jealous, is all. The major is a man worth claiming."

Lizbeth felt her cheeks heat. Though she knew Meg hadn't meant to embarrass her, she still had. Hoping to transfer their focus to someone else, she looked around the kitchen. "Meg, have you seen Cassie? I just realized she usually comes down here to take her break right about now."

Looking pensive, Meg motioned them toward the door. "Lizbeth, no one's seen her today."

"Why not? Is she sick?"

Meg shook her head. "She's gone. All her things too." After looking over her shoulder, she lowered her voice. "Cook says Cassie probably took off with an admirer or something, but I don't know. That don't seem like her."

"That isn't like her at all!" Cassie was always full of good humor, but she wasn't flighty. Lizbeth knew she wouldn't have left without giving notice and careful planning. "Has anyone told Aileen? What did she say?"

"I guess Cook told her, but you know how Mrs. Howard is. If it don't concern paying guests, she don't pay too much attention."

Biting her bottom lip, Lizbeth nodded. "She can be that way, I suppose."

"No, she is that way," Meg corrected. Softening her voice, she said, "Look, don't worry about Cassie. I'm sure she's fine. I know you thought she was a good girl, but she had an eye on the gentlemen. Most likely she found her own Major Kelly and let herself get swept off her feet."

Lizbeth would have argued about that some more, but she was aware that Julianne was listening to every word and Meg was beginning to look uncomfortable. "Thanks for the tray and for letting me know about Cassie," she said at last. "I'll let you go before Cook gets upset."

As if on cue, Cook called out, "Meg, they don't pay you to stand around and do nothing."

Meg grinned. "I'll see you later. Work calls. Plus, you've got a tray to deliver."

After smiling at her again, Lizbeth led Julianne out of the warm kitchen. "I'm sorry about that."

"Think nothing of it. I'm sorry about your friend."

"I am too. Well, I'm surprised. No matter what Meg said, I can't see Cassie running after a man without careful thought."

"Maybe she had a reason you didn't know about."

Looking at Julianne, Lizbeth realized that could be the case. Though she and Cassie had been friends, they'd been close work friends. Lizbeth had certainly never told Cassie about her past. It only stood to reason that Cassie hadn't felt compelled to share all her secrets. "Maybe she did at that," she said softly.

Julianne placed one elegant hand on her arm. "Are you all right? If not, I can carry the tray to Captain Monroe's room."

There was no way she would allow that to happen. "I'm fine. Though I am worried about Cassie, I'm not going to borrow trouble. I'm just going to have to assume she's moved on to some place better." She determined to ignore the fear that invaded her thoughts.

Looking relieved as they walked through the lobby, Julianne nodded. "Perhaps that's the best thing to do at the moment."

Lizbeth was just about to change the subject when Aileen called out her name. Unable to avoid her, they stopped again.

Her cousin was beaming. Beaming! She looked as though she were half floating with excitement. After quickly introducing her to Julianne and setting the tray down on a nearby table, she said, "Aileen, what has happened? You look so happy."

"Major Kelly's family just arrived."

Lizbeth was so surprised, she pushed all her worries about Cassie's whereabouts from her mind. Even she knew Ethan wasn't close to his family. She needed to warn him so they wouldn't catch him off guard. "Where are they?"

"Visiting him, of course. I escorted them to the captain's room myself."

"You did what?" Oh, he wasn't going to be happy.

"I had no choice, Lizbeth. That was Mr. Michael Kelly! He must own half of Texas."

"Did you warn the major first?"

"Of course not." She sighed and then spoke with even more emphasis. "One more time, Lizbeth, Mr. Michael Kelly is here, with Mrs. Kelly and their other children. Of course I'm going to do whatever they ask. Besides, they're his parents."

Reluctantly, Lizbeth conceded that her cousin had a point. It wasn't a hotelier's job to screen guests' visitors—only to do what was asked quickly and efficiently.

Amusement lit Julianne's eyes. "Something tells me neither Major Kelly nor the captain is going to be excited to entertain guests."

"We better hurry."

Aileen trotted along as Lizbeth picked up the tray, and they headed down the secret hallway that wasn't much of a secret anymore. "Dallas is so excited. They requested three more suites too."

So they were staying. "Aileen, you had better prepare yourself to face the wrath of Major Kelly."

"What wrath? He's the most gentlemanly man who stays here."

Lizbeth felt like pointing out that his good manners didn't necessarily mean he was honorable at every occasion. After all, he was a gambler. He'd also fought in the war and survived a prisoner of war camp. A man didn't come out on the other side of those things without being tough.

Julianne paused a couple of feet before Devin's door. "Thank you for informing us, Mrs. Howard, but we will take it from here."

Aileen drew to a stop. "I was going to open the door for you."

"We'll simply knock."

"Lizbeth—"

She knew what Aileen wanted. She wanted Lizbeth to let her peek inside the room so she could report what was going on to her husband. But there was no way that was going to happen. Ignoring Aileen's look of longing, she walked down to the captain's door and knocked.

When it opened, six faces stared back at her. One of which was scowling.

"At last you have returned," Ethan said, his voice sounding as sharp as one of Bertha's butcher knives. "Do come in. You are just in time to meet my family."

28

Time might as well have stood still for his family. As Ethan stared at his brother, sister, and parents, each one decked out more elaborately than the last, he wondered if any other family in the state of Texas had been so blessed. The Kelly family had managed to survive the war without losing a member, losing their home, or, it seemed, their pride.

He'd only come to terms with the fact that despite his problems adjusting to civilian life, he had been just as blessed.

As he watched Lizbeth and Julianne enter the room, Lizbeth carrying a tray of food, he could sense their surprise and wariness. He hated it. Lizbeth's green eyes were clouded with worry. She was worried about him, about how he was feeling. After what she'd just revealed.

Before he could begin introductions, his mother stepped forward.

"I must say the service here couldn't be better. Set everything up along the back counter. Then you may go." Her voice lost a tad bit of warmth when Lizbeth and Julianne froze in confusion. "If you are waiting for a tip, you are going to have to do something more than stare back at me like deer lost in the glade."

Had his mother not noticed the women weren't wearing maids' uniforms? Before Ethan could say a word, Lizbeth nodded and lifted the lid off the tray. Seeing her jump to his mother's bidding was more than he could take. Furious, he crossed the room and stopped her. "Don't," he said. When she flinched at his harsh tone, he gentled his voice and curved his hand around her own. "You are my guest now."

"I don't mind."

"But I do."

"Ethan, what is the problem?" his mother asked.

"Everyone, this is Lizbeth Barclay. She is a friend of mine. Also, may I present Miss Julianne Van Fleet of Boerne?" When they gaped at him, he continued the introductions. "Lizbeth, Julianne, please meet my parents, Michael and Genevieve Kelly. And these two are my siblings, Phillip and Margaret."

He noticed his brother and sister were studying both him and the women with interest. When Julianne curtsied, Margaret stepped forward and smiled. "It's a pleasure to meet you, Miss Van Fleet, and you too, Miss Barclay."

Julianne inclined her head. "Thank you."

Lizbeth curtsied but didn't say a word. It was obvious she was uncomfortable.

"I'm completely confused. Why are they

bringing food in here if they don't work at the hotel?" his mother asked.

"I was an employee here until very recently," Lizbeth said.

Julianne moved to Devin's side and was now speaking to him softly. Before Ethan had allowed his family to enter, he'd assisted Devin back into bed. This was after he'd considered refusing to see them at all.

It was Devin who had insisted they come in. He said he had no modesty after the war and could not care less who saw him in bed—though he still wished Julianne and Lizbeth didn't have to. Because Ethan couldn't argue that point, he'd allowed his family to enter and explained how Devin was still recuperating after being shot. Of course, his family had looked somewhat alarmed, but they'd handled the news with grace. The Kelly family prided themselves on being able to adapt to any situation with ease.

Since then, Devin had been reclining in bed, just as if he usually received guests while lying down. Now, though, it was easy to see he wasn't pleased with Ethan's mother's assumptions about Julianne and Lizbeth. That was good, because Ethan was just as appalled. It was time to get his family out of the room and figure out why they'd suddenly decided to track him down.

"We need to allow Devin to rest," he said abruptly.

After studying Ethan's expression, his father nodded. "Yes. Of course, son." His father walked to Devin's side. "I will hope and pray you continue to heal, Captain. It was an honor to meet you."

Ethan could hardly believe his father's words. This was the first time in Ethan's memory his father wasn't acting as if he were the most important person in the room.

After his mother and siblings said their good-byes, his father opened the door and ushered the three of them out. Then he paused, obviously waiting for him as well. "Ethan?"

"I'll be right there. Close the door, please."

To his surprise, his father did as he asked. And his mother didn't even offer a word of protest! What in the world was going on? Feeling as though he were in the middle of a strange dream, Ethan turned to Devin. "Obviously I need to see to my family. After I ascertain why they have decided to pay me a visit, I'll send those telegrams posthaste."

Amusement lit Devin's eyes. "Thank you. Now, ladies, I think it would be best if you left as well."

"I am not leaving," Julianne said. "I came here to help you, and that is what I intend to do."

"I am better now, Julianne."

"All the same, I am staying."

"I'm going to go back to Mrs. Harrison's,"

Lizbeth said quietly. "I have a lot to do. Enjoy the time with your family, Major Kelly."

Knowing his family was lingering in the hall, waiting on him, Ethan nodded. "I'll call for you later. We have much to talk about." He was no longer concerned about gossip.

Lizbeth nodded before slipping out the door.

Ethan felt a loss—and the loss of everything he'd wanted to say deep in his heart. Lizbeth was embarrassed that Devin and Julianne knew about her past, having no idea Julianne had a past too. She'd acted as though his family should treat her like their servant too. It was all a mess. A complete and utter mess. He wanted to protect her more than ever. Be there for her. Reassure her that nothing she could say or do would distract him from convincing her to marry him.

But first he had to deal with his family. And, yes, go after Bushnell.

"I'll be back as soon as I can," he told Devin.

"I'd rather you take your time, Major. You have quite a list of people who need your attention."

Ethan felt like rolling his eyes. What Devin had said was a complete understatement.

Walking out into the hall, he studied his family. They were all standing rather leisurely, somehow managing to appear as though they loitered in hotel hallways on a regular basis. Knowing he had perfected that same way of behaving made his temper flare. Here again was another example of how he'd thought he was so different from his family, when in fact he was just like them. "Follow me," he said at last.

"Ethan, your men might be used to following your directives without question, but I assure you this family is not," his father pronounced. This was more like him. "Where are you taking us?"

"To my room. It's just on the second floor. We can confer there."

But still his father hesitated. "Ethan, I would rather not discuss our business while sitting on the edge of a bed."

"I have a sitting room. All of you will be completely comfortable." And he will have gained a few moments to accept the fact that his family had descended upon him without notice.

When his father looked as if he was tempted to question him further, Ethan started walking. He knew he was walking too fast for the women, for his mother most especially. But he couldn't bring himself to care. His mind was feeling too muddled. Why had they shown up? And what was he going to say about Lizbeth?

Seconds later, Phillip caught up with him. "So, who is that woman with the dark curly hair and green eyes? I am sure she is more than a mere maid."

What she was, was complicated. "Lizbeth is no one you need to worry about."

"If she matters to you, I will," Phillip said, surprising him. "Besides, you know Mother is going to have a dozen questions about her. You should prepare yourself."

In the face of everything they were going through, such worries struck him as laughable. "She can ask all the questions she wants. I'll be all right."

Phillip slowly smiled. "You are better. The shadows in your eyes have faded."

"I have recently realized that myself."

"I hope that means we'll be seeing more of you."

As much as Ethan wanted to make that promise, he couldn't quite do that. He needed to know why his family had come to *him*—and see how they treated Lizbeth. If he couldn't be assured she would be treated with care, Ethan knew he would keep his distance as much as he could. Hoping to ease the tension between them, he changed the subject. "Phillip, how have you been?"

"You know. Doing the same. Working hard." Sounding aggrieved, he continued. "I've had to help Father find workers. We have to pay field hands now. Not much, of course, but that is a concern."

Ethan didn't dare touch that. His schooling at West Point had taught him a lot about how others viewed slavery. By the time he'd left the academy, he, too, had disdained the practice and privately promised himself he would do everything he could to help end it. He'd fought in the war to uphold the honor of the South, not to celebrate the inhuman practice of owning another man.

"How is Margaret?" he asked, eager to change the subject again.

Phillip shrugged. "About the same."

"Couldn't you share something more? Don't forget, I have not seen her in six months," he said as they walked up the stairs. He was aware of his father escorting their mother and sister at a far slower pace. "Is she well?"

His brother frowned. "She lost George. Remember?"

He had been in such a bad place when he'd been home, Ethan wasn't even sure if he'd been aware of how much she'd been grieving. "George McDonald, yes?"

Phillip nodded. "He was a fine fellow. He died two months before the nuptials were set to take place. Margaret already had her wedding gown and everything."

Ethan couldn't believe he hadn't known of all that, and since seeing Margaret, he had all but forgotten her loss. Forgotten his family *had* been touched by death. He didn't want to admit that. "How did he die again?"

"George had to report to camp for training.

Then, right before he went out into the battlefield, he contracted some kind of stomach ailment. Margaret heard he'd died within two weeks of contracting it."

"It was most likely typhus." Far too many men had died from poor sanitary conditions.

"Whatever it was, he died. As you can imagine, she's still having a difficult time getting over his death."

"I'm sure she is," he said softly, realizing yet again that he wasn't the only person in the family who had suffered. He'd been so consumed with fighting his own demons that he hadn't spared a thought to theirs.

Which brought him back to his family's sudden appearance.

"Why did Father bring all of you here?" he asked, realizing he needed to prepare himself before all four of them were confronting him with something that would likely catch him off guard.

Phillip slowed his steps. "Not sure if I should be the one telling you."

Whether it was because he was still coping with Devin's injury, absorbing Julianne's arrival, or felt as if he still wasn't doing his best for Lizbeth, his temper snapped. "You are almost thirty years old. When are you going to be old enough to speak for yourself? Tell me."

They were walking down his hallway now.

Every door was closed, no one else in sight. But the hall had never felt so long. Ethan was both eager to pull his brother into the privacy of his room yet also dreading the moment.

"Father wanted to be the one to tell you."

"What would it matter if he wasn't? Do you really think the world would end?"

Looking stung, Phillip stepped back. "Of course not."

"Then what has you so afraid?"

Phillip clenched his fists. "I am not afraid of anything."

If he wasn't, he was a fool. "What is the reason, then?"

Their parents and his sister would be joining them within a minute or two. Ethan pulled out his key, inserted it into the lock, and resigned himself to waiting.

"They want you to return home," Phillip said under his breath.

That was it? "I'll come home as soon as I'm able." He smiled encouragingly. "I promise."

"No, you don't understand, Ethan. Our father is dying. The doctors don't give him more than six months to live. We need you back. I . . . I can't do it all on my own."

An ache settled deep in his heart as shock overcame him. But though he knew he'd have to later come to terms with what he'd just heard, Ethan didn't dare give in to it now.

Therefore, he pushed back the pain just as he had done during the war over and over again. "Have you even tried?"

Phillip flinched. "I have, but it's never been good enough. I've never been good enough, at least not in Father's eyes."

He grunted. "I think we both know that is a lie. I've been the embarrassment to him."

"They have missed you, worried about you, and prayed for you," Phillip corrected, his voice thick with emotion. "But never, never did they feel embarrassed."

"I had nightmares. I couldn't adjust when I returned." Lowering his voice, he said, "I was weak."

"You were human, Ethan. You fought with honor. You are a much-lauded survivor of a prisoner of war camp. Everyone in Houston speaks highly of you." He chuckled, the laugh sounding harsh and dark. "I promise, you are many things to our parents, but a disappointment is not one of them."

What if his brother's words were true? What if his father didn't regard him as a black sheep but as a prodigal son? "I don't know what to say," he said at last.

"No? Well, why don't you simply answer me instead? What is it going to take to bring you home, Ethan?" he asked between gritted teeth. "Would our father dying do it? Or does it need to be something more important to you? Maybe the idea of running your family's legacy?"

"That isn't more important than our father."

"Really? What about Mother begging? Would that encourage you to put us first?" Phillip stepped closer as he walked through the threshold into Ethan's suite. "Or do you make sacrifices only for strangers or your fellow comrades from prison?"

Ethan gripped the frame of the door as he struggled to answer. Quite simply, he didn't know.

29

Ethan never imagined he'd feel sorry for his father, but he was coming close to it at that moment. Standing in his suite next to his brother, and looking at his sister and parents standing together next to the windows, he felt a tension in the air that was almost claustrophobic.

When he'd entered his room, he'd been determined to merely stand and wait for his father to come to the point of his visit all on his own. Michael Kelly had always liked to be in charge, and Ethan had no desire to take that away from him.

But after watching him clumsily attempt to get to the point of his visit and fail, Ethan realized he couldn't do it. He couldn't act as though he weren't his father's son. He was. And that meant his father deserved his respect, even when he didn't feel comfortable giving it to him.

"Sir," he finally began. "I'm sure you are busy. Perhaps you could share why you have decided to visit me here."

"Yes, I'm sure it is difficult wondering why we have descended upon you without notice," his father said stiffly.

"I don't care about that," Ethan retorted, suddenly realizing he meant it. "You are my family. I might not have shown it of late, but I still love and care for you."

He could practically feel his siblings' approval beside him. Ethan didn't know if that mattered to him. But after getting to know Lizbeth, he realized he'd taken them for granted.

Only after talking to Lizbeth and realizing just how much she'd had to do on her own, how much she'd had to survive without any help or comfort . . . Well, it made him ashamed. Yes, he'd been hurt and imprisoned. But he'd also always known that, when push came to shove, he would never have to stand completely alone. Now he wanted to stand by her side and give her the support and love she needed.

And, perhaps, also reach out to the people in this room. It was time to stop focusing on their differences and pay attention to what they had in common. Because, at the end of the day, he was incredibly blessed to still have his family. They were imperfect, but so was he. Therefore, if there was even a chance to have a kind of new relationship with them, he had to try.

"We want you to come home, Ethan," his mother said, her cultured voice breaking the silence. "The war is over now. And . . . and we need you with us."

"Yes," his father said. "You have your life to reclaim. It's time you came home for good."

Home. The word brought up images of a wide front porch, the grove of pin oak trees, the stable full of fine horses. The deep burgundy rug that lay in the center of the house's formal drawing room. His great-grandmother had brought that rug over from England.

It all brought forth a wave of sentimental longing. He wanted to be a part of the family again. But was he ready to move home right away? He just wasn't sure. He also didn't want to say anything about his father's illness until he brought it up himself. Not trusting himself to speak, he remained silent.

"Ethan, what do you have to say?" his father prompted.

"I want to help, but I may need more time. I have a rather full life here."

"Doing what?" Father ran a finger along the top of the marble-topped dresser. "Gambling? Living in a hotel?"

Ethan couldn't help but smile. "I would hesitate to call my success at the tables a failure. Besides, I don't gamble as frequently as you might imagine. I've also come to the aid of my friends. Helping them in any way I can."

"But what about when your family needs you to come to their aid?" Phillip asked. "Do we not count?"

Margaret stood up and walked to his side. "Ethan, won't you reconsider? Just because there's been strain between us, it doesn't mean we can't make amends. Doesn't everyone deserve a second chance?"

Ethan swallowed. His sister's words were much like what he'd been meaning to tell Lizbeth. That she was worthy of a second chance. That just because her life had changed didn't mean it no longer had value. "Yes," he said at last.

When Margaret launched herself into his arms, he held her tight. In spite of himself, tears pricked his eyes. "There, now," he murmured, pressing his lips to the top of her head. "Everything will be okay."

But instead of nodding, she shook her head. "It won't. Father is dying."

Though Phillip had prepared him, he still flinched. He lifted his head and stared at his parents across the room. "Is she telling the truth?"

Their father nodded. "I . . . I have some kind of disease in my organs. The doctors say I won't last much longer."

"But, Margaret, we weren't going to tell him yet. Remember?"

"He needed to know, Mother."

Phillip looked at their parents with a pointed expression. "It's time for us all to be honest with each other, I think."

His parents exchanged looks. Then their father nodded. "Phillip is right. We came here to ask you to come home because we need you to run the ranch."

Looking at Phillip, Ethan said, "Are you sure you won't resent me being there?"

"I'll be grateful, Ethan."

"Faye's husband died, son," Mother said. "She is free now. Maybe that might make a difference?"

"Why would I want her back? She married another man while I was a prisoner of war. I didn't even know of it until after the fact."

"We can find you someone," his mother said. "So many women are available now."

"I already have found someone," he said. "I've already found Lizbeth."

"And who is that?"

"She's the girl we thought was a maid," Phillip supplied. "That woman with the dark curly hair."

"She's pretty," Margaret said. "She seems sweet."

"She is."

"Does this mean you're considering my request?" his father asked. "Would you return home?"

"Would you accept Lizbeth on my arm?"

The tension in the room grew taut as his parents exchanged glances again. Then his mother walked to his side and clasped both of her hands in his. "With open arms," she said.

Her expression was completely serious. In that

moment, Ethan realized she was sincere as well. If he could convince Lizbeth to marry him, he could move them to the ranch and she would be secure. Settled.

Squeezing his mother's hands lightly, he said, "I'll come home soon. I need to take care of a few things first, but I'll come back. It's time."

When she pressed her lips to his knuckles, he could almost feel a collective sigh of relief fill the room.

Funny, but he might have felt a bit of relief too.

"Here you go, Devin. Are you ready for some nourishing soup?" Julianne asked as she carried a bowl to his side.

Devin yawned as he struggled to sit up. After everyone else left his room, he'd been so exhausted, he'd told Julianne he wanted to rest his eyes for a bit. To his dismay, he'd slept almost two hours.

During that time, Julianne had straightened the room, eaten some of the food she and Lizbeth had brought in, and then eventually had gone to get fresh water and some soup for him. She'd left him a short note, describing her errand.

He'd found it the moment he woke up. Then, while he was waiting for her return, he'd used the time to analyze his degree of pain . . . and make plans for retaliation. After so many years of war, he didn't take putting the law into his own hands lightly. But Bushnell had been more than a thorn in his side. He was a threat to all of them. He'd tried to kill him. He'd also treated Julianne disgracefully and, it turned out, violated Lizbeth. Surely there wasn't another man in his life who deserved retribution more.

However, focusing on such dark thoughts had drained him. He'd felt desolate and bitter. After taking a few sips of the broth, he set the bowl on the table by the bed.

Julianne's appearance was truly a ray of light. "I'm ready for your company," he said lightly.

She paused, not even hiding her surprise. Then she smiled. "I'm glad."

Oh, that smile. Just like that, life seemed better. Struck by a new sense of optimism, he inhaled deeply. She had such an effect on him.

Would he ever be able to look at Julianne without being completely struck by her beauty? It wasn't likely. Though he'd learned long ago that one's outward appearance didn't make or break a person, few people were blessed with a beauty like hers.

However, he had decided that was a good thing. He liked the idea of being a little tongue-tied around the woman he had chosen to love.

Yes, love. He'd come to terms with the depth of his feelings for her sometime around the moment he was bleeding and struggling up the front steps of the Menger Hotel. He'd had a momentary epiphany about the connection between bleeding to death and the pain in his heart. He'd decided if he was going to bleed out, he might as well die honestly. And that involved telling himself that he had loved his family. He'd loved his country. The men he'd fought beside and suffered next to in prison barracks.

And a beautiful woman who had suffered in her own way, but was still walking and breathing and looking her detractors in the eye.

Julianne picked up the bowl and carried it across the room. Then, with a rustle of taffeta, she returned to his side. "I'm so glad you slept. How are you feeling?"

There was no way he was going to share with her the ugly thoughts he'd been entertaining about Bushnell's fate. "Oh, you know," he murmured. "I feel like I've been shot."

She didn't smile at his quip. Instead, she leaned closer, bringing with her the faint scent of roses he now recognized was as much a part of her person as the striking auburn hair that framed her face.

"When did the doctor say he was going to return?" she asked.

"He didn't. Hopefully he won't be back."

"You dislike doctors that much?"

"I dislike being poked and prodded that much."

As he'd hoped, she perched next to him on the bed. Examining his bandage, she murmured,

"I never took you to be squeamish, Devin."

"I'm not. I just don't necessarily trust saw-bones. I saw too many drunken ones on the battlefield." Belatedly realizing the images in his mind weren't fit for feminine ears, he shifted restlessly. "Don't mind me. Everything seems to irritate me today."

"I'll watch myself, then."

"Everything except you." When her eyes warmed, he said, "I just don't like lying here like an infant." He didn't like being weak, and he really didn't like being weak in front of her. He was sure she was one of the strongest women he'd ever met.

After smiling softly at him again, she turned her attention back to his wound. Her fingers were light as she loosened the gauze strips and inspected his bare skin. "Everything seems to be doing all right."

He noticed she didn't look squeamish. "Do you have experience tending wounds, Julianne?"

She leaned back. "Some."

The very fact that she looked so uncomfortable talking about her skill made him curious. "How?"

"Like many women, I volunteered in the local hospital during the war."

"I didn't know." He really didn't know much about her, he realized. Suddenly, he wished she would tell him everything about herself. He wanted to know it all—her favorite foods, her favorite colors, how she'd gotten her beagle. What she dreamed about. He wanted to know it all.

She smiled slightly, though the warmth didn't reach her eyes. "Did you think I only waited for Daniel to visit me?"

"Of course not." Although his thoughts had been perilously close to that conclusion. "I guess hearing about your work at the hospital took me off guard because you look so delicate." He was not lying.

"If I ever was delicate, I learned to overcome it rather quickly." She walked across the room, gathered fresh gauze and scissors, then returned to his side. "At first Mrs. Mills acted as if my reputation was going to infect the injured men like a leper's disease might. But after some time passed, any help was welcome."

"I would have liked to see you tending to the men. I bet they thought you were an angel coming to them."

"Aren't you full of poetic words this afternoon?" She shrugged. "I don't know what they thought."

"Really? Most soldiers weren't shy about flirting with women." In fact, he would have been hard-pressed to imagine her not being inundated with all sorts of heartfelt sentiments of love and devotion.

She tensed as she seemed to take a moment to

get her bearings. "I have neglected to tell you where I was," she said in a halting way. "You see, Captain, I tended to the men who were most grievously injured. Most of them died," she added, her voice thick with emotion.

He knew about those wards, of course. Doctors separated the worst of their patients so as not to hurt the morale of the healing. On paper it made sense, but in practice Devin had always thought it bordered on cruelty for the men in those rooms.

He'd visited his men in those places more than once. He could still recall the dark feeling of doom and the smell of death lingering in the air. Never would he have imagined anyone putting a delicately raised woman in such a place.

"You were assigned there?" He didn't even try to temper the indignation in his voice.

"Mrs. Mills knew those men needed kindness too."

"Of course they did. But that was no place for a sheltered woman. I'm sorry, Julianne. I hate that you experienced that."

"I'm not. It was worthy work."

"Of course it was." He was making a mess of things. "How about this? I'm proud of you. Will that do?"

Her eyes lit up. "Yes, Devin, I think that will do just fine."

30

It was almost dark by the time Lizbeth returned to the Menger Hotel. She'd considered staying away until morning, just so she wouldn't have to speak to either Dallas or Aileen again. Or see Ethan's face, now that he'd had more time to think about her ruin. Or the strain in Julianne's eyes. She didn't have the strength to fight another verbal battle, especially when she had no idea what she could say.

But while she did, indeed, have legitimate reasons to give the hotel a wide berth, she hadn't been able to do that. Not when Captain Monroe still needed help, knowing Julianne must be very tired by now.

And chances were good Major Kelly wasn't going to be able to do much for either of them for a while. He had his family here, and they looked both formidable and demanding. Lizbeth imagined they were going to require every bit of his time. She had decided to offer to sit with the captain so Julianne could get some rest. Spending the evening feeling useful would be the best thing for her state of mind.

To her surprise, the lobby of the hotel was bustling, a rare sight so late in the day. Several couples who looked well-to-do were sipping tea in the lounge areas while a great number of soldiers was standing near the entrance of the bar, their blue uniforms a stark reminder of who was in charge.

Lizbeth turned from them before one could catch her eye. She knew her habit of avoiding Yankee soldiers as much as possible was rather futile, but it couldn't be helped. Her brain and body would likely always tense up around any man in that blue wool uniform.

Her cousin was standing near the entrance, looking as if she would love nothing more than to exit the premises as soon as she possibly could. When she spied Lizbeth, she gestured for her to come closer.

"What's going on?" Lizbeth asked.

"It seems Major Kelly's parents have a great many friends in the area. When their appearance became public knowledge, scores of people descended on us. We are now filled to the seams. Every guest room has been taken."

"Dallas must be pleased."

Aileen shrugged. "I don't know if he is or not. By and large they are demanding in the extreme."

"It's a well-run hotel, Aileen. You and Dallas do a good job of managing it."

She looked just about to say more when Dallas approached. As usual, he was dressed in a three-piece suit. Unusually, however, he was sweating. She could see it on his brow.

Though she didn't owe him anything, she smiled. "Good evening, Dallas."

"Lizbeth. Hello."

"I hear you are filled to capacity."

His cursory nod stilled. Then he stared at her as though she were his new lifeline. "Are you here to work?" he asked.

"I am not."

"Any way I could persuade you? Since both you and Cassie left, we are extremely short-handed."

Ignoring the jab at her, she asked, "What happened with Cassie? Do you know where she went?"

"She left without a word," Aileen said. "I must admit to being surprised. It seemed out of character."

"Do you think something could have happened to her?" Lizbeth asked, feeling her anxiety rise again. "Maybe we should go to the sheriff."

With an impatient move of his hand, Dallas waved off her concern. "Cassie's departure is hardly noteworthy. Maids leave all the time without notice. What matters is that we are now extremely short-handed."

As much as he was heaping on the guilt, she wasn't going to feel a bit of it. "I hope you'll fill the jobs soon, Dallas."

He coughed, whether from embarrassment or irritation, Lizbeth didn't know. When he regained his composure, he said, "We have an important family staying here, you know." Looking around the crowded lobby, he added, "All their important friends too. Good service would cement the Menger's reputation as one of the top establishments in the state."

Lizbeth almost smiled. It was hard to imagine such things still meant so much to some people. "Since you're so busy, I had better let you both return to your duties. I only stopped to say hello to Aileen."

"You mean you came here to gloat. Now that you are connected with the major, I guess you're feeling high and mighty."

"Stop, Dallas," Aileen said, surprising Lizbeth. "As I told you earlier, we need to move forward. All of us do."

Dallas looked angry, but he held his tongue.

Knowing it wasn't the time to ease the tension between them, Lizbeth left for the captain's suite. When she arrived, she knocked on the door.

Almost immediately, Ethan opened it, then stepped into the hall. He closed the door quietly behind him. "I thought you would stay the night back at the Harrison."

"I thought I might be of some use here," she explained. "Since your family is in town, I assumed you would have other obligations to attend to."

"I already met with my family." Looking a little put upon—and a little bit resigned too—he smiled. "I believe they are currently holding court in the dining room. They have a great many friends here in San Antonio. Fortunately, one couple kept them occupied while I took care of some telegrams Devin asked me to send."

"I saw Aileen and Dallas on my way through the lobby. They said your family has created quite a stir."

He chuckled. "That's one way of putting it." Sobering, he continued. "I stopped here at Devin's room to check on him. I was planning to visit you next."

"Now you don't have to." Feeling conspicuous and a little embarrassed that she came when it was becoming obvious Ethan didn't want her to stay, she cleared her throat. "I will be seeing you, then. Julianne must be caring for Captain Monroe."

"She insists. But please allow me to walk you back. I want to speak to you about what happened earlier."

"There's no need."

"There's every need." He held up a hand. Almost reached out to touch her . . . then seemed to reconsider. "Please, stay here a second while I tell Devin and Julianne what I'm doing."

"All right."

"Don't you leave," he warned.

His expression was so hard, she almost smiled. "I promise. I won't go anywhere."

True to his word, Ethan stepped back into the hall mere minutes later.

"How is he?" Lizbeth asked.

"He already seems much better. Julianne has put on a pair of spectacles and is reading to him."

Ethan sounded bemused. "Are you surprised they are doing something so mundane or that she wears glasses?" she asked as they walked through the hotel lobby.

"A little bit of both, I guess," he replied as he led her outside. "I'm ashamed to say I made far too many hasty decisions where she is concerned. At first I was sure she was nothing more than a pretty face."

Lizbeth might have felt jealous if the same thing hadn't crossed her mind. "They seem well suited. Perhaps they will have a long and happy future together. After all, people do say opposites attract."

"I don't know if we are opposites, but I hope you and I might find a future together one day as well," he said as they continued to walk down the street.

"Oh?" She couldn't be sure he was still talking about marriage.

"Yes. You see, it's a long story, but I think I finally mended things with my family." He took a breath. "Actually, I told them I will eventually return home for good."

"That's wonderful." She meant that sincerely. "Family should stick together." She was happy for him, but feared his new bond might ultimately force him to move on to a woman who was more of his social equal.

"They would like me to take over the running of the ranch and our holdings."

"Ah." He would be leaving soon. No doubt when they were apart he would wonder why he'd ever felt so attached to a maid. It was a struggle to keep her composure.

He looked down at her. "You don't seem to be sharing my enthusiasm."

"No, I am happy for you."

"Lizbeth, when I return, I want you by my side. I told my brother and parents that."

Shocked, she almost stumbled. "Ethan, I don't know—"

"Shh. You don't need to say anything yet. Just know that I haven't given up on us. I am looking forward to my future, Lizbeth. Just as importantly, I want you to want to be there with me."

It was on the tip of her tongue to say she wanted to be by his side as well. But those painful years during the war and experiencing so much loss made her wary.

"Say you'll think about it," he said.

"I'll think about it." Then, because she didn't want him to imagine she wasn't touched by his words, she curved her hand around his elbow and smiled up at him. No matter what, she wanted him to know she was proud to be walking by his side.

After a moment, the muscles in his arm relaxed and he smiled too.

It was so lovely, a new warmth filled her insides. Right at this moment, they were together. Her hand was on his arm. That was enough for now.

31

Johnson's Island, Ohio
Confederate States of America
Officers' POW Camp

They'd become a greeting party of sorts. Whenever one of them heard word of additional soldiers arriving, five of them would stand at the entrance of their barracks and welcome the newly imprisoned.

As the dozen or so men walked toward them, their expressions as ravaged as their bodies, Devin figured he'd done nothing harder in his life. He had nothing to offer them except acceptance. Sometimes that was received gratefully.

Other times? The men lashed out at them in anger. Resentful of their circumstances. Scared they wouldn't survive. Worse, that they would while their comrades who hadn't been picked up would die while fighting. It was a difficult transition to make, leaving the ranks of the brave for the company of the survivors. Devin knew. He'd experienced every range of emotion during his long months of incarceration.

Officer Crosby stopped at the entrance and looked at Devin with a practiced eye. "You ready for them, Monroe?"

Devin nodded. He wouldn't go so far as to say Crosby and he were close, but they had definitely come to an agreement over the last two months of Devin's captivity. They treated each other with respect, sometimes even bordering toward the friendly.

Devin thought the man was a lot like him. Unlike some of the other guards, Crosby had fought with valor during much of the war. He seemed to find the lack of exercise as difficult to bear as the whole feeling of helplessness that pervaded their surroundings.

Sometimes, too, Devin would catch Crosby eyeing the other guards with something close to impatience and disdain. And no small wonder. Devin realized some of these men wouldn't have lasted an hour on the battlefield. They were as unruly as they were lazy.

Crosby pulled out a heavy brass key ring and unlocked the doorway. "Listen up, you Johnny Rebs. You are under our jurisdiction now. Best mind yourselves and watch your backs. Save yourself some pain and worry and listen to Monroe here. He'll make sure you get on all right."

All at once, the dozen new prisoners turned to Devin and stared. Their expressions ranged from cautious hope to pure disdain.

Devin was used to that too. Some of the incoming prisoners were sure any man who survived imprisonment must be a traitor. Some-times, after the guards left, the new prisoners would take out their anger and pent-up fears on him. He'd learned the hard way never to face a new band of men alone.

When Crosby left, locking the gate securely behind him, Devin spoke. "I'm not going to tell you welcome, because we all know this is no place where any of us would choose to be. Instead, I'll just introduce myself. I'm Devin Monroe, Captain, C.S.A. Behind me is Major Ethan Kelly, Lieutenant Robert Truax, Lieutenant Phillip Markham, and Sergeant Thomas Baker."

A man wearing captain's bars eyed him suspiciously. "How come you're greeting us? You work for the Yanks or something?"

Before Devin could answer, Markham stepped forward. "We have the dubious honor of being some of the longest residents of this place. We got sick and tired of watching each man new to our ranks enter here looking like they were weeks away from dying."

The captain eyed Phillip, then nodded. "Name is Underman. Randolph. I'm out of Kentucky."

Markham nodded. "Captain Underman, I'll do my best to help you and your comrades survive here."

"Is it possible?" another man asked, this one a colonel. His expression was slightly incredulous. "We heard no one survives here long."

"We do our best to beat the odds," Devin said. "Now, come along and we'll make sure you have cots to sleep on."

"Do you observe rank here?"

Devin barely refrained from rolling his eyes. In almost every group of new prisoners, someone always made sure Devin knew he didn't intend to follow the directives or advice of a lowly captain. "We try to honor each man's worth, Colonel."

"What does that mean?"

"It means we've learned that the men's ranks usually stem from honor and bravery on the battlefield, not while sitting in a prisoner of war camp."

"Rank and file means everything, Captain."

"Not here, it doesn't," Ethan Kelly blurted.

The colonel swung around to face him. "I know you. You were at West Point."

"I was. Markham was as well. I don't recall you being there, however."

His expression tightened. "I did not have that benefit."

"Seems like you've still done all right for yourself."

The colonel lifted his chin. "One learns quickly to prevail no matter what happens. All that matters in life is who comes out on top."

Phillip Markham, the man who'd always been their voice of honor, eyed him coldly. "No, sir. All that matters is who survives."

"That's the same thing."

Phillip shook his head slowly. "I beg your pardon, but I must disagree. That's not the same at all. It's not even close."

32

The following evening Devin was feeling even more like himself again, and with Julianne at last getting some sleep in her own room, he and Ethan were spending a few late-night hours in the Menger bar. Though it was connected to the hotel, it was everything the lofty Menger was not. With its wide plank floors, polished copper bar, scuffed tables and chairs, and dim lighting, it was a man's retreat. Devin imagined scores of men over the years had found solace here, especially the men who had been to war.

Returning to civilized society was a challenge. Sometimes men needed to be around masculine comforts and away from elegant wallpaper, etched drawings, genteel voices, and feminine sensibilities. Devin had found it to be something of an oasis in the midst of so much fussiness. He was now used to soldiers' plain speaking. And many men like him were in San Antonio. Former officers, former Confederate soldiers— they were a rough-and-tumble lot. After spending years in only the company of men, they were uneasy at spending too long a time in feminine company.

Oh, some men were the exception. Devin figured Ethan was one. He was a true gentleman, and no matter how hard he protested that he didn't fit the title, it remained true.

But that didn't mean he didn't enjoy holding court with Devin in one of the bar's back tables. Smoking cheroots, sipping whiskey, and trading stories with other men who had survived.

Devin had just accepted a second round of drinks from the barkeep, paid for by a cavalry officer from Louisiana, when Mrs. Howard opened the bar's ornate door.

Right away, the atmosphere in the room changed. It was obvious her presence wasn't welcome.

Women weren't wanted here, that was true. But it was more than that. Ethan had told him there was something condescending about her, and Devin could tell many of the men in the room didn't care for that. As for Devin, he only needed one reason to stay as far away from her as possible: she'd sided with Bushnell instead of Lizbeth.

Leaning back, he watched Mrs. Howard make her way through the maze of tables. She ignored the men who stood up when she approached or nodded in her direction. Beside him, Ethan fidgeted.

"Looks like we've got company," he muttered.

Devin didn't reply, only picked up his cheroot and inhaled. When she stopped in front of their table, obviously ill at ease, he barely got to his feet. Then, after exhaling his smoke in a way that would make his mother cuff his ears, he raised his eyebrows. "Mrs. Howard. To what do we owe this honor?"

Ethan, who had stood up politely, tossed him a look as he gestured to the chair that had just been vacated by the Louisianan. "Evening, Mrs. Howard. Care to join us?"

She looked taken aback. "Uh, no, thank you, Major Kelly." After clearing her throat, she spoke again. "I am sorry to disturb y'all, but you have visitors."

She hadn't tried to contain the sarcasm in her voice, and Devin didn't attempt to hide his lack of respect for her. "Who is it?"

"A pair of, uh, men."

She had purposely not said gentlemen. Well, so be it. At the moment, he wasn't feeling like much of a gentleman either. "Well, where are they?"

"I wasn't sure where you were. Or if you wanted to see them . . ."

"Mrs. Howard, if you could show me where you left them cooling their heels, I'd be obliged," Ethan interjected as he stood up once again and circled the table.

Looking relieved to no longer be dealing with Devin, she smiled hesitantly at Ethan. "Yes, of course, Major. If you will follow me. I asked them to wait in the lobby."

After giving Devin a pointed stare that said to

settle down, Ethan followed Mrs. Howard back through the smoky bar and out the door.

When the door firmly closed behind him, two men at the bar clinked glasses. That gesture returned the festive air back to the room.

And with it, the tension Devin hadn't even been aware he'd been carrying dissipated. He smoked his cheroot and sipped his whiskey while he waited. One or two men paused near his table, obviously eager for him to extend an invitation for them to join him.

He didn't.

After exchanging the minimum of small talk, he used the time to think about Julianne. She'd looked very fetching that afternoon when, over her objection about his readiness, he'd taken her for a short stroll on the street in front of the Menger.

She'd worn a dark-gray dress that should have looked drab on her. Instead, it only served to accentuate her auburn hair and blue eyes. She had held his arm and smiled at him as though he were the only person in the state. Under her spell, he'd told her a story or two about growing up with his brothers and how he'd gotten into far too much mischief. Despite her concern for his health, she'd laughed and teased him, coaxing him to chuckle too.

Their interaction didn't go unnoticed. Men eyed him enviously. She didn't seem to notice. He had, though. He hadn't needed their approval, but he'd understood their envy. He'd been amazed he had the honor of her company.

Before they returned to the hotel, Julianne mentioned she needed to go home, at the same time trying to extract from him a promise to fully heal before coming to Boerne to see her. He convinced her to let him pay for her room at the Menger a few nights more. He couldn't bear the thought of her returning to her house before he had Bushnell taken care of. He'd managed to scare her enough to stay.

He wasn't especially proud of that, but he was glad it had served its purpose. He wasn't going to play the fool again. No matter what, he would make sure she was safe.

And as soon as he did that, he was going to continue to court her. He still wanted to marry her. More than once in the last two days, he'd offered to marry her immediately. Of course she'd refused, but she looked at him in a way that told him a part of her had wanted to say yes. It had made him gratified.

When the saloon door flew open again, Devin put down his glass. Tension snaked up his spine as he watched closely for the newcomers.

When he saw who it was, he grinned. Ethan had entered with Robert Truax and Thomas Baker.

Tossing his cheroot in the brass spittoon nearby, he stood and strode over to meet them. "You are a sight for sore eyes, gentlemen," he exclaimed as he held out his hand.

Robert shook his hand first. "I would hug you, but I hear you're filled with holes," he joked.

"Only two—the bullet went in my shoulder and then out. However, they are sizable."

Baker grinned. "I'm sure they are impressive wounds, Cap. I'm just glad that bullet didn't kill you." And with that, he wrapped his arms around Devin and lightly hugged him.

Devin might have been embarrassed by the affection they were showing if these men weren't his closest friends in the world. In addition, he knew he owed them more than he could ever repay. These men had put their lives on the line for him multiple times and had suffered next to him on Johnson's Island. Never would he shy away from their friendship. "It's good to see you both. A nice surprise too. I didn't expect to see y'all for at least another day."

"I told them the same thing," Ethan said.

"You know the story. When one of us calls, the others come running," Thomas said. "No exceptions."

"I rode out yesterday after receiving your telegram, Ethan," Robert said. "And somehow Thomas and I arrived at the same time."

"Come on, let's sit down before somebody decides to take our spot," Ethan said as he beckoned them back to their table. Devin appreciated that. For the conversation to come, they'd need that corner out of hearing of other patrons.

The men didn't need any further encouragement. After calling an order for two additional whiskeys, they settled themselves, each covertly taking stock of the others.

"No offense, Cap, but you look like death warmed over," Baker said.

"I look better than that," Devin protested.

"Not by much. Shouldn't you still be in bed recuperating?"

"I should not. I got a bullet hole, not an amputation."

"Doc say you're gonna be all right?" Truax asked.

"He did. So stop staring at me like I'm gonna pass out."

Ethan laughed. "The problem is neither of us looks as fit and hardy as these two. Once we get hitched and set up a home, I'm sure we'll look like we're in glowing good health too."

Thomas smiled. "The major doesn't lie. Laurel changed my life."

Robert smiled. "Indeed. It's amazing what marriage and a home can do to you."

"And how is the lovely Miranda?" Devin asked. They all knew of Miranda because she was once their good friend Phillip Markham's wife. Phillip had died on Johnson's Island, and Miranda had mourned extensively. When they'd heard men and women were ruining Phillip's reputation and making Miranda's life unbearable, Robert traveled to Galveston to try to help her. While doing so, the two of them had fallen in love and soon after they married.

Robert smiled. "With child."

That news made every jest and ribald comment evaporate from his head. "Many felicitations," Devin said sincerely. "I hope she is feeling all right."

"Mrs. Truax is having to adjust to being a pampered lady of leisure. Between me and the rest of the staff, she's only allowed to take her daily walks and take care of herself."

Ethan chuckled. "How is she handling that?"

"To my surprise, she simply bats her eyelashes, smiles at me, and says, 'Yes, Robert.' Then she does what she wants. Within reason, of course."

Devin grinned. "Sounds like the South needed her in the army. She could have taught us all a thing or two about dealing with superior officers."

"She could at that," Robert said softly. When their drinks arrived, he took a sip of his whiskey, then looked at both him and Ethan. "Speaking of officers . . . What is going on with Bushnell?"

"He's the one who shot me," Devin said.

Thomas Baker gaped. "I knew he was an idiot

and a blowhard, but this doesn't even make sense."

"It caught me off guard too, especially seeing as he shot me in the back."

"And he's still alive?" Truax murmured.

"If he was here in San Antonio, he wouldn't be. But he isn't," Ethan said. "That's why we called for your help. We need to go after him and see that justice is served."

"I'll be glad to hand out justice," Baker said with a satisfied look. "No one is going to get away with shooting you in the back, Captain."

"This isn't just for me, Baker," Devin said. "It's for a Miss Van Fleet and Miss Barclay too."

Robert looked at them both. "What does Bushnell have to do with them?"

"Unfortunately, far too much," Ethan said. Succinctly, he told them about Lizbeth—the fact that Bushnell had both marked and violated her, and then most recently had nearly forced his way with her in a hotel room.

Then Devin shared how he met Julianne, how she had come to his aid when he was shot, and that she'd been Bushnell's mistress during the war. He also explained why she'd allowed such a man into her life.

Both Thomas and Robert gaped.

"I don't know what to respond to first," Baker said. "This Lizbeth, is she all right now?"

"She is. I've got her resting and relaxing at a

small inn nearby. She was fired for entering my room uninvited, despite her reasons."

Robert's eyebrows rose. "What kind of an establishment is this? I would string up any blackguard who tried to take advantage of Miranda or any of the staff at our inn."

"The couple who runs the place are relatives of Lizbeth's," Ethan said tightly.

"And that's supposed to help me understand?"

"Suffice to say she's under my care now."

"And Julianne? Where is she?"

"She is staying here at the hotel." Devin hesitated, then decided he might as well come clean about everything. "She's come to mean a lot to me. I . . . well, I intend to marry her one day."

Silence met his pronouncement. As each of the men digested his news, Devin felt his pulse slow and his body tighten. He knew what was going on—his body was preparing to fight. He had felt much the same way before every battle during the war.

And that made him realize he was making the right decision. He had fallen in love with Julianne Van Fleet and wanted her to be his wife. He didn't care what her past was. He didn't care what she'd had to do to survive. All he cared about was that she *had* survived.

Even if these men who meant so much to him

didn't agree, he knew he wasn't going to change his mind about Julianne.

But then, to his surprise, Ethan raised his glass. "Here's to the lovely Julianne, men. May she be loyal, strong, and true."

Baker and Truax raised their glasses too. "Yes, here's to love and marriage and finding women to put up with us," Robert Truax added, finishing off the toast. "We aren't easy to live with . . ."

"But I reckon one day we'll be worth the trouble," Thomas said with a wink.

Devin raised his glass as well. "And if we aren't, may they never tell us to our faces," he said with a laugh.

"To Julianne!" they called out as they clinked their glasses together.

Few moments had ever felt so right.

33

They had been discussing Devin's departure for a solid hour. Julianne knew Devin wasn't pleased with the way she was reacting, but she couldn't help herself. As far as she was concerned, if Daniel Bushnell was out of sight, he should be out of mind as well. "I don't understand why you are doing this," she said at last. "I don't understand what purpose going after Daniel serves."

Devin abruptly stopped his pacing and stared at her incredulously. "Well, first, there is the matter of honor," he said slowly, as if he were speaking to a small child. "He tried to kill me, Julianne."

"But he did not succeed."

His eyebrows rose, he snapped his mouth shut, and then, with a mutter under his breath, he began pacing the length of his hotel room. *Pacing,* just as if he didn't have two stitched-up bullet holes in his shoulder.

"Devin, maybe you should sit down for a spell?"

"I am fine."

"Not exactly. Your wound is still healing."

He stopped again. Stared at her and smiled somewhat grimly. "Exactly. I am wounded."

Maybe they were finally getting somewhere? "That's why—"

"Julianne, I'm not the type of man to be shot in the back and turn the other cheek."

She knew he was strong. She knew he was a leader. She knew he'd probably killed or maimed more men during the war than he could count. But that was during war, when he was fighting for a cause. Now was different. "You should speak to the sheriff," she said reasonably. "Then he would take care of Daniel for you."

"He's not going to do anything."

"Of course he will. You are well respected—"

"Don't you see? That's one of the problems. It shouldn't matter who I am or how much influence I have. And that is what it will come down to. Even if the sheriff does bring Bushnell in, he's not going to bring him to trial."

"You don't know that."

"I know how things work, Julianne. And you do too." His lips pursed. "He's a complete reprobate. He took advantage of you. But he has money, and money is influence."

Though it made her skin crawl, she was strong enough to take responsibility for her actions. "I knew what he wanted, Devin. And, while, um, I can't say my experiences with him were pleasant, I'm not going to lie and tell you he raped me. He did not."

But instead of the lines in his expression

easing, he looked even more disturbed. "You are not the only woman he took advantage of, Julianne."

"I realize that," she replied, knowing they were both speaking of Lizbeth. "But that was years ago and during the war."

"He should still pay."

He opened a drawer and pulled out his pistol. "Some deeds are too terrible to excuse, no matter what the situation. He violated Lizbeth and he used you unforgivably." When she started to protest again, he interrupted her. "I'm not the only one who feels this way, Julianne. The other men agree with me."

Watching him carefully inspect his Colt, Julianne suddenly realized what he meant. "I told Ethan I was Bushnell's mistress myself, and it's right that he knows. But you told your other friends, didn't you?"

"I had no choice. They needed to know."

He had no choice? Realizing Devin still wasn't meeting her eyes, she swallowed hard.

"And did you tell Lizbeth Barclay too?"

"Of course not."

"Because it would upset her too much?"

"Because I may not be a gentleman, but I know better than to speak of such things to young women."

Because Lizbeth would be scandalized that Julianne had done such a thing, and would hate her because of who that man was. Julianne wouldn't blame her either.

Devin walked to face her. Placing both hands on her arms, he held her secure in front of him. "Julianne, I care about you. I don't care about your past, and I don't care who knows. You are still the loveliest, strongest woman I've ever met in my life. Never doubt that."

He sighed. "Now, what I brought you here to tell you is that Robert visited a number of the less-savory gambling establishments in San Antonio late last night, finding men there you would never want to know. Near dawn he discovered that Daniel's kidnapped one of the maids from the hotel. An hour ago, he also learned where he's no doubt taken her."

Remembering the conversation with Meg in the kitchen, Julianne gasped. "Is it Lizbeth's friend Cassie?"

He nodded slowly. "Ethan is about to tell her."

And just like that, all her arguments died inside her. "That poor girl."

"Robert believes Bushnell is holding Cassie in a house just to the east of here. He's no doubt terrorizing her. We have no choice. He must be stopped."

Devin was right. Daniel did need to be stopped.

Eying him carefully, Julianne realized this was the man she'd fallen in love with. Devin Monroe didn't sit idly by while women were abused.

He didn't persuade others to put themselves in danger. He certainly didn't hope for problems to be taken care of by someone else.

And now that they knew it wasn't just a faceless woman in jeopardy, but one of Lizbeth's friends, well, there was no choice, was there? "I understand," she said at last.

Looking as if she'd taken a load off his shoulders, he released a ragged breath. "Thank you. Now, will you still be here when I return?"

"I'll be here."

What other choice did she have?

Ethan knew stranger things had happened, but mending the rift with his family had been unexpected and had caught him off guard.

If he weren't a believer, what had happened here at the hotel would have made a believer out of him. No other reason could explain the way his family had reached out to him, the way he'd been able to forgive them, or the way they'd all come to an understanding. While their relationships might not ever be the same, Ethan realized they didn't need to be. They simply needed to exist.

Wasn't that how he felt when he was liberated from Johnson's Island? All the men released had been thin, exhausted by war and prison conditions. They were scarred and weaker than they'd ever been. But in place of muscle and good health had come an awakening of their spirit and a new appreciation for small blessings and true friends. In his more introspective moments, Ethan realized he wouldn't be the man he was without surviving that imprisonment.

After gathering his gun, Bowie knife, and ammunition, he prayed. Prayed that the Lord would one day understand why he was joining his three blood brothers to ensure justice had been served to Daniel Bushnell.

Just as he was rising, he heard a faint knock at his door.

It was Lizbeth.

"I was just on my way to find you," he said.

"I hope that means you have a few minutes to talk."

"I do have a few minutes, but only that. Something has happened. Come in." As she entered the room, he took a moment to admire her. Lizbeth was wearing a light-blue dress. It was made of a fine wool and was immensely flattering. Her hair was arranged in a mass of curls, framing her face. He didn't know if he'd ever been more struck by her beauty than he was at that moment.

If he hadn't, he was certainly a fool. Her goodness shined through her, and that was what had drawn him to her. Only now he saw things so clearly. It wasn't that she needed him and he needed to do something good without expecting anything in return. It wasn't that she was merely pretty. No, it was the simple knowledge that she was better than him. Being around her could make him better. And, he suspected, he could do the same for her.

It was only a shame that he was coming to this realization just when he was about to leave her.

She noticed his weapons on the bed. "You look like you're preparing for a duel."

He turned to face her.

"Lizbeth, we've known from the beginning we would need to deal with Bushnell. Devin and I called in two of our comrades from the war, Robert Truax and Thomas Baker, to help us. They arrived last evening, and then Robert discovered where Bushnell is no doubt hiding." He drew in a breath. "He has Cassie."

Immediately tears formed in her eyes. "I . . . I was afraid of this. From the moment Meg told me Cassie had gone so suddenly, something inside of me knew he had her. He must have forced her to take her belongings, to make everyone think she'd left on her own. How can anyone be so evil, Ethan?"

He reached for her hand and clasped it in between both of his. Tried to steady her and pass on his strength, though what he really wanted to do was hold her close and promise that everything was going to be all right. "We're going to find them."

Her hand trembled. "He could have other men

with him," she warned when she looked back into his eyes. "You could get hurt."

"I know," he said softly.

She looked even more worried. "I don't want anything to happen to you."

"I don't want anything to happen to me either." Trying to smile, he said, "We have so much to look forward to, Lizbeth. But I have to do this. How can I not?"

"You're right. Cassie needs you. She needs someone to help her."

Ethan felt in his heart everything that she wasn't saying. That she'd needed someone, but no one had been there. That reminder made his insides ache. He realized then that he needed to bring up what had happened to her during the war.

Steeling himself for her reaction, he said, "I also want to avenge what he did to you." Though he hated to see the pain he was causing her, he continued. "Bushnell hurt you unbearably. He scarred you. In more ways than one."

As he'd learned she often did when she was nervous, Lizbeth pressed her other hand against the jagged scar. "He did. But I'm all right now."

"Lizbeth, he needs to pay for what he did to you. He used his uniform to his advantage. There . . . there are no words to describe how despicable his actions were."

"Ethan, I want you to go after him. I want you to rescue Cassie. But . . . well, let's not dwell on what happened to me anymore. It's over and what was done was done. Nothing is going to ever change it."

It wouldn't. But bringing the man to justice would make him feel better. "Lizbeth, I have something to confess to you. I've been trying to find a way to tell you . . ."

"What is it?"

"I . . . well, first, as I told you, I want a future together, and my family wants me to move back and run the ranch. I meant what I said. I'd like to do that with you by my side."

She stared at him, wide-eyed. "You said they would accept me. Isn't that still true?"

"Absolutely. They'll accept you because they know you have my heart."

She smiled tremulously. "Why the long face, then?"

"Because there's something else I must tell you, but I don't know how to say it."

"I think you should just tell me then."

Feeling as if he were standing up to be court-martialed, he forced himself to say the next few words. "Lizbeth, you need to know . . . Well, I led a raiding party to your house."

"What?" she whispered.

"Soon after Bushnell's. I know it was soon after his visit because the scar on your face was still fresh." Though she was staring at him as if she'd seen a ghost, he drew himself up, straight and tall. "I was the officer in charge, Lizbeth. I gave the order to search your property."

"The man who stood in the shadows . . . That was you?"

He nodded. "I had orders to get whatever I could. We were freezing. Starving. Men were depending on me."

Her hands fisted. "But I was cold too," she said in a small voice. "I was starving too. You took the last of everything I had."

"I've dreamed about it since. It's haunted me."

"When did you realize I was the same woman?"

He wished he could lie. But he couldn't. He owed her every bit of the ugly truth. "The moment I saw your scar."

Pure pain filled her eyes. "Why didn't you tell me this days ago?"

"I didn't want you to hate me. I didn't have the words to try to excuse myself. I'm afraid I still don't."

"That is why you are going, isn't it? Not just because that man ruined me, but because you feel like you did too."

"To some degree, yes."

"Did you tell the other men? Is that why they are going?"

"They would have come because of Devin's injury. But I did tell them about what Bushnell did to you. They feel you need to be avenged too."

"Really? They are willing to risk their lives for something that happened to me long ago?"

"It is because of you. And Devin. And to help the woman in Bushnell's clutches now." He paused, then continued, knowing that Lizbeth needed to know everything if she was ever going to trust him enough to one day be his wife. "There's one more thing you need to know, Lizbeth."

Her eyes widened. "What else could there be?"

"Julianne was Bushnell's mistress during the war. She was starving and so was her grandmother. He used her need to his advantage."

"Julianne was his lover?"

"To an extent, yes."

"And you've known about this as well?"

Her eyes were shimmering with unshed tears. It was almost too hard to bear. "I learned a few days ago."

She said nothing for a long moment. Then, folding her arms across her chest, she spoke. "I suppose I should thank you. All this time I have been comparing myself to you and have come up lacking. But now I realize you are just as flawed as I am."

Each word stung. Hurt. But she was hurting, he reasoned. In time, she would come around. "Lizbeth, when I return, I promise we can discuss this further."

"I don't think that will be necessary, Major Kelly."

"What does that mean?"

"It means I am done being lied to and coddled for my own good. I need to start new."

"I want to start new with you. Lizbeth, I have fallen in love with you."

She shook her head. "No, love isn't like this."

His relationship with Faye came to mind. He'd thought she'd been his perfect match, but now he knew the truth.

"I've never been in love before, not like this. But I think you are wrong. I think it is exactly like this. It's messy and hurtful. Awkward and confusing. It's not neat and perfect. But don't you see? All these flaws and cuts are going to mend and make us stronger."

"Like mine?"

"Like yours."

Lifting her hand, she traced her scar with one fingertip. "Ethan, don't you see? This hasn't made me stronger."

He approached her. He yearned to reach for her. To hold her close and tell her everything was going to be fine if she would just trust him again. "That isn't what I meant. You know it."

"Isn't it?" She wiped a tear from her eye. "You say you love me, but you are about to commit murder. You say you want to protect me, but you've kept secrets to protect yourself. You say you respect me, but you've shared my shame with men who are strangers to me. You say you want to be my friend, but you introduced me to a woman who willingly entered into a relationship with the man who haunts my dreams. You don't know how to love. Or if you do, your concept of it is so stretched and scarred . . . well, it's only a faint parody of love."

He was having a difficult time speaking. "Lizbeth, please try to understand."

"No, you try to understand. You try to see things from my viewpoint. Then maybe one day you won't look upon your secrets with anything but shame."

Ethan knew he wasn't going to have to wait years for that to happen. He was ashamed at that moment.

It threatened to suffocate him.

"When I return, I'll find you."

Her eyebrow arched. "And if I refuse to see you?"

"Then I'll come the day after. And the day after that."

He strode from his room then, wishing he could yell or scream or break windows or do something. Anything to make the pain more bearable.

But he had a feeling nothing was going to do that. Nothing short of going back in time.

34

The four of them set off just after four o'clock. Late enough in the day for Bushnell to have been lulled into thinking no one was going to search for him while still giving them the ability to easily scan the perimeter and watch one another's backs. They'd all learned it was a good idea to be ready for anything, just in case their best-laid plans went awry.

Whether it was by one of their designs or because they'd unconsciously fallen back into habits they'd adopted during the war, they were riding two by two. A good fifty yards separated the pairs. If one of them was shot, enough space was between the groupings to allow the others a fighting chance.

Ethan was in the lead, Truax by his side. Ethan was there because he knew the area better than any of them. Truax, because he'd been the one who had talked to the old-timer who'd ratted out Bushnell.

Devin took the rear next to Thomas Baker.

As usual, Baker was riding his horse as if he'd been born on it. He looked supremely comfortable on the animal. Of course, anyone would, Devin reckoned. That horse was a fine-looking appaloosa gelding. White with gray-blue spots on its hindquarters.

Devin was riding Midge. She was his favorite mare. She'd miraculously survived the remainder of the war while he'd been in prison. At the war's end, she'd been escorted to his cousin's house. She and her husband had taken special care of the mare, spoiling her with fresh grass and lots of lazy days.

Though he would have missed her, Devin would have left her there if she'd shown a preference for it. But it seemed she, like him, considered them a matched set. The pain in his shoulder was a clear reminder that he'd been a benefactor of her loyalty. She'd delivered him, bleeding, to the Menger just a few days ago.

She wasn't as spry as she used to be, but she was stronger and smarter. He trusted this horse as much as he trusted Ethan, Baker, or Truax. He felt she had just as much heart too. As if she sensed the importance of the day's mission, she was trotting at a good clip. Maybe Midge was like him; she needed to be out in the world every now and then, just to prove to herself that she still had what it took to survive.

"Feels like old times, doesn't it, Cap?" Baker said after they'd ridden a couple of miles. "Even our formation is how it used to be."

Devin nodded. "I was just thinking that myself. Actually, I was just thinking Midge seems a little eager to prove herself this afternoon. I guess she needed to get out of the stable for a while."

Thomas looked at Devin's horse with a fond expression. "She's still got it, don't you, girl?"

Midge perked up her ears, as if she knew Thomas was speaking to her. Devin scowled at Thomas. "I think she's flirting with you."

He grinned. "Nah. She knows I'm a married man now. She just recognized my voice. I cleaned her hooves and brushed her coat more times than I can name."

Devin had forgotten that Thomas had often done such tasks for him. Most of the officers he'd served with had servants with them to take care of their horseflesh. Others had just found a private to do his bidding. For some reason, Devin had always taken care of his belongings himself . . . and then Baker had.

"How come you always took care of Midge?" he asked curiously. "Was it because she was that good of a horse? Did she matter to you that much?"

"You mattered, sir," he said lightly. "That's why I did it."

"Ah." Now, what did one say to that? Even after all this time, Baker's honesty could still get him choked up.

"So . . . Miss Van Fleet must be quite a lady."

Devin looked at Thomas sharply, ready to scold him if he was being disrespectful, if he'd had a change of heart from the night before. But the look in Thomas's eyes said he was being completely sincere. Embarrassed that he had been rushing to her defense for the wrong reasons, he nodded. "She's very fine."

"And you're going to marry her?"

"Yes, I told you men that in the bar when you arrived. I just have to convince her sooner than later."

"Cap, you were on the Red Roan Ranch when I was so besotted with Laurel I could hardly see straight. You know I'm not going to judge."

"We have a different relationship than you and Mrs. Baker. Julianne and I . . . well, we've had a complicated beginning."

"Yeah, I can see how meeting Laurel while I was working on a prison chain gang was real simple and easy in comparison."

Devin grinned again. "Point taken." Last summer Thomas had gotten into some trouble and landed in a small-town jail because he owed some money. Instead of reaching out to the rest of them, he'd planned to serve out his time . . . until Laurel Tracy paid for him to be her indentured servant for the span of one year.

"Is marriage agreeing with you?"

"Very much so. But that isn't to say we don't have our own obstacles to overcome every now and then."

"As you know, Julianne has a history. Though

I've told her I don't blame her for what she did— and I don't—sometimes I find I still care. I'd be lying if I said it didn't bother me at all."

"Ah. Yes. I can see how it would bother you."

"You do?" For some reason, he'd been hoping Thomas would be on Julianne's side.

"Well, sure," he said as he scanned the horizon again, his expression sharp. "I mean, I'm sure you've told her about all the things you did during the war to survive." He lowered his voice. "And the way we handled things on Johnson's Island."

Devin was shocked. "You don't share such things with women. Don't tell me you've told Laurel about the things we did."

"Of course I haven't," he retorted, giving Devin a look equally as shocked. "She'd have nightmares."

"Then why are you bringing them up?"

"Because your Julianne probably wishes you didn't know about what she did to survive."

"That was different." Because his actions didn't involve losing his good reputation, he admitted to himself in a burst of shame. "Anyway, uh, I upset her for another reason. I mean, it's related, but different." Lord, but he was no good as sharing secrets!

"What did you do?"

"She knows I told y'all she was Bushnell's mistress. She's embarrassed, of course."

"And feels you betrayed her."

"Because I did." Maybe it was being on Midge and riding next to Baker, or maybe it was because Devin knew it was time to admit some things to another person. Whatever the reason, he felt compelled to continue to spill his innermost thoughts. "She seemed to let it go before I left her just now, but I don't know if she'll ever completely trust me after this."

"I guess we'll see," Thomas replied, his voice suddenly quiet and still.

Wrestled from his musings, Devin looked up in surprise. There, about a half mile up the road, was the dilapidated two-story hacienda they'd needed to find. Finally, they could do something to right so many wrongs.

He and Thomas guided their mounts up to Ethan and Robert. The horses exhaled softly but stayed completely silent.

"Do you think Bushnell has spotted us yet?" Baker asked as he gazed intently at the house.

Robert shook his head. "I doubt he's looking out the windows. No doubt he'll be focused on the woman he kidnapped."

The tension among the four of them rose. Devin clenched his jaw as he imagined how Bushnell was abusing Cassie. And, yes, how he'd no doubt hurt Julianne. Although she'd never said he beat her, Devin suspected it. He remembered what she said that day before he stormed out of her parlor.

"I came to know more about Bushnell's ways than either of us would care to discuss."

"I've loathed few men more," Ethan said, no doubt voicing what all four of them were thinking.

Thomas shared a look with Robert. Devin wondered if they were thinking about their wives and how they'd feel if Bushnell were taking advantage of them the way he was no doubt taking advantage of Lizbeth's friend.

It was time to end this. End the pain. End the worry Bushnell had perpetrated upon so many.

Taking care to keep his voice down, Devin said, "Major, we planned to arrive two in the front, two from the back. Is that still how you would like us to proceed?"

"Yes. We need to capture him. If he realizes we're here, I wouldn't put it past him to leave Cassie and sneak out."

"All right, then. Let's proceed." Devin felt his horse's muscles tense in anticipation. It mimicked his own body's response. Years of riding into battle on horseback brought back muscle recognition.

"Gentlemen, thank you for your support and your friendship. I am grateful for it," Ethan said. Then, after he pulled out his pistol and cocked it, he spoke. "Forward!"

Holding the reins tightly in one hand and his Colt revolver in the other, still ignoring the pain in his shoulder, Devin kept to Ethan's side as Robert and Thomas veered toward the back.

Whatever was destined to happen couldn't be put off any longer. It was time.

35

"I never imagined a filled hotel could feel so empty," Julianne murmured to Lizbeth as she stared out the window. "I hope the men are all right."

"And Cassie," Lizbeth added. "I hope she will be okay." Though they'd already cleaned Captain Monroe's room from top to bottom, Lizbeth still was moving restlessly around the space, wiping shelves that didn't need dusting and polishing furniture that already gleamed.

It was a testament both to her nervousness about the mission and to her respect for the men that she was cleaning the captain's suite in the first place. After all, Aileen employed a capable staff to do such things. A staff she was no longer a part of. However, doing something as simple as cleaning both Ethan's and the captain's suites had felt like the right thing to do.

When she'd mentioned her idea to Julianne, the other woman had been eager to help, and even went with her to collect cleaning supplies. Though there was quite a bit of tension, no doubt because of their past experiences with Colonel Bushnell. Not that Julianne knew Ethan had spoken of Lizbeth's relationship with him. Neither had made mention of the past. It seemed it was far easier to discuss dirt and cleaning solutions.

But now, hours after the men had left, it was apparent neither of them could think of anything other than the men and the mission they were on.

Lizbeth walked toward Julianne. "They are capable men, don't you think?" she asked hesitantly. "I'm assuming they know what they're doing." What if they did something reckless and made things worse for Cassie?

Julianne turned to face her, a faint smile on her lips. "You really don't know about these men, do you?"

"I know Ethan." Well, as much as he'd allowed her to know him. "And Captain Monroe a little bit. Their friends must be nice too," she added weakly. Even to her ears, her praise of them seemed rather distasteful.

Julianne's smile widened. "They are more than that, Lizbeth. After Captain Monroe first called on me at home, I asked some former soldiers about him. Oh, the stories they told!"

"He was that impressive?" Lizbeth tossed her dust rag on a side table. Though she knew war wasn't a glorious enterprise, she still couldn't help but let her imagination take flight. The captain in his uniform, leading men into battle, must have been a sight to see.

"He was extremely impressive! It seemed

his bravery and honor had no bounds, and that transcended to his best friends too. Major Kelly, Lieutenant Truax, Sergeant Baker, and Captain Monroe were a band of brothers whom many believed could take care of most anything." She sighed. "Even all this time after the war, people still talk about their bravery. Isn't that something?"

Lizbeth nodded. "It is. I'm glad you shared that with me. Even if the soldiers exaggerated those tales, I feel better about the men's chances of surviving today."

After a pause, Julianne said, "I should probably tell you, I heard about Captain Monroe and the other men from Bushnell too. During the war, Daniel wrote me about their battles. He mentioned all of them with pride." She rolled her eyes. "Of course, he listed himself too. And he wasn't on too many battlefields—not at the beginning, anyway. He was too busy strutting around and making connections so he could raise his rank."

There it was. Julianne's past was now out in the open and as unavoidable as the bed in the middle of the room. Choosing her words with care, she said, "Ethan told me about your past relationship with Bushnell. I, uh, honestly don't know what to say."

All traces of light vanished from Julianne's expression. "You don't need to say anything. I don't expect you to feel anything for what I did but contempt."

That seemed harsh, even though Lizbeth had been feeling very close to that. "I wouldn't categorize my feelings that way," she said hesitantly. "But I will admit it's hard for me to imagine any woman entering into a relationship with that man willingly."

"I understand."

Lizbeth doubted it. "He ruined me."

"He did. And you are right. He hurt you in many ways. He should and will pay for his actions." Her voice softened. "But let me ask you this . . . Did he ruin you forever?"

"How can you ask that?" she blurted. "He raped me. He cut me. I wear this scar on my face. Isn't that enough?"

"Of course it is," Julianne said in a rush. "You have every right to hate him. I, for one, loathe him." She took a deep breath. "But what I am trying to say is that when I look at you, I don't see a broken woman deserving only of pity. I see someone who is strong and capable. A survivor. I wondered if you ever saw that too." She shrugged. "I just thought you should know."

Lizbeth was shocked. Could it be that she was more than a victim?

"Do you think it's ironic that of all the people in the state, the two of us met, and that we have developed relationships with men who were in a prison camp with Bushnell? It brings a new definition to a small world, I think."

Julianne's gaze warmed. "It's ironic and disturbing and a great many other things. But maybe God thought it was fitting too."

"How so?"

"Well, how could one attempt to describe such a man? With the four of us, there was no need. We all know exactly what he was like. And because of that, maybe in time we can all help each other move forward."

For the first time since Ethan told her how he'd come to her ranch after Bushnell was there, Lizbeth smiled. "This is true. At least there's that."

"I couldn't help but notice you seemed upset with Major Kelly today. Was it because of what he told you about me?"

"No." She bit her lip. "He'd been keeping a secret from me. He led a group of men to my ranch just two weeks after Bushnell came. He recognized me when we met again last week, from my scar. But I didn't recognize him."

"Did he hurt you too?"

"Oh, no. Nothing like that."

"Did his men?" she asked quietly.

"No. They weren't especially kind, but they weren't cruel," Lizbeth answered, remembering that time as if it had happened just days ago. "The men were on a requisitioning raid. They took what few belongings I still had and then left. My head knew they had no choice. But my heart? Well, it was breaking. But of course, I was already broken." She shivered. Truly, that time in her life was so bad, she had rarely allowed herself to think of it.

Julianne plopped down in one of the chairs they'd just fluffed. "I bet you couldn't believe it when you realized he'd seen you before."

"I was certainly shocked. He said he remembered me because of my scar."

"What did he say?"

"He said he dreamed about that raid. That he's always regretted it."

"Was he sincere?"

Of that, she had no doubt. "Oh, yes. But I was so upset with him for not telling me he'd been there I didn't care if he felt bad." Feeling worse by the second, she mused, "Actually, I thought I was going to be upset with him for the rest of my life."

"Because he took your belongings?"

She shook her head. "No. And not because he kept his raiding my home a secret from me. Because he saw me at my worst. Because he saw me damaged and despondent and lonely. And instead of helping me, he only took more. But now? Now I don't know why I thought it mattered so much. If it wasn't him, it would have been someone else."

"Someone recently told me writers and poets make wars seem glorious but only fools think that way."

Lizbeth smiled awkwardly. "That's true, I suppose. Right when war broke out, my parents dressed me up to go to the officers' dances. The men in the uniforms looked so handsome and brave. I think I truly believed they would look the same in battle."

"I can only think there's a reason the Lord put us through so much. Maybe he needed us to meet each other. Or to be the right women for these men, Devin and Ethan."

"Do you think we are the right women?"

"I think we might be the right women for two men who also thought their lives were going to be quite different."

Lizbeth felt the tears come. "They could be injured right now. Or dead."

"Don't think that way. We have to keep our hope."

"But what if they are?"

"Then I guess we'll accept it. But they aren't, Lizbeth. They are fighting for their own reasons. Not just for us, or even to rescue poor Cassie. And I happen to think they are too good for the Lord to take them while fighting a man like him."

Lizbeth was awed by the passion in Julianne's voice. She was speaking from her heart, and it was obvious she believed every word she was saying. Clasping Julianne's hand, she said, "We need to keep praying. For our men, and for Robert and Thomas. And for Cassie to realize that even if the worst has happened, she can be a survivor too."

Julianne smiled. "I can't think of a better activity to do right at this minute. They need our prayers, and we need the Lord's comfort."

36

Standing on the outside of the hacienda with Devin, reeling with the knowledge that he was about to end another man's life, Ethan waited for the moment that usually came on the eve of a battle. There was always a time when all the chaos in his mind shut off, doubts faded away, and his body settled.

Right then and there, his body and mind would meld and all the hours of preparation would pay off. He would suddenly feel nothing but cool intent. Nothing would matter except for the job at hand. That was when he had been able to raise his rifle, to surge forward, to command other men to stay strong and risk their lives for the cause.

But now, as he stood at the door of the hacienda, his body tense and his mind churning with a dozen mixed emotions, Ethan realized this was a completely different situation. Nothing in his life had prepared him for what he was about to do.

Probably because everything about this mission was personal. He knew Daniel Bushnell. He knew him well. Not only had Ethan slept in the same tents and barracks as him, he'd also shared bread and hardtack and water. Ethan had sometimes laughed with him. He'd sometimes argued with him. He'd usually followed his orders.

And while it was true that he'd never cared for Bushnell, Ethan could admit that he'd never had an overwhelming urge to do him harm.

That had all changed when Devin was shot.

And when Lizbeth told them what he'd done to her.

Even when he'd come to terms with just how badly he'd used Julianne.

Since then, anger and the need for justice to be served had boiled inside of him. Daniel had used his rank and the integrity of everything they stood for and twisted it all to his advantage. As far as Ethan was concerned, Daniel Bushnell had dishonored everything he, as a Southern gentleman and a man of honor, had stood for.

Every time he allowed himself to think of Lizbeth being brutalized by him he could hardly contain his anger.

"Ethan, you okay?" Devin asked, his voice low.

"Yeah. I . . . well, I can't seem to settle."

"This is right," Devin said. "Justice needs to be served. Not just for Lizbeth and for Julianne, not just for Cassie, but for the countless women he's taken advantage of . . . and intends to continue to violate."

"Not to mention that he tried to kill you."

His own words and Devin's explanations rang in his ears. At last, he found the quiet sense of peace he had been looking for. He breathed in. Out.

Then, without another second's doubt, he kicked the front door. He half expected it to hold firm. But instead it cracked. One more forceful kick and it sprang open. "Bushnell!" he called out.

Behind him, he heard Devin cock his gun, ready to shoot. But when Bushnell didn't appear, they entered, immediately each intent on a different angle. In front of them, Ethan heard the faint shuffle of someone scurrying around.

"Don't make us hunt you down, Daniel," Devin called out. "We're all too old for that."

Pistol raised, Ethan tensed, again waiting for a reply. He scanned the area, carefully looking for places where someone might be hiding. But he saw nothing. Heard nothing more than his own harsh breathing.

All that remained was an eerie feeling in the air. By mutual agreement, they spanned out farther into the house. Robert and Thomas had joined them after entering through a back door.

Mexican red tiles made up the floor. They were hard under his feet. Each step echoed through the house. They might as well have brought in a score of soldiers. Seconds passed.

"We sure he's here?" Baker whispered.

"I am." Robert stepped forward. "His horse is outside. I'll go find him."

"Not alone," Devin murmured.

He paused, then nodded. "All right, Cap," he murmured. There was a new slight edge to his tone, though Ethan couldn't discern whether it came from Robert being amused that Devin felt he needed help or whether it came from appreciation of the other man's concern.

Maybe it was a combination. They needed to remind each other that they weren't as battle-ready as they'd once been. Reflexes were slower, their responses a bit sluggish.

Just as Ethan was about to join Robert on the stairs, an earsplitting scream pierced the air.

"Cassie," he stated, though none of them had needed an explanation.

Thomas let out a string of curses as Robert rushed on ahead by himself, all of Devin's warnings either completely forgotten or destined to be completely ignored.

As one, Devin, Baker, and Ethan raced up the stairs and down the hall. Each of them had their pistols drawn. Ethan's arm felt like it was on fire, the muscles were so tense. Their pace slowed, each man keeping an eye out for Bushnell, the woman he held, and ready for the possibility of any other men they didn't know about ambushing them.

When they reached the end of the hall, Robert stood outside a door. It was obvious he was impatient to go inside.

"At least you waited here," Devin muttered sarcastically.

Before Robert had time to say a word, Ethan pounded on the door. "Open up, Bushnell. You're outnumbered and outgunned. We both know you never could hit a target without taking five minutes setting up the shot."

"My pistol's already pointed at the door," Daniel replied. "The moment you open it, I'll shoot. Don't make me kill you."

When Cassie screamed again, Robert surged forward. Ethan had to put a hand out to stop him. They still didn't know what they were getting into.

But when she cried out once more, Robert tore forward. "Her death ain't going to be on my hands," he said as he pressed his shoulder into the wood. It didn't give.

"Step aside," Devin ordered as he raised his Colt and shot the lock. It swung open. "Bushnell, we're coming in!" he yelled. "Put your weapon down."

Ethan felt as if he were in a tunnel as he charged in after Devin and Robert.

Then he halted, stunned as he saw the sight in front of him. Daniel Bushnell was in his shirtsleeves and trousers only. His feet were bare. He held a knife in one hand and a pistol in the other. On the bed lay Cassie. Her torn dress was shoved up on her thighs, her lip was bleeding, and she was gazing at them in desperation.

It was so much like everything he'd envisioned happening to Lizbeth that Ethan felt himself sway.

Just as Bushnell raised his arm.

Finally, Ethan's heartbeat slowed and the doubts faded away. He raised his pistol and fired.

Bushnell jerked when the bullet hit its mark. Cassie screamed when he fell on the bed, obviously dead.

Only then did Ethan realize he hadn't been the only man to fire. The three men at his side had done the same. One of them—or maybe all of them—had ended Bushnell's life.

37

The moment Julianne saw Devin enter the lobby of the Menger Hotel, she burst into tears.

Devin froze. "Julianne?" he rasped as he curved an arm around her shoulders and lowered her onto a nearby settee. He turned to briefly speak to Lizbeth and then helped her to her feet, guiding her to the hallway that led to his suite. "Sweetheart, what's wrong?"

Sweetheart? Had she ever been anyone's sweetheart? That, of course, made the tears fall even harder.

They continued until Devin unlocked his door and pulled her inside. Only when Devin stepped toward her with his palms up, as if he were attempting to still a skittish colt, did Julianne finally get control of herself.

"Don't mind me," she said, doing her best to dab at the tears on her cheeks. "I'm just so relieved you're okay."

His expression eased as warmth entered his eyes. "I'm okay," he affirmed. "I'm fine."

He wasn't hurt. "Oh, thank the good Lord!" Beyond caring about how she looked, or retaining any composure at all, she rushed toward him and launched herself into his arms.

After the slightest hesitation, he wrapped his

arms around her tighter. "Julianne, careful now," he drawled, hesitation thick in his voice. "I've been on horseback for hours. No doubt I smell to high heaven."

She thought he smelled like man and leather and fresh snow. That wouldn't make a bit of difference to her, not in the slightest. "I couldn't care less," she murmured as she pressed her cheek to his chest. "I'm just so grateful you are here in one piece."

His arms tightened around her. "I am that."

She leaned back so she could see his face. "You really aren't hurt? You haven't opened your wounds?"

"I promise. I'm no worse for wear."

Now that worry had been put to rest, she dared to bring up the other concern. Because she knew him well enough to realize he wasn't going to easily give her any details, she kept her question simple. "Did you find Daniel?"

"We did, Julianne. You won't have to worry about him anymore."

Her body tightened. "What does that mean?" He might not want to tell her, but she needed to know the truth.

Sighing, he ran a hand down her hair. "You aren't going to let me cloak what happened in vague assurances, are you?"

She knew from his tone that he wasn't actually angry. "I cannot. Devin, tell me the truth. Is there a chance he could show up at my house again?"

"There's no chance at all. He's dead, honey."

Her breath hitched. Her mind spun as a mixture of emotions settled inside her. She was relieved, and maybe a little sad for the news too. Daniel Bushnell had done a great many terrible things. But no matter how others might perceive how he treated her, his money had saved her during the war. People could think what they would, but she would always be grateful she'd been able to survive.

"Did you do it?" she asked.

A muscle in his jaw jumped. It was obvious he was uncomfortable. Which made her feel terrible. Why did she even want to know? She *didn't* need to know. It wouldn't change her feelings for him. "Listen, forget I asked. It doesn't matter."

"I didn't kill him, Julianne. Rather, it wasn't only me."

That's when she knew she was a liar. Because she felt pure relief. Not because she would feel differently about Devin, but because she didn't want him to have to carry that burden. And she could tell by the set of his shoulders, the way his eyes looked tired, that he would have held that burden close to his heart. Maybe he would even eventually resent her for it.

Reaching up, she rubbed her hand against the scruff on his cheek, trying to console him in a way only a touch could do.

He closed his eyes for a brief moment as though he was drinking in her touch. "What happened was inevitable. When we got there, it was obvious he wasn't going to come out of that house alive."

Remembering there was another victim, she braced herself to hear the rest of the news. "What about Cassie? Was she really there? What happened to her? Will she be all right?"

For the first time since he walked into the room, his expression eased. "Cassie was there, but I think she is going to be okay. Right now Baker and Truax are escorting her to her family. She . . . well, Daniel had beaten her badly. She was bleeding. We got there just in time."

Julianne shivered. "The poor girl. I hope she'll recover eventually."

"I hope so too. Of course, we're living proof that a person can recover from some of the most adverse situations. We'll simply have to pray that Cassie will somehow find the strength and courage to do that."

Julianne liked how he'd phrased his statement. It was true, she realized. Not only did one's body have to recover from trauma, but the mind and heart did as well. Of course, faith played a big part in that recovery. "Lizbeth and I knelt and prayed for her and for you men for hours."

He ran his fingers through her hair again. "I'm

grateful you did. I needed your prayers. Maybe God heard them and took pity on us all."

"God didn't need to take pity on you. You and Ethan were in the right. You saved that young woman."

His expression softened as he looked down into her eyes. "I have to admit I was more than a little wary. I feared you wouldn't want to see me when I returned. Will you ever forgive me for sharing your past with Robert and Thomas?"

Julianne was surprised he had to ask. Couldn't he tell how much he meant to her from the way she greeted him? But then she remembered what kind of man he was. He was a man used to taking nothing for granted. "I have already forgiven you."

"That quickly?"

"The moment you rode off, I realized anything could happen to you. It made me so scared. That's when I started to realize keeping secrets about my past from your friends doesn't matter all that much. I can't change the past. It's a part of who I am, and most everyone knows about it. For better or worse, while I'm not proud of what I did, I have decided to stop cowering in shame. So many other people had to survive far worse things."

"I can promise you they have." He rubbed his hands over her arms. "Julianne, I'm so sorry I made you regret trusting me."

"Like I said, it's over now. I don't want to dwell on regrets."

"I don't either."

He was still holding her arms. They were still facing each other, barely inches apart. Her face was tilted up to his. Devin was staring down at her, his blue eyes looking languid and almost dark.

And just like that, the tension between them dissipated. Gone was the stress and the worry and the sense that they could be pulled apart.

In its place was something new and strong. A pull that had nothing to do with lies or truths and everything to do with something far more basic and primal.

"Julianne," he rasped. His hands curved around her body again, pulling her so close she was sure she could feel his heartbeat.

Maybe it was because she wasn't inexperienced. Maybe she'd lived long enough to know what he wanted from her. But there was a difference for her that was unchartered. Because she felt something new. She desired him too. It had nothing to do with debts or promises or contracts or guilt.

It was all about what was in her heart. She'd fallen in love with him. Even though she would have told anyone before she met Devin that she didn't believe in love, she realized now that she couldn't have been more wrong.

She had simply not been ready.

Licking her lips, she suddenly felt shy. What should she say? How should she convince him that he didn't need to hesitate? That she would never confuse what was happening with them with what she'd done with Daniel?

She felt his gaze fasten on her mouth. And just when she decided to say something, anything . . .

It turned out she didn't need to say anything at all.

He pressed his lips to hers. Then, with a moan, shifted her, lifted a hand to curve around her jaw, then proceeded to kiss her in a way she hadn't known was possible.

If she didn't know better, she would say his kisses were drugging. Encompassing. All consuming.

But really, what they were like was Devin. Powerful and brave. Direct and to the point.

Perfect.

Much, much later, he lifted his head. Searched her face. "Too much?"

Since she felt as though she could barely stand on her own feet, she sighed. "Oh, no, Devin. I think it was just right."

He smiled before he leaned down and kissed her again.

38

Devin had returned to the Menger over an hour ago. After he talked with Julianne, he told Lizbeth they had found Cassie, and that Robert and Thomas were taking her home to her family. He also said Ethan was fine and only a few minutes behind him. Before Lizbeth could pepper him with questions, he'd turned back to Julianne and they'd retreated to his suite.

She didn't even know what had exactly happened with Bushnell. But she assumed by Devin's demeanor that their mission had been accomplished.

Then, a bundle of nerves, she settled on a chair in the corner of the lobby and watched the front door. Each time the door opened, she leaned forward, anxiously hoping to see Ethan stride through. Looking strong and proud and so heroic.

But as the minutes passed, and the hour grew late, she realized he wasn't going to come. Worrying her bottom lip, she wondered if he was in a saloon.

Just as quickly, she disregarded that idea. That wasn't who he was any longer. Determined to find him, she decided to begin at the first place he would have gone—the stable.

When she walked into the barn, the warm,

musty air kissed her skin. It felt warm and inviting inside. Welcoming. Feeling optimistic, she walked down the center aisle. Each stall was filled. When the horses saw her, they shifted restlessly. A few whickered a greeting.

A palomino pushed his nose out between the slats of his stall, begging for a pet. Unable to help herself, Lizbeth slid a hand through and rubbed his soft nose. When he stepped closer, gently nudging her hand, she laughed. Just as she moved away from the horse, she heard a board behind her groan.

She turned, expecting to see one of the four grooms the hotel employed.

Instead, she found Ethan. He was leaning against one of the back stalls, half hidden in the dim light. He was standing quietly. Completely silent.

Everything about him seemed to be the exact opposite of the man she'd first talked to in his room. Gone was his proud and sardonic bearing. Gone, too, was his aura of confidence.

In its place was a man who looked exhausted by life.

She approached him carefully. She didn't want to intrude, but she didn't want him to be alone either.

He stood motionless, watching her approach. When she stopped in front of him, he finally spoke. "Lizbeth, why are you here?"

How could she not be? Keeping her voice purposefully light, she said, "I was looking for you, of course."

"Why? Do you need something?"

His voice sounded brittle. She decided to temper it with a bit of levity. "As a matter of fact, I do. I need you."

He straightened. A hand that had been shoved into one of his pockets fell to his side. "I beg your pardon?"

"I've been waiting for you in the lobby, Ethan. I've been waiting for over an hour. I thought you would walk inside directly after Devin, but you didn't arrive. That's why I ventured out here. I started to worry about you."

"I didn't know how to face you. And, well, I'm not fit for company right now."

"Only horses?" she asked lightly.

"I don't know if I'm even fit for them. Gretel doesn't seem real fond of me at the moment either."

She couldn't let another moment pass before she said what was really on her mind. "I'm really glad you are all right. Are you hurt at all?"

"No. I'm just fine. We got Cassie. She's with Baker and Truax."

"Yes, I heard that." Staring at him closely, she noticed Ethan didn't seem happy about their mission. "What's wrong? Did Bushnell escape?"

"No, we found him. He was where we thought

he'd be." He ran a hand along his brow. "He drew his gun, so I raised my gun as well. Actually, all of us did. He didn't stand a chance."

She released a ragged sigh. "So he's gone?"

"He's dead. It happened fast. So fast. After all that worrying and planning, it felt almost too easy." He grimaced. "I'm sorry. Like I said, I'm not fit for company right now."

He turned from her, but he didn't walk away. Lizbeth knew there would come a time when the harsh reality of what he was telling her would no doubt hit her hard. Maybe she would scream and cry. Maybe she'd dissolve into tears. But all she could think about at the moment was Ethan.

Carefully, she ran a hand down his back. "You're worrying me."

"Don't. I'm fine."

"What's going to happen next? Are you going to get into trouble?"

"No. After we, uh, left that house, we took Cassie to a doctor and I went for the sheriff. Between the four of us and Cassie's recounting of all she went through and what happened when we arrived, the sheriff seemed more relieved than anything."

"So he won't be taking you in for questioning or anything?"

"I don't think so." Ethan turned and tried to smile, but he couldn't seem to manage it. "Lizbeth, honey, I'm real glad you came out here. I'm sorry you had to go looking for me, but I think it might be best if you went on back inside."

"And do what? Wait for you some more?" she lightly teased.

He rubbed a hand over his face. "No. Of course not. I'll come find you at Harrison House tomorrow before I leave."

She gaped at him. "You're leaving?"

"Yeah. Like I told you earlier, my parents want me home. They left this morning. I was going to linger here a bit, but I think it's best if I go on my way."

She noticed he was avoiding her eyes. He thought she was still upset with him.

Impulsively, she reached for his hand and then pulled him down until they were both sitting on the ground, side by side. "Ethan, I know you want me to leave you in peace. And I will. But first, will you give me a couple of minutes? I'd like to tell you a story."

He shifted, stretching his legs out in front of him. "What's it about?"

Everything in his tone said he could not care less about any tales she might be telling. But maybe he'd think differently when she was done.

That is, if she could put everything she wanted to say in the right words.

"It's about a girl," she said.

"Okay . . ."

"Just hush and listen." She waited a beat to make sure he kept his silence, then stopped worrying about the right words and aimed for the right thing to say. "When she was a teenager, she had bright dreams for herself. She was going to find herself a handsome man. He was going to be perfect too. He was going to be wealthy and kind and polite and even kind of fun. But most importantly, he was going to think she was something special."

He cleared his throat. "Ah. Did she find him?"

"Not exactly." She took a breath, hoping to settle the emotion rushing through her. "See, the war came. Her parents died. Other family members went off to fight and didn't come back, and no handsome man appeared in sight. Then, well, things got worse."

"Lizbeth—"

His voice was strained. She ignored it.

"She ended up alone. In a small house on a small ranch. On the outskirts of San Antonio, in a place called Castroville. Every day she just tried to survive. And then . . . when men did show up? Well, they didn't come to make her life better. They just made everything worse." She swallowed hard. And though it felt as if she were choking on her words, she continued. "And so she tried a little harder to survive."

"And then?" Ethan asked softly.

"And then the war ended. So she had to work

in a big hotel and forget about her dreams." She smiled softly. "She was very good at that. As the months passed, she forgot she'd ever cared about love and marriage. Actually, she forgot she'd ever had any dreams at all."

She turned slightly. Took one of his hands. "And then she met him."

He blinked. "Who?"

"The man she'd always dreamed of. And he was just as handsome and kind as she'd dreamed he'd be. But he wasn't perfect." Laughing softly, she continued. "Not by a long shot. But that was okay, because she wasn't perfect either."

Ethan stared at her. Tightened his grip on her hand. "What happened next?"

"He realized that was okay too." Staring down at their linked hands, she whispered, "Ethan, I don't care what you had to do today. I don't care why you kept secrets or why you did what you needed to do in your past. I don't even need you to be different or better."

His eyes turned glassy. "What do you need, then?"

"You, Ethan Kelly. I only need you." Smiling softly, she said, "Do you think you can one day need me too?"

Instead of offering her words, he reached for her and pulled her close. Bent his head so it rested in the nape of her neck and held her tight.

Then, just when she was about to relax against

him, offering him comfort, Lizbeth felt his lips brush her skin. She pulled back slightly, intending to flash him a smile, but that idea evaporated as he whispered her name and then kissed her neck again.

She trembled, then gasped as Ethan traced a slow, lingering path along her throat. His mouth was warm. Each place it touched felt like a brand, making her aware of little besides how close she felt to him, how treasured. How very wanted.

When she shivered again, he lifted his head. "You okay, Lizbeth?" he drawled. His voice sounded deep, almost languid.

Wonderful.

As his question registered, she knew only one way to answer. And that was to circle his neck with her arms and raise her lips to his.

With a sigh, he pressed her close and kissed her at last. It was lovely. Perfect. No, it was even better than that. It was worth waiting for.

39

Johnson's Island, Ohio
Confederate States of America
Officers' POW camp

"Something is going on," Robert Truax whispered when he joined the ten or so men gathered around the wood-burning stove in the middle of their barracks. Though it was June, the air was still chilly. "None of the guards are around."

Intrigued, Ethan put down the figure he'd begun trying to whittle. It had been a hopeless task. He wasn't an artist and had no vision for how an ordinary stick could be made into a thing of beauty. But like Thomas and his constant attempts to better himself, he'd decided to at least attempt to push himself to learn something new.

That said, he was thankful to be concentrating on something else. Looking at the other men, they seemed to be having the same reaction he did. Some men were curious about Truax's information; others simply looked happy to have something new to talk about.

"I saw seven of them leave today on a skiff," Thomas said.

"They were probably going out to scout," someone said.

Thomas shook his head. "Nah, that weren't it. The guards wouldn't ask seven men to do the job of two."

"You forget who we're talking about," General McCoy said with a grin. "Our guards need double the time and double the manpower to do most anything."

"Yessir," Baker agreed. "But they had knapsacks. I've never seen them leave the island like that before. I don't think they're coming back."

Ethan's mind began to race. It was summer of 1865 now. The war had been going on a long time. Far longer than anyone had anticipated. And, if he was being completely honest, the South had hung in there longer than he ever would have imagined.

Turning to one of the newest members of their group, he said, "Where were you taken captive?"

"In Georgia, sir."

"Tell me the truth. What was Lee saying about our chances? What did you hear?"

His gaze darting around the assembled lot of them, the man sputtered. When he met General McCoy's eyes, he paled. "I couldn't say, sir."

"Come on. I've been here over a year. You were out there until just six weeks ago. What was happening?"

Again the man looked like he might throw up.

Baker shook his head. "He ain't going to tell

you a thing, Major. Speaking against the cause is a treasonous offense."

Of course, Baker's voice was laced heavy with sarcasm. Baker was known for saying too much about half the time. He would never let a probable consequence interfere with spouting his thoughts. But he was the exception, not the rule.

"We were losing," another newcomer said. "Our men were sick and starving and had more problems than a mammy could shake a stick at."

"Watch your mouth, Lieutenant," Bushnell barked.

"Leave him alone, Daniel," General McCoy said. "Kelly asked for the truth and he received it."

"What are you thinking, Kelly?" Devin asked.

Ethan was afraid to give voice to his hope. But he couldn't very well expect other men to speak their minds if he was afraid to do the same. "I'm wondering if something significant happened," he said.

What he was too afraid to share, however, was that he couldn't help but think about what was going to happen to all of them if the South had lost and the war was over. Rules of engagement stated they should be escorted out, but few things happened during the war that followed any such rules.

Devin was staring at him intently, no doubt

wishing Ethan would finally say what all of them were thinking. Then the door to the barracks burst open and they all turned in surprise.

There was Dunlap, the guard who had been there the longest and was far and above the men's favorite.

"Dunlap, you decide to join us for a spell?" Truax asked.

But instead of teasing Truax right back, Dunlap swallowed nervously. "Afraid I don't have time to be sitting around with you men today."

"I saw a half dozen of you Yanks leave on a skiff," Thomas said. "What's going on? Do they have to go fight again?"

Dunlap ignored Thomas's question. "I came for General McCoy."

"Only McCoy?" Bushnell asked.

"Uh, yes. He's the highest-ranking officer Reb, right?"

"That is correct," Bushnell said haughtily.

The general slowly got to his feet. "Where are you taking me?"

"The commander has requested your presence."

His expression tightened, but he walked to Dunlap's side. "Am I coming back?"

Dunlap's mouth pinched. "I believe so, sir."

"All right, then, let's see what he wants," he mumbled as they left the room.

After the door slammed behind them, conversation stumbled forward again, each person

415

guessing why the commander needed General McCoy.

"This ever happen before, Kelly?" the Georgian asked.

Ethan shook his head. "Not that I can recall."

After another twenty minutes or so, conversation petered out and they all huddled together in silence. The tension in the room increased as each minute slowly ticked by.

After another thirty minutes passed, Ethan was so stressed out he picked up his stick and knife again.

Just as the door opened.

They turned as one to greet General McCoy, who quietly closed the door behind him. It was so silent, Ethan was sure he wasn't only hearing his own heartbeat, but the hearts of the men surrounding him too.

McCoy stood at attention.

One by one, each man in the room got to his feet and stood at attention too.

General McCoy's expression was carefully blank, though Ethan was fairly certain he had seen pain in his eyes before he hastily covered it up.

"Gentlemen, it is my duty, as the highest-ranking officer of the Confederate States of America here, to inform you that the War of Northern Aggression has ended. Last month, in the town of Appomattox, Generals Lee and Grant met and signed the treaty. Tomorrow morning Dunlap will take the lot of us on a boat to land, where we will be given tokens for a one-way train ride to Kentucky. After that, we are on our own."

"It's over," Robert Truax murmured.

"Almost over," Thomas said, never one to look at anything through an optimistic light.

General McCoy stared down the line of them. "I would be remiss if I didn't say it has been an honor and a privilege to serve with each of you. God bless and Godspeed on your travels home."

When he saluted again, every man assembled saluted him back, holding their hands and posture steady for several seconds.

After everyone relaxed, the general pulled cigars from beneath his cot. "My Mimi sent these to me months ago. I've been saving them for a special occasion. I can't think of a better time than now. You're all welcome to join me."

Most of the men followed suit, opening boxes and envelopes and pulling out cheroots and cigars, packages of tobacco, and, in some cases, pilfered containers of whiskey and moonshine.

Soon, only a few men remained in the barracks. Ethan was glad of that. He needed time to think and to come to terms with the wealth of emotions rushing through him. After all, was there anything more disturbing than despair mixed with joy? So many men had died for the cause. Just as many were maimed and disfigured. Now many would say they'd died for nothing.

Had they? Ethan didn't know. He supposed only history would tell that story.

He thought about all the hardships they'd endured. The things each of them had had to do, the women who had gone hungry and been at the mercy of the elements without their men at their sides.

The door opened, bringing in the crisp scent of fresh air.

"There's quite a party going on outside, Major," Devin Monroe said. "You coming?"

"I don't know."

"I think you should," he said, his voice light. "The stars are out and the air is clear. We have much to celebrate. After all, tomorrow is a new day."

"I don't feel like celebrating much right now."

Looking concerned, Devin eyed him carefully. "What's on your mind?"

To anyone else, Ethan would have smirked and said something meaningless. But he couldn't do that to Devin. Neither of them deserved that. "Everything. I've been thinking about how much we've all suffered."

"You speak the truth. We have suffered."

"We buried so many men here too. We'll never see them again."

"That's true. We'll only see them again in heaven."

Ethan was incredulous. "Do you still believe in heaven?"

"I never stopped." Devin breathed deep. "I might be wrong, but I like to think the Lord has something better for us than killing and sickness and captivity and pain. He's already sent Phillip Markham there. Too many others to count as well. One day, if it's his will, I'll join them. And maybe you'll be there too. And Baker. And Truax. And we'll all stand together and look down upon this island and nod our heads."

Devin wasn't making sense. "Why? Why would we nod our heads when we see this place?"

"Because when that day comes, we'll understand. We'll understand why this war happened, why we were brought here to Johnson's Island. Why we survived and lived for many years after." Striking a piece of flint, he lit his cigar. He puffed on the end, illuminating the air with a faint glow, surrounding them with the faint scent of sweet tobacco.

And then Captain Devin Monroe continued. "One day we're going to understand why he put us here." He lowered his voice. It turned thick with suppressed emotion. "And when we do?"

Ethan Kelly knew the answer then. "That will be enough."

Discussion Questions

1. The scripture verse from Luke (Luke 17, 5-6) about the mustard seed guided me while writing this story. Were you familiar with this verse also? How might it apply to your life?

2. This novel features four characters who suffered and yet survived during the Civil War. With which character did you identify most? Why?

3. The themes of coincidence and God's will are explored throughout the book. How do you relate to these ideals? Have you ever experienced something that you considered to be particularly coincidental?

4. I really enjoyed writing about a band of brothers who vowed to be there for each other for the rest of their lives. Who might you consider to be part of your own band of brothers?

5. Did you find the flashbacks at the prison camp to be helpful or distracting to the story? Why or why not?

6. What do you think will happen to each of the four men now that they have found happiness?

7. Of the four couples in this series, Robert and Miranda, Thomas and Laurel, Ethan and Lizbeth, or Devin and Julianne, which would you be most interested in reading a novella about?

Acknowledgments

Although my name is on the book's cover, there are a great number of people who made this book possible. I owe a great deal of gratitude to everyone who worked so hard to make this novel as good as it could be.

First, I'm so very grateful for my husband Tom who helped me create Captain Monroe and his remarkable band of brothers one evening while we were making dinner. He and I both loved the idea of creating a hero who was larger than life. I owe Tom my thanks, too, for visiting Johnson's Island with me. I also want to thank my girlfriend Mendy who toured the Menger Hotel with me in San Antonio, and my first editor Becky Philpott who had tea with me at the Menger and encouraged me to set a novel there.

I owe a great deal to my editor Karli Jackson for her help in fine-tuning this book and Jean Bloom for helping me get the timeline and organize the many, many details in this story. Also important was my first reader Lynne Stroup, who spent a great many hours helping me turn in a very long book on time.

My heartfelt thanks also go out to Kristen Golden and Allison Carter. These ladies in publicity and marketing work wonders! I also want to extend my appreciation to all the bloggers and reviewers who have embraced this series and encouraged everyone to give it a try.

Last but not least, I would like to give a little shout out to my father, who has been camped out up in heaven for over twenty years. It's because of my Dad's love of Louis L'amour, old westerns, and Palominos that I love them too. Thank you, Dad, for instilling in me a love of all things Texas. I think this series would have made you proud.

With blessings and my thanks,
Shelley

About the Author

Shelley Shepard Gray is a *New York Times* and *USA Today* bestselling author, a finalist for the American Christian Fiction Writers prestigious Carol Award, and a two-time HOLT Medallion winner. She lives in Loveland, Ohio, where she writes full time, bakes too much, and can often be found walking her dachshunds on her town's bike trail.

Visit her website at www.shelleyshepardgray.com
Facebook: ShelleyShepardGray
Twitter: @ShelleySGray

Center Point Large Print
600 Brooks Road / PO Box 1
Thorndike, ME 04986-0001 USA

(207) 568-3717

US & Canada:
1 800 929-9108
www.centerpointlargeprint.com